ROUGH WORLD
THE FINAL JOURNEY

V. KIM KUTSCH, DMD

ROUGH WORLD MEDIA, LLC

ROUGH WORLD: The Final Journey
All Rights Reserved
Copyright © 2017 V. Kim Kutsch

Cover art by Taylor Bill
Cover art © 2017 Taylor Bills. All rights reserved - used with permission.
www.illustrationplanet.com

ISBN: 9780997497243

ROUGH WORLD MEDIA, LLC

www.roughworldmedia.com

PRINTED IN THE UNITED STATES OF AMERICA
Signature Book Printing, www.sbpbooks.com

I dedicate this book to all adventurous children, young and old. It's a rough world out there, so be safe and trust one another.

PREFACE

The places and characters in this novel are the product of my grandson James's video game creation *Rough World* and his cartoon strip characters Some Random Guy and his friend Tannic. This is the third book in the trilogy. The story doesn't follow James's depiction of Rough World precisely. I took artistic liberties to weave a story from his basic ideas and added some of my own. This is a work of fiction. The places and the characters are not real. But as I wrote these books, the characters became very real to me. They came to life and became a part of my own life. I hope you enjoy this continuation of the Rough World story. It's fiction, of course, so this story never really happened. Of course, there's always the random chance it could have happened. I mean, just a random chance . . .

PROLOGUE

Some Random Guy studied the clock. He couldn't hear it ticking, but the second hand was sweeping around the dial with a slow, steady motion. He counted. Ten more minutes and sixth period would be over. It wasn't that he was bored, not exactly. It was just a case of senioritis. He was ready to be done with high school and move on to college. His thoughts drifted forward to the weekend. He and Danika and Tannic would probably hang out and see a movie, eat some pizza, maybe play video games. It had been like that since they last returned from Rough World six years ago. Danika had become one of his best friends. Tannic already was, of course, but Tannic's problem was that nobody but Some Random Guy and Danika could see him. To everyone else, it just looked like Danika and SRG were hanging out together. But they thought themselves as the Three Amigos. They did everything together.

The kids at school thought that Danika and SRG were an item because they were always together. But there wasn't any romance involved, to Danika's dismay. SRG looked at her as one of the guys and Danika could handle herself with the best of the guys. She was a serious gamer and the only person who gave SRG a real challenge on any video game. But secretly she had a crush on him. It had started the moment they left Rough World Two. Well, it might have started a little earlier, somewhere along the road through their Rough World adventure. But now there was nobody in the world she'd rather spend time with than SRG. She hadn't told anybody about this, though it seemed obvious. But he was a guy, and guys could be pretty oblivious. She dropped clues about her feelings, but they just sailed over his head.

The three of them also shared a serious secret together. When they got back from Rough World, they didn't tell anyone about the experience. Even now, it was something they alone shared. No one else would understand or believe it anyway. But they knew it was real. Their adventure had forged a bond of friendship between them that would never break. And they'd made a pact that day: They would always be friends and they would never tell anyone else about their experience in Rough World. And they agreed that they would never play Rough World again. It was still a popular video game, but SRG took his copy out of the family room and hid it deep in his closet. He buried it behind a pile of other remnants of his childhood. The game was too dangerous to even consider. Since that fateful day of the lightning strike, his copy of the game could transport them into Rough World for real. They'd been lucky to survive it twice. He'd tried to forget about it, but either way he never wanted to see it again. But yet he couldn't get rid of it either.

He looked at the clock again. Three minutes now. The class was Global Politics, and Mrs. Hathaway was seriously nice, but he just wanted to be somewhere else. He was tired of politics. He wanted to be studying math and science in college. He was already thinking about majoring in computer programming, and he had told his parents as much, but he hadn't told them that in his heart he wanted to create videos games. He was worried they wouldn't see that as a real career. Oregon State University had a good information technology program, he liked the campus, and it was close to home. So he was pretty much decided on it.

He looked at the clock again. Then he almost laughed out loud. All the random thoughts you have while waiting for the bell to go off. It was funny. He wondered if college classes would be more interesting, or if he'd be watching the clock there too. Two more minutes now, and he'd meet Danika and Tannic at his locker. It was Thursday, and they needed to make plans for the weekend before his parents did it for him. His parents were good at that.

Danika was in Spanish class and Tannic was attending calculus. Danika was thinking about studying media and maybe becoming a writer. She'd been looking at Linfield College. It was a smaller, private school, and she really liked the people there. And she wouldn't be more than an hour from SRG.

Invisibility caused some problems for Tannic. He'd audited classes all the way through high school, with no one knowing but SRG, and he planned to continue his education at OSU. They were hoping to start a company together after college. Tannic would be what they called the "silent partner"—the invisible partner, in this case—but he would at least have the chance to participate.

Tannic's situation was all that stupid wizard's fault. Rufus had never been great with magic, but he'd really bungled the situation when he started obeying the evil Queen Diana. She'd wanted to get rid of the heirs to the throne by sending Tannic and Danika into the great unknown. Instead, they'd randomly arrived in Albany, Oregon. If their father had lived, they'd still be in Fairhaven and Diana wouldn't have crowned herself queen. But time and fate work on their own agendas, and here they were.

Danika had shown up first. She was only four years old at the time when she was discovered wandering alone and was adopted by the Karsten family. Now the world knew her as Katie Karsten, but SRG and Tannic knew that she was really Danika Silveren from Fairhaven. Tannic arrived by way of the same magic spell—kind of. He hadn't drank all of the potion so he was mostly all there, just invisible.

The bell rang and snapped SRG out of his random thoughts. He grabbed his backpack and books, jotted down next week's assignment, and joined the throng of students heading out the door. The hallway was packed with bodies. It was the last class of the day for most of them. He slowly squeezed his way through the crowd to his locker. Danika was waiting patiently for him. Tannic was nowhere in sight.

Chapter 1

The Prom

"So, are you going to the prom?" Danika asked.

"Nah, I don't think so. I'm not into dancing. Are you?" Some Random Guy responded.

"Uh, I haven't decided yet. Chase Cooper asked me to go with him, but I haven't given him an answer yet."

"Why not? Don't you want to go?" he asked.

"Well, we are seniors. I've never gone to a prom, and this will be my last chance . . ." There, she'd said it. She let it hang in the air for a moment. How could she be more obvious? But it just floated randomly through space, seemingly unnoticed by SRG.

"Wow. I'm kind of surprised. You don't even wear dresses, I never figured you for the type of girl who would want to do that. I mean, I'm trying to picture it. Actually, you'd look pretty funny in one of those gowns," he teased.

Tannic arrived just in time to watch Danika storm off.

"What got into her?" SRG asked innocently. Then he caught himself and looked around quickly to make sure nobody was watching him. They couldn't see Tannic and it would appear that he was talking to himself, like a crazy person. He lowered his voice and looked at Tannic.

"Dude, are you really that dense?" Tannic asked.

"What? What are you talking about?" SRG answered the question with a question.

"You really don't get it, do you?"

"Get what?"

"Seriously, you don't get it? She wants you to ask her to the prom, stupid! Haven't you ever noticed how she looks at you? How she always wants to hang out with you? The way she's turned down every boy who's ever asked her out on a date? She's even picking a college that won't be too far from where you go! Hello! Do you not get that?"

"Not really, I guess. What are you trying to say?"

"Okay, let me spell it out for you slowly, Einstein. My sister has a crush on you. She's had it since fifth grade. She wants to go to the prom with you, Compadre! She's been waiting for you to ask her!"

"Whoa, are saying what I think you're saying?" SRG swallowed as the realization slowly sank in.

"I can't believe you haven't realized. I mean, I know my sister well, but I've known this for years!"

SRG had a bewildered look on his face. "I never really thought about it. I mean, we're like best friends, not like . . . that kind of thing," he answered. "I guess I never really thought about her that way. Whoa! I mean, wow!"

"Compadre, it's obvious to everybody but you how she feels. She drops hints all the time. I can't believe you didn't notice."

"We've never talked about it. At least I never . . . wow . . . so what do I do now?" SRG asked nervously.

"If I were you, I'd go apologize and then ask her to the prom. I mean, if I were you."

Some Random Guy studied his best friend. He searched his face for an answer. He still felt caught off guard and confused. "I've never been to a prom. I wouldn't even know what to do." A nervous panic rose in his stomach. He looked at Tannic again.

"Trust me, you'll figure it out. You just dress up, go out to dinner, and then dance a bit. I think that's all there is to it," Tannic said. "I mean, I've never been to one either, but it's not like I can ask anybody out."

"Okay then, I'll do it. I'll do it right now. I don't want Danika being mad at me. If that's what it takes, I'll take her to the prom!"

Some Random Guy marched with determination down the hallway to Danika's locker. She was putting her books away and organizing her backpack. He could feel her irritation as she threw a couple of books into her locker with more force than necessary.

"Danika?" he asked softly.

"What?" she barked.

"Well, I, uh . . . I just had this kind of crazy idea. I mean, I was thinking . . . maybe . . . since this is your last chance to go to a high school prom and all . . . that maybe . . . uh . . . " Some Random Guy swallowed hard. "Maybe you and I could go to the prom together. I mean, if you wanted to or whatever. Something like that. I think."

"SRG, are you asking me out to the prom?" She studied him for a reaction.

"Uh, yeah. Yeah, that's what I was thinking," he replied nervously.

"Well, I'm sorry, but you're too late. I just told Chase I'd go with him."

SRG was crestfallen. He couldn't believe it. Now he was really confused. He turned around, and everybody was staring at him. He'd just asked a girl out for the first time in his life, and she had rejected him, and in public. And it was Danika, of all people. He was stunned.

"Uh, okay, well, I just wanted to make sure you got to go to the prom," he stammered and walked away.

"SRG! Wait! I was just messing with you. You hurt my feelings. Of course I'll go to the prom with you. I really want that. I've waited forever for you to ask me out," Danika shouted.

Then the kids in the hall all broke into cheers and SRG felt his cheeks redden. Why did he feel so embarrassed?

Tannic had evidently heard the cheering. SRG walked uncertainly as he approached his locker but developed a little swagger as he reached Tannic, who was leaning against it.

"So?"

"So, I asked her, and she said yes. Can you believe that? Danika and I are going to go to the prom together. Wow, I'm not even sure where to start," he pondered. He stared over Tannic's shoulder into empty space with a dumbfounded look on his face that slowly turned into a wry smile.

"Talk to your mom tonight. Tell her what happened, and I'm sure she can help you get this all organized. I mean, your mom will know what to do."

Some Random Guy shook his head in agreement. He'd never been to a prom before. He didn't even know where to start. But Tannic had the right idea. Surely his mom would know what to do. And she'd probably enjoy the heck out of it.

That night Some Random Guy sat patiently at the dinner table while his two younger brothers, the knuckleheads, talked about their day at school. What they were studying. What they did during recess, what they ate for lunch. Who got into trouble on the school bus. Random stuff that he didn't really care about. He had one thing on his mind. Then his dad talked about work and what was going on in the company, some of his frustrations, the challenges with the new product. SRG looked patiently for an opening to bring up the prom, but it never came. As soon as his dad finished, his mom starting talking about her day, and then the knuckleheads added more about their day, and just like that dinner was over. Everyone left, and SRG sat there alone. Finally, he stood and started helping his mother clear the table. This was novel for him. She looked surprised.

"Oh, you don't have to do that, Honey. I'm sure you've got homework."

"Uh, actually, I'm happy to help, and I've finished my homework, and there's something I need to talk to you about . . . " he said hesitantly.

She looked at him curiously. "What is it? Is everything alright? Something happen at school?"

"Yeah, well, uh, actually, I, uh, asked Danika . . . er, I mean Katie . . . to go to the prom with me . . . " he answered tentatively again.

Mrs. Guy lit up. "Oh Stevie, that's wonderful! And she said yes?"

"Of course, Mom! Come on . . . have a little faith in me."

"I'm sorry, I just meant, well, never mind. I'm just a little surprised. You've never gone to a prom before and you've never asked Katie out on a real date before. I'm just a little surprised, that's all, happy, but surprised."

"Yeah, well, I'm a little bit surprised too. But I asked her and she said yes. And now I've got a problem," he explained. "I have no idea what to do next." He looked at Tannic, who was leaning quietly against the wall in the kitchen, smiling like a Cheshire cat.

"Don't worry. Let me get your father in here. We know exactly what to do. Oh, this is so exciting!" She was clapping her hands as she scurried out of the kitchen. Within a minute she returned with Some Random Guy's dad in tow. He looked more amused than anything.

"Okay, so where do we start?" SRG asked somewhat anxiously.

"Simple. You'll need to rent a tuxedo and then plan dinner at a nice restaurant. Not pizza, someplace nice and kind of fancy. And you'll need to get her a corsage. I can help you pick one out. Do you know what color her gown is going to be?" his mom asked.

"Mom . . . "

"Don't worry, I'll call Mrs. Karsten and we'll get that organized. You'll probably want to take your dad's truck—my minivan wouldn't be too cool." She paused. "On second thought, you could call your grandpa. I'll bet he'd let you drive his Mustang for this special date. That would be really cool."

"It's not a special date Mom. It's just the prom," Some Random Guy clarified.

"The junior-senior prom. And how is it not a special date?" she asked, not waiting for an answer. She looked at his dad, who winked back, and they both smiled with a knowing look in their eyes. They spent the rest of the evening helping SRG plan. Every detail was covered. He was grateful to have parents to help him sort things like this out.

Friday was a painful day at school. He felt like a fish out of water. For the first time in his life, he had no idea how to act. Suddenly he was a nervous wreck whenever Danika was around. She was the happiest he'd ever seen her, and he was scared to death. It didn't help that he hadn't gotten a wink of sleep: he'd tossed and turned all night, agonizing about the prom. And Danika. What was happening to him?

He couldn't focus in class, and by lunchtime he could hardly keep his eyes open. He sat with Danika in the cafeteria, barely eating. He was lost in thought, still wondering how he was supposed to act, and why he felt like he should act differently in the first place. Danika had been one of his best friends for seven years. He'd always felt completely comfortable around her. So why did he feel so weird now? *It will pass*, he finally told himself. *It's just a prom.* He just needed to get used to the idea of it. It wasn't like Rough World or anything, it was just a dance. That's the lie he told himself. It sounded good.

His mom had called Mrs. Karsten last night. She'd jumped the gun: Katie hadn't even gone shopping for a gown yet. But his mom couldn't help it, she was too excited. Raising three boys, she had missed out on girly things like getting a daughter ready for a prom. But Katie had been around the family for years now, and they all adored her. She'd always secretly hoped that something like this might develop, but she would never meddle in her son's life. At least, she believed that about herself.

Danika and Some Random Guy met after the last bell and made plans to meet at his house later, play video games, eat pizza, and generally hang out. His parents had a "date night" out, and they had lured him into keeping an eye on the knuckleheads with the promise of pizza. They were happy that Katie was coming over to help him babysit. Well, more like preventing the total destruction of the house than babysitting. Still, he and Danika and Tannic could keep a casual eye on his brothers. And as long as nothing got broken, they would be okay.

Chapter 2

A Daring Gamble

Danika arrived at 6:30. It was only a short walk from her house. SRG's brothers were arguing, typically, about something insignificant, but they weren't breaking things yet. The doorbell rang, and the pizza was there before she, Tannic, and SRG could even start playing. It was hot out of the oven, and the warm aroma quickly filled the house. His brothers ran down the stairs and grabbed their meat lovers' pizza from SRG as he was still paying the delivery boy, vanishing back upstairs in a second like a pack of wild dogs with a fresh kill. SRG brought the three-cheese pizza into the family room to share with Danika.

Tannic didn't eat. It was kind of strange, but like his invisibility it was something they'd all gotten used to over the years. He didn't usually comment on it, but tonight the pizza smelled really good, and just once he really wanted to take a bite and taste it for himself. Pizza didn't exist in Fairhaven, so he'd still never tasted it. He swore that if he ever made it back there—and was a whole and complete person again—the first thing he would do would be to make a pizza and eat the entire thing himself. Maybe two pizzas. Shoot, maybe even three.

Danika and SRG both started eating, though. SRG ended up with a string of soft cheese hanging from his chin, and Danika picked it off and put it in his mouth. She looked directly into his eyes. He froze for a second. She'd never done anything like that before. Normally she would have slugged him in the shoulder and told him he looked like a dork with cheese hanging from his chin. Something had changed. *It must be that prom thing.*

In the pause, Tannic walked over to the television and turned on the console. He started digging through the pile of video games and didn't notice the events on the couch. "You guys want to play a video game or watch a movie?" he asked. "How about Super Smash Brothers 15?"

"I don't know. We've played all these so often, I'm kind of bored with them," Some Random Guy replied through a mouthful of pizza. "We need a new game. Throne Master is coming out soon. That should be really cool."

"Yeah, I'm kind of bored with all those games too," Danika agreed.

"What, then? Do you want to watch a movie?" Tannic asked.

"I don't know. We've seen all of these at least a couple of times. We need some new movies too. What's on TV?" Some Random Guy asked. "We could always look for something on Netflix."

"It's Friday night, Compadre," Tannic answered. "Not much on TV. I don't really feel like a movie, anyway."

"Okay, so it's back to video games," SRG concluded.

"Hey, I have an idea," Danika teased with an evil look in her eyes. "But it's daring . . ."

"Okay, Danika," Some Random Guy replied, taking the bait. "I live on the edge, after all," he boasted. "'Danger' is my middle name."

She gave him an odd look and then grinned devilishly. "We could play Rough World. We haven't played that game in what, six years?"

Some Random Guy leapt from the couch and almost spit out his pizza. "No way! That's not funny, Danika. We are not doing that. Not now, not ever!" He could feel his heart race at the suggestion. The rush of adrenalin made him feel sick to his stomach. "That's not funny," he repeated, trying to calm himself.

She was taken aback. "Well, it was just a thought. And obviously a daring one, Mr. 'Danger Is My Middle Name.' We could just turn it on and see if we can still talk to Dr. Denton. We could find out how he's doing, what he's up to," she added.

"Oh man. I don't want to see that game again, ever," Some Random Guy responded.

"Me neither, Compadre," Tannic agreed. "We need to leave it alone, in the past. Sorry, Danika, but that's a really bad idea. It's too dangerous."

"Oh, you guys are no fun. We don't have to play it, we can just turn it on and talk to Doc. Come on, be a little adventurous for once," she goaded.

"Uh, adventurous? Really, Danika? Are you forgetting what happened the last time we were in Rough World?" SRG replied. "We almost died. For real. In fact, I did die for a moment!"

"Oh, come on. We don't have to go there. We can just turn the game on and check in with Doc. What harm is there in that?" she asked.

"I don't know, Danika," SRG hesitated. "I just don't think that's a good idea."

"Yeah, count me out. Color me invisible," Tannic said, breaking the tension. SRG laughed out loud.

"Okay fine," Danika answered. "I'll turn it on myself, and I'll talk to Dr. Denton, since you two guys are clearly too scared," she challenged them.

"No, it's too dangerous!" Some Random Guy argued. "I can't let you do that."

"Yes you can, and I've made up my mind." She addressed him firmly and folded her arms. "I know you still have it hidden in your closet. We'll just talk to Doc. It'll be okay, you'll see. Come on . . . "

SRG sighed. "Okay, well, if you really insist . . . I'm not letting you do it alone. But for the record, I still think it's a huge mistake."

"Me too," Tannic agreed.

"If you absolutely insist on it, then we're all in this together. But we're only talking to Doc, we're not playing the game. Are we all clear on that?" SRG asked.

"Sure, whatever," Danika responded.

"Yeah, okay," Tannic added after a flash of hesitation.

"Okay. I'll have to go find it. I haven't looked at it in years, and I'm not even sure I still have it. My mom might have donated it to goodwill." SRG walked slowly up the stairs to his bedroom. His feet were stalling while his mind was racing.

He secretly hoped he would discover that his mother had given the game away, but he knew she hadn't. The game was something that still had a hold on him. He never wanted to see it again, but he couldn't get rid of it either. Still, it took a couple of minutes of digging in the back of his closet before he found it, in the furthest corner, at the very bottom of the pile. A dusty game cover of Rough World. He gently wiped the dust off and took it back to the family room. Danika and Tannic were waiting anxiously on the sofa.

"I still don't like this idea," Some Random Guy declared. "I should have destroyed the game, but I buried it deep in my closet. We should rethink this."

"Ah, come on. Let's talk to Doc!" Danika insisted.

Tannic walked slowly across the room and plugged the game into the console. They all tensed in anticipation as the Rough World screen came to life. The first scene appeared, and they saw a person moving about in the lab. It wasn't Dr. Denton. After a couple of seconds, they recognized his nephew Cody.

"Cody, can you hear us?" SRG asked.

Cody jumped and turned around to face the screen. He stared for a couple of seconds.

"Who . . . who is that? How do you know me?" He studied their faces. They were six years older and they looked different now. "Wait a minute, SRG? Is that you? Danika? Tannic? I hardly recognized you. You gave me a start!" When they nodded, he grinned. "Wow, I can't believe it. Doc talked about you all for years, wondering how you were. You made it home safely?" Cody asked.

"Yeah, it's us!" Danika answered. "We made it back in one piece. His plan worked perfectly. So where is Doc? Is he around?"

"Oh, that's a long story. I'm afraid things haven't been good in Rough World since you left. Your success inspired the citizens to take on Mr. Eville. It took several years for them to plan and get organized, but eventually there was an uprising in the Jagged City, and basically a war broke out. And I know you won't be surprised to hear it, but they recruited Doc to become the leader of the rebellion. It started out well, but in the end Mr. Eville sent his army of Minotaurs to quash the uprising, and they killed a lot of people. The war didn't really last that long. Then about a month ago, his henchmen kidnapped Doc. From what I've heard, Mr. Eville is holding him captive in a dungeon in World Three, Level 10. But I haven't heard from Doc himself, and I haven't been able to get a word to him. I've gone underground, actually: I just slipped back into the lab to get some supplies for the resistance army. They're reorganizing as we speak. You're lucky you caught me. But enough about our problems, what's going on with you guys? Please give me the short version, I shouldn't stay here long. Mr. Eville's army is still hunting for me."

Danika and Tannic looked worriedly at SRG. His mouth was dry. He swallowed hard. "So what you're saying is, Doc's in serious trouble?" he asked.

"Well, you know Mr. Eville. He'll keep Doc alive as long as he has some value, but after that who knows. I'm sure he's being tortured, though. There's information they want to get out of him, and I know he'll never reveal anything." Cody's face was clouded with worry. "But I really have to get going. Maybe we can talk again when it's safer, after this whole thing blows over."

"Wait, Cody." SRG studied Danika and Tannics' faces. He took a deep breath, and his voice cracked as he spoke. "Doc's in trouble and he needs our help. He did everything he could, he risked his own life, to make sure we got home safely. We can't let him down either. I said I'd never do this again, but now I don't have a choice, I have to go help him. I have to."

"Me too," Danika answered without hesitation.

Tannic sighed. "Compadre . . . me too," he said reluctantly.

"Wait a minute," Danika interrupted "What about your brothers? Can we just leave them alone here? How long will we be gone? Your grandpa calls them range animals, and I think that's pretty accurate. We're supposed to be babysitting them, remember? Maybe one of us should stay here just to make sure they don't destroy the house and cover for the other two."

"No way, this was your idea Danika. If we go at all, we all go together. I guess we just have to hope that we get home before my parents do and that the knuckleheads don't break anything major. I mean, theoretically that could work, right? Nobody even has to know we left."

"Uh, Compadre, there's a pretty good chance we won't get home," Tannic said somberly. "Did you forget that?"

SRG sighed. "I know, but how can we not help Doc? I couldn't live with myself."

"Me neither," Danika responded immediately.

"Yeah," Tannic sighed. "Me neither."

"Okay then, its settled. We all go together. We'll take our chances. We're going to rescue Doc or die trying. Cody, do you remember how to reverse the polarity on our controller and transport us to the lab via the TENT technology?" SRG asked.

"Sure, I know exactly how. But I'm not sure what you can do by being here. And, I mean . . . are you sure you want to? Things are crazy here. Mr. Eville's army is everywhere. It's really dangerous right now."

"I know that. But Cody, we already defeated Rough World Two, which means the game should send us directly to World Three. Then we just have to make it through to Level 10 to rescue Doc, and then we get another shot at defeating Mr. Eville in his private office and freeing the citizens of

Rough World. Once and for all." SRG laid out the whole strategy without even thinking about it. It sounded perfectly logical and easy. Only, this was Rough World, and nothing was easy in Rough World. Ever.

"Well, that could work," Cody agreed. "But you'd have to defeat all the levels of World Three, and no one's ever done that—you were the first team to defeat Worlds One and Two. World Three's not a place anybody should choose to go."

They looked at each other again, for a long moment, then nodded their agreement. Danika spoke first this time. "We've made up our minds, Cody. Transport us to the lab. We've got to save Dr. Denton or . . . " Her voice faltered. "We owe him that."

"Okay, if you're sure. Just give me a couple of minutes to set up the polarity reversal. Then you'll all need to have your hands on the controller." Cody moved swiftly about the lab, gathering electronics, changing wiring, assembling equipment. Eventually he returned to face the screen.

As they waited, SRG hesitated and then asked one last time "Are we sure about this?" Danika and Tannic shook their heads in agreement. But it had all happened so fast, they weren't really sure. "Okay then, we're all in it together. And we're going to need each other to survive World Three. I just hope my brothers don't destroy the house before we get back."

"That's if we get back, Compadre," Tannic added solemnly.

Some Random Guy frowned in worry and then nodded. Danika cuddled closer to him on the couch and took his hand.

"You guys ready?" Cody asked. "Put your hands on the controller and I'll flip the switch!"

They all closed their eyes as their hands squeezed together on the controller. "Here goes nothing—" were the last words out of SRG's mouth. There was a flash of light and a loud boom.

They opened their eyes to a thick fog with a familiar, dense smell. As it thinned, they saw that they were standing in Dr. Denton's lab once again. Cody was standing in front of them, still speechless.

"That was just how I remembered it," Tannic noted.

"Yeah, I can't believe we're back here for real," SRG said.

Danika didn't say anything.

"There was one thing I never told you that I really liked about Rough World," Tannic suddenly confessed. "Here, I get to be a whole person again. Everybody can see me. I like that."

SRG blinked. "I never really thought about that. Maybe because I've always been able to see you. That must be nice."

"It is. I kind of missed being real," Tannic concluded.

"So what's the plan?" Cody asked.

"Well, one of us should stay in the lab while the other two work their way through the levels. How safe is it for you to stay here too?" SRG asked.

"Hey, nothing's safe here in Rough World. But as long as you guys are here, I'll stay and take my chances. It's probably the best bet we have for saving Doc. He'd be so proud if he knew what you're doing, but he really wouldn't want you risking your lives."

While Danika was distracted examining the equipment Cody had set up, SRG looked at Tannic and nodded toward the door. Tannic nodded back and raised his eyebrows at Danika. SRG shrugged his shoulders. Then quietly in unison, they moved to the door, unnoticed by Danika. Tannic picked up the Dragonwrigley sword from where it leaned against the wall as SRG opened the door. They both bolted outside.

"Do you think that was the right thing to do?" SRG asked, feeling guilty about sneaking out on Danika.

"One of us had to stay behind. She'll be safer with Cody. I definitely don't want her out here with us. I'm sure the lab is safer," Tannic reassured him.

"Yeah, you're probably right. But we did forget something in our haste. We didn't get the special weapon for this level. And if you're the main player, I have no idea what my special power will be."

In Rough World the main player carries the Dragonwrigley sword to defeat the enemies, while the partner player carries a unique special weapon that is different for each level. The partner also is given a special power throughout the game.

Tannic frowned. "It's too late now. I guess we'll have to make do. Maybe we'll discover your power. Anyway, we'll get by with the Dragonwrigley. By the way, this thing is heavier than I remembered."

"I felt the same way. So did Danika. Where do you think we are?"

A desert landscape and tall rock walls faced them in every direction.

"It should be Level 1 of World Three. It's definitely someplace we've never been before. I wonder what the common theme for the levels will be."

* * * * *

Without warning, a team of Minotaurs burst into the lab through the inner door. One grabbed Cody. Another spotted Danika, who had just realized that she had been abandoned by the boys. She ran to the outside door and pounded on it furiously. "Help! Tannic! SRG! Help me!" she screamed at the top of her lungs.

They were still standing outside of the door when they heard her scream. Without thinking, Tannic heaved up the Dragonwrigley and swung it. Sparks flew as the blade crashed into the metal door, and then it slowly creaked open. Danika came running out and into SRG's arms. The Minotaur stepped up to the door and looked at the three of them. It grunted before Tannic could raise the sword again, shook its head, and shut the door. They heard the latch click.

"Wow, I had no idea the Dragonwrigley would open the door," Tannic said in amazement. "I just reacted. Did we try that on World One? I can't remember now. I didn't think we could open it from this side."

"Me neither," SRG answered. "I don't think we ever tried that before. But here we are now, the three of us, on our own. I think we can assume the Minotaurs took Cody hostage."

"But what do we do now? I mean, there can't be three players in the game," Tannic said.

"Hey, we're all here aren't we?" Danika asked. "There isn't supposed to be a force field surrounding Mr. Eville's desk either, but he has one. He released special enemies on World Two that weren't even supposed to be in the game. Remember the Dragon Fish? Who says we can't have three players? Mr. Eville? The cheater?" she asked sarcastically.

"Well, we're all in this together, the Three Amigos," Some Random Guy boasted nervously as they fist bumped. "Come on . . . let's go."

Chapter 3

Dr. Denton's Incarceration

Dr. Denton looked up at his captor. He could barely make out the Minotaur's expression. It was dark in the dungeon. And it smelled. Of smoke from the fire pit, of sweat, and of Minotaur. But it smelled mostly of fear, his own fear. He thought about his nephew Cody and his lab. He thought about Mr. Eville and the citizens of Rough World. He thought about the sequence of events that had led him here. It was the three kids he had helped, Some Random Guy, Tannic, and his sister Danika. If they hadn't randomly shown up in his lab six years ago, he probably wouldn't be in this dungeon right now. But he had helped them, and they had given the people hope. They'd inspired a generation. He had no regrets. Even if he died now, he would do it all over again.

His thoughts were interrupted by a blinding flash of pain as the Minotaur struck him with the cat-o-nine tails. The cat was a short whip that had nine strands with knots tied in them. It was a cruel punishment that had been used first by navies and then adopted by pirates. It left a stinging pain and sometimes broke the skin, depending on how hard it hit. The Minotaur had swung it hard enough to get Doc's full attention and leave small welts on his back. They stung, and he broke into a sweat again. The beads ran down his face and burned in his eyes. He blinked hard as his vision blurred.

Doc was stretched out facedown over the rack. He was helpless. The Minotaur had used many forms of persuasion to get him to talk. But he hadn't said anything. He screamed out in pain when he needed to. But to Mr. Eville's dismay, he hadn't given up anything.

As he blinked sweat from his eyes, he looked around at the dungeon again. He couldn't see everything, but what he could see was enough to send chills down his spine. In the far corner stood a vertical rack with ropes and pulleys attached to it. In the center, a fire burned slowly, with what looked like branding irons heating in the coals. Along one wall, he could make out a line of doors covered in iron bars. He didn't know if he was the only prisoner or not. He hadn't seen or heard anybody else.

A rat ran across the floor in front of him. It stopped and quizzically cocked its head at him before scurrying onward and disappearing into a hole in the far wall. He blinked hard again to make his eyes stop stinging. His thoughts drifted to Mr. Eville.

Beezil had been a childhood friend of his. They'd been in the same class and on the same sports teams. They would play together after school and sleep over at each other's houses. They'd been inseparable. But that all fell apart after Beezil's father died. Beezil's family sold their house and moved to the bad part of the Jagged City. He'd been lonely and trapped in a mean environment, and things went downhill for him. He fell in with the wrong people. It wasn't long before he joined a gang and got involved in petty crimes. It was a pattern of events that repeated itself in every society: eventually he moved on to more serious crimes, and then he formed his own gang. They took control of the south side of the city, fighting for turf against the rival gangs.

It was about then that Beezil started using Minotaurs as enforcers. They were strong and lacked any real sense of morals. Right and wrong didn't matter to them, which was a real advantage for Beezil's plans. He kept gaining power, through brute force and intimidation, until the day he realized that true power lay in politics. When he finished school, he set his sights on the mayor's office. He fought a bitter campaign against the incumbent mayor, and in the end Mr. Eville prevailed. Rumors of cheating—fake voters, ballot-box stuffing—circulated for years afterwards, but the investigations all stalled out and nothing was proven. Of course, it was Mayor Eville who was investigating himself, and he found no evidence of wrongdoing.

From mayor he moved on to governor, gradually seizing more power until he finally just declared himself lord and ruler of Rough World. His Minotaur henchmen immediately squashed any potential rival or threat to his power, and he had been in complete control for years. That is, until Some Random Guy and Tannic showed up on the scene and completed World One. That was a defeat for him, but he had tricked them in the end, taking Tannic hostage and keeping a firm grip on his power. It would have stayed that way too, but a few months later Danika arrived in Rough World alongside SRG, and together they defeated World Two. Then Doc helped them outsmart Mr. Eville. But that was six years ago.

As word spread of their success, the three children had become folk heroes. They showed the citizens that Mr. Eville could be defeated. He was not invincible. And if three kids could defeat him, a well-organized militia of citizens surely stood a good chance. They had recruited Dr. Denton to be their leader. He was, they were sure, the smartest person in Rough World, and would know what to do and how to do it. And maybe he would have; but he didn't get the chance. Beezil's goons squashed the uprising like a bug on the sidewalk, and just like that the short-lived war was over. Then they came after Dr. Denton. The Minotaurs captured him in his lab and brought him to this dungeon. The uprising soon dwindled as the citizens faced a superior strength and a better-armed enemy. The Minotaurs were relentless, and everyone involved in the short-lived revolution died or were forced underground, constantly hiding from pursuit. They were just trying to stay alive until they could reorganize and make another coup attempt. And that was where things now stood.

Dr. Denton lay face down and thought about all of these events until he was interrupted again by the cat. He screamed as the nine tails stung his back and brought tears to his eyes. He clenched his teeth from the pain and then spit onto the floor.

"Anything to say yet? No? Well, don't worry, I'll get you talking soon . . . heh, heh, heh," the Dungeon Master laughed. "And if I can't make you talk, perhaps the good Captain Killbeard will get some words out of you. Heh, heh." He swung the cat back again, preparing for another round.

Doc was puzzled. "I thought he was dead," he murmured. "Who? Killbeard?"

"There's a headstone with his name on it . . . World Two."

"Har, har! And you believed that? He's very much alive, that I can assure you!"

Captain Killbeard was the most evil pirate that had ever lived, in Rough World or anywhere else. Blackbeard and Bluebeard looked like Girl Scouts compared to him. He was a liar, a cheat and a scoundrel. He would just as soon cut your tongue out than look at you. Then while you were reeling helpless on the ground, he would belly laugh and kick you with his wooden leg. Just the mention of his name brought a hushed fear to anybody in Rough World.

* * * * *

The door of Mr. Eville's office flung open and Darwood ran in. He was out of breath, and he stopped abruptly at the desk and blurted, "Sir, we have a situation!"

"Oh, what is it now, Durwood? The uprising is squashed. Dr. Denton is my prisoner. I have everything under control. What could be so urgent that you need to interrupt my afternoon?" Mr. Eville demanded.

Mr. Eville persisted in his little game of calling Darwood by the wrong name just because he could. He had a habit of doing little things to make sure you knew he was always in control. This bothered Darwood, but today wasn't the time to bring it up. "I just got word from World Three, Level 1, Sir. There are players in the game! It seems that some old trouble has returned. The Minotaurs that brought in Dr. Denton's nephew reported seeing a teenage girl in the lab when they broke in. She fled into Level 1, where two young men were already waiting with the Dragonwrigley. The Minotaur wasn't certain, but thought it looked like Tannic and that scoundrel SRG!"

"What? That's not possible! Call the Minotaur here immediately, Durwood! I want to talk to him!"

"Yessir," Darwood replied. He made the call on his cell phone, then turned it off. "He'll be here shortly Sir. He's already in the building. But if I might add, Sir, it has to be them. Think about it: they're in World Three. No one else has ever completed World Two, even though that was six years ago. So who else could it be?" He was interrupted by a knock, and the Minotaur walked slowly into the office.

Mr. Eville leaned forward in his chair behind his large walnut desk, a concerned look on his face. He stroked his chin. "Tell me what happened," he grumbled. This day wasn't turning out the way he had planned. If it really was those kids, he'd have his hands full. But he'd have a few surprises for them in World Three. *Oh, yes*, he thought to himself, *they haven't seen anything yet. They shouldn't underestimate Beezil Eville.*

"Well, uh, Sir, we broke into the lab and Cody was there, like you said. We grabbed him. But there was a girl there too. I didn't know who she was. I ran after her but she got out the door and into Level 1. I looked out the big door and there were two boys standing there too. They looked like those boys that beat all those levels before. One of them had the big sword. I closed the door and locked it. Did I do right, boss?" the Minotaur asked. He looked visibly strained to have spoken politely and clearly for so long.

"Yes, you did very well." He continued, almost to himself. "Hmm, so all three of them are back, are they? This is good. I'll be able to get rid of them for good this time." He let out a sinister laugh.

"Uh, Sir, isn't that a problem?" Darwood asked.

"Isn't what a problem, Durwood?" He frowned.

"The three—I mean, aren't there only supposed to be two players? How can all three of them be in there? What will happen?"

"Huh. I have no idea. It's never come up before. Must be a glitch in the programming. But it doesn't matter. This just gives me the chance to eliminate all three of them at once. It's perfect." He nodded with satisfaction. "That is all, you may both leave. Oh, and Durwood?"

"Yessir?"

"Keep me informed of events in World Three. No doubt they'll finish themselves off quickly enough, but let me know if I need to step in personally—I do have a few extra tricks up my sleeve."

"Will do, Boss!"

Darwood followed the Minotaur out and closed the door gently behind him. Mr. Eville leaned back in his leather chair, propped his alligator boots up on his desk, and surveyed his inner sanctum with pride. He had picked out everything in this room: the deep plush carpeting, the dark walnut paneling. His awards hung on one wall. The only thing that soured his expression was the Transport Chamber, the grim reminder on the far wall that somebody could defeat him and dethrone him by winning the game. But he would never let that happen. The Transport Chamber had only been used twice, more than six years ago now. He would make sure it wasn't used again for a long, long time.

The bottom drawer of the desk creaked as he pulled it open. He hesitated and glanced at his wristwatch before deciding to pour a drink. Then he leaned back again and sighed deeply. This was only a minor setback. And he would relish the opportunity to get even with those three. He'd waited a long time, and his revenge would be that much sweeter. And defeating them would send a loud and clear message to the citizens of Rough World. They wouldn't attempt any more uprisings, not soon, maybe ever. He pulled the cork from the clear glass bottle of Kimhomen, and poured himself a healthy dram. He raised the Glen Cairn whisky glass to his nose and inhaled the peaty aroma. Light danced in the amber liquid as he swirled the glass. He took a sip and savored it. *This will pass*, he thought. *I can relax. I have Dr. Denton, and nobody has ever defeated World Three. This will work out even better than I had planned.* A contented smile shaped itself on his face.

* * * * *

The dungeon master glared at his prisoner in frustration. The cat was usually very effective, but no matter how hard he worked his prisoner over with it, Doc wouldn't reveal anything about the uprising. Doc hadn't talked at all except for that one question about Captain Killbeard. It wouldn't do. Mr. Eville expected results, and his own reputation was at stake. He looked around the dungeon for a better method of persuasion, and his eyes settled on the branding irons heating up in the fire. He walked slowly and deliberately across the room, paused for dramatic effect, and picked one up. Its business end glowed an angry red. Turning it over in his hands, he looked up at Dr. Denton and smiled. His craggy yellow teeth shone in the flames.

"Still not talking, huh? Perhaps this little toy will loosen your tongue. Har, har!" He laughed as he walked back to Dr. Denton. He raised the iron and lightly brushed its hot end across Doc's face to make sure he understood what was coming next.

Doc closed his eyes and held his breath. The heat seared his face, and the pain was far worse than the cat had delivered. His mouth went dry and he coughed. His mind was racing. He wouldn't be able to keep this up forever, but he didn't want to give any information to Mr. Eville. He would rather die. But that was starting to look like where he was heading anyway. He just had to hold out as long as he could. At some point they would break him. The acrid smell of his own fear reminded him that he was just a scientist, not a secret agent trained to resist interrogation.

As he thought through his options, a second shadow grew next to the Dungeon Master's. He twisted his head, but he couldn't see who else had entered the room. His neck was stiff with pain from his time on the rack, and he couldn't hold his head up. He let it drop again, his muscles complaining loudly in his ears, and braced himself for the next pass of the iron. Then he heard a voice he recognized.

"Oh, Dinrod, is this really necessary? I don't want it. Truly I don't. But you're leaving me no choice. If you'd just be reasonable, we could end this now. I just need to know where the uprising's underground headquarters are. That's all. And you know I'll find out sooner or later. And when I find it I won't need you anymore. Come on, be reasonable," Mr. Eville urged.

"Beezil, listen." Doc's voice was gravelly. He coughed again and forced his head up. "I don't know anything. I'd tell you, but I was never invited to their meetings. I honestly don't know. I spent all my time at the lab. Please. I'd tell you, but I don't know anything. Please." He hung his head again in defeat.

"I'm so sorry that you insist on inconveniencing me. I was ready to let you out of here." Mr. Eville brought his head close and lowered his voice. "We both know you're lying to protect them. That's an honorable thing, truly it is, but is it worth dying for? Because that's the only option you're leaving for yourself."

Mr. Eville nodded to the Dungeon Master, who returned

the iron to the fire and picked up a fresh one. He walked back to Doc and ran the iron down his back, close enough to the welts to burn the skin. Doc screamed. His shrieks and the smell of burnt flesh filled the dungeon. Mr. Eville shook his head. The Dungeon Master brought the iron back to its starting point.

"Wait, wait!" Doc pleaded. "Okay, I'll tell you whatever you want to know, just stop, please."

Mr. Eville smiled. "That's more like it. You see? It doesn't have to be like this at all. We were friends once. Perhaps we can be friends again."

"I'll help you, but we'll never be friends," Doc spit out in disgust. "Never!"

"Well, I'm just glad you see it my way. Now tell me where the uprising is hiding out, and I'll stop the torture. I'll squash this little rebellion, take care of those pesky kids, and everything can go back to normal. Oh, I'll probably still need to keep you here for a while. Just as a precaution, but—"

"What did you . . . what kids?" Doc asked wearily.

"Oh, I'm sorry. Did I forget to tell you? It seems that scoundrel SRG and his little friends Tannic and Danika are back. They're lost somewhere in World Three as we speak. Soon I'll be rid of them for good. Har har! This is turning into a wonderful day!"

Doc's mind raced. It couldn't be. He hadn't heard from them in six years. What would they be doing here? Then it sank in. There was only one reason they'd have come back. Somehow they'd found out and they were here to rescue him. He took a deep breath and released it as he hung his head down in dread. He had no choice now. He would have to see this through.

"I'm afraid I misspoke." He coughed again. "I can't tell

you anything. I wouldn't even if I knew something. But if you kill me, you'll never find out at all. Not about the uprising, not about what I know about creating electricity. You can't win."

Mr. Eville sighed dramatically. "I'm so sorry to hear that, Doc. I really am. I thought we were getting somewhere. So long, Dinrod. It was nice knowing you." He paused. "No, I take that back. It wasn't nice, I was just being polite. You've chosen your own fate. Goodbye, Doc." He nodded to the dungeon master, and then the clack of his alligator boots on the stone floor was the only thing piercing the silence until it faded away.

"Well, my friend. It looks like we still have some work to do." The dungeon master returned to the fire to exchange irons again. When he brought the fresh iron in contact with Doc's back, the skin sizzled and Doc screamed as loud as he could. Then he slouched, and his world went black.

* * * * *

"Shh. Did you hear that?"

Danika and Tannic looked at SRG blankly.

"Hear what?" Tannic asked.

"I swear I just heard Doc's voice. It was weird."

"What did he say?" Danika asked.

"He didn't say anything. It was a blood-curdling scream, way off in the distance."

"I didn't hear anything, Compadre. Don't worry. It's probably just some strange bird we'll meet on this level. Have faith, Compadre. I'm sure Doc is fine. We just need to get through the first nine levels. Let's get with it."

Chapter 4

WORLD THREE LEVEL 1

The Grand Canyon

"**D**id you see anything else with the Dragonwrigley? A special weapon of any kind?" Tannic asked.

"I didn't really look. I was just trying to open the door without Danika noticing," SRG replied.

"So you admit it! You left me there on purpose!" Danika fumed.

"Listen Sis, it made me crazy watching you in World Two and not being there to protect you," Tannic confessed. "We both thought you'd be safer in the lab with Cody."

"Who says I need protection? I *carried* the Dragonwrigley last time! Anyway, the lab didn't turn out to be very safe anyway," she added.

"The lady has a point," Some Random Guy agreed.

"Okay, fine. Anyway, before we go any farther, maybe we should crack the door open again and take a quick look. In case there was another weapon."

"Good idea, Good Buddy," SRG said.

The door was behind them, just apparently hanging in thin air. You could walk around it on all sides, but to get back into the lab, you had to walk through it. And after a few minutes it would disappear and be gone altogether. They knew this from all of the previous levels in Worlds One and Two. Tannic hoisted the Dragonwrigley high over his head and brought the blade down against the door with all his might. Sparks flew, the latch gave way, and the door teetered open again. Some Random Guy stepped in and immediately stepped out again, now holding a rope with a grappling hook on the end.

Tannic's face turned white. "I hate heights," he moaned.

"No, no, Tannic, you're not afraid of heights. You're just afraid of hitting the ground. Remember?" SRG smiled.

"Something tells me I'm going to hate this level."

"We don't even know what it is yet. Come on, let's go find out!"

The trail they took wound through a rough and barren landscape. Sagebrush and a fine yellow grass carpeted scattered patches of the otherwise dry soil. SRG tried to remember if it was the white or the yellow flowers of Rough World sagebrush that were poisonous. He was fairly certain it was the yellow ones, but the last time he'd seen either was so long ago, back in World One, that he couldn't honestly be sure. He decided to avoid all the sagebrush, just in case. He didn't mention it to Tannic or Danika, so they continued in silence.

The sun was beating down from high in the sky, and it was hot. Tannic had the lead with the Dragonwrigley. SRG had the rope coiled over his shoulder and the hook in his right hand. Danika, in the rear, seemed deep in thought. But they were all on edge and keeping an eye out for anything that looked dangerous.

Eventually the trail led through a thin stand of juniper trees. They were little more than head-high, but even the sparse shade brought welcome relief from the sun. SRG was thinking random thoughts about sunscreen when the land opened out in front of him and the trail stopped abruptly at its edge. They halted. The view was breathtaking. Before them lay the largest, deepest hole in the ground they'd ever seen. It was miles across, and its sides revealed layers of rock in colors so bright and varied that you couldn't have painted it any prettier. It defied description. They couldn't see the bottom, but they could hear the sound of a river raging far below.

Tannic gulped out loud and just said "Wow!"

SRG wiped the sweat off of his brow, took a deep breath, and let it out. "It . . . it looks like the Grand Canyon. I mean, I've never been there but it looks like the pictures I've seen."

Danika looked up from staring into the chasm. "Wait a minute—have your grandparents been to the Grand Canyon?"

"No, I don't think so, I don't know. Why?—oh, wait," he said, remembering. "Don't start with that again. My grandpa didn't write this game."

"Well, you have to admit. It didn't make any sense, but it did seem pretty suspicious," she replied.

"What are you two talking about?" Tannic asked.

"Oh, back on World Two, I seemed to know things about every level because they were like places my grandparents had visited, and my grandpa had told me about them. Danika thought my grandpa must have had something to do with creating Rough World."

Tannic burst out laughing. "Are you kidding? I've watched SRG's grandpa play video games. He dies in the first level! Always. It doesn't matter which game!"

"I know, right? But she had me doubting it myself for a while."

"Well, I still think it seemed suspicious," Danika concluded.

"Just let it go Danika," SRG exclaimed.

"So what's the plan, Compadre?"

"I don't know. Where would you hide a Rainbow Star in the Grand Canyon?"

They looked across the vast expanse below them. It wasn't a promising question.

Finally, Danika spoke up. "A lot of them have been hidden in ruins or temples. Is there anything like that here?"

"I don't know. There are some native ruins in the southwestern part. What was the name of the people?"

"Anasazi," Danika replied. "Lucky I paid attention in history class. Maybe we should look for some of those ruins." She sighed. "It would have been nice if Doc were around. At least he could have filled us in about the levels."

"Yeah. We'll have to figure this out on our own. We have a rope and grappling hook. I'm guessing that means we need to climb down into the canyon. What do you guys think?" SRG asked.

Danika opened her mouth to respond and was interrupted by an arrow whizzing past her head. It stuck quivering into a juniper trunk. They all ducked and looked in the direction it had come from.

Within seconds another arrow arrived, and then a third almost on its tail. They lay sprawled out on the ground, panicked.

"What do we do now?" Tannic whispered.

"You have the Dragonwrigley this time," SRG replied. "See if you can get a clear shot at them. We'll look for a place to climb down, in case you can't. Wait." He paused, thinking. "Those last two arrows came almost at the same time. That means there's more than one person firing."

Tannic crawled back to put himself between his friends and their enemies. He gripped the sword tightly, the blade pointed toward the unseen foe. He inched forward on full alert for any movement in the brush. He didn't have to wait long. A juniper tree twenty-five feet away shook as a Minotaur tried to sneak past it. Tannic stood up and swung the sword toward the creature. A flurry of fireballs caught the beast mid-stride, and it collapsed to the ground. But before Tannic could react, he heard the next arrow. When he saw it, it was protruding from his chest. He looked at it, puzzled. It didn't hurt. It didn't even seem real. Then he watched as his body went limp beneath him, and then his world went dark.

SRG crawled to the canyon rim and found a spot to climb down. He was lowering Danika over the edge when he glanced back and saw Tannic take an arrow to the chest and fall to the ground. A Life Wedge glowed for a moment above Tannic's head and then faded away. SRG's mind flashed back to six years before, and the reality of what they were doing hit home fully. He shoved Danika over the edge and she fell ten feet to the outcropping below. He tossed the grappling hook after her. She picked herself up and started dusting herself off, and was about to yell at SRG when she saw the worried look on his face.

SRG wasn't sure what to do. He didn't have a weapon. Tannic was down. Then he saw the Minotaur sneaking through the brush. He didn't have a choice. He jumped over the edge and thudded down next to Danika. The Minotaur would be on them in seconds. He looked for a place to hide, but they were completely exposed.

"Why did you push me? What's going on?" Danika demanded.

"It was a Minotaur. Tannic is down. He lost a Life Wedge. We have to hide, quick."

"Hide? Hide where?"

"I don't know," SRG replied. He looked over the edge. It was at least a hundred feet straight down to the next ledge. It would take a coordinated effort with the rope and grappling hook for the two of them to reach it, and it would take much too long. They were running out of time. His heart was pounding as his mind searched for other options, but he didn't find any. He looked back at Danika. She was gone.

"Danika!" He hissed. "Where are you?"

"Right here, silly."

"No you're not. I mean, I can hear you." He looked around. "I can't see you. What's happening?"

"I'm right here. You can't see me? I'm—"

The shadow of the Minotaur interrupted her, covering them like a black cloud. It stood on the canyon rim just above them, dressed in buckskin leggings lined with fringes, a breastplate made of what looked like grass reeds woven in an intricate pattern, and a headdress of bright feathers punctuated with a small pair of antlers that rested between the Minotaur's own horns. It grunted, glaring at SRG, and nocked and arrow and pulled it full draw. SRG froze. As Danika watched, one of the Life Wedges above his head began to light up. The Minotaur released the arrow and at the same moment fell face forward over the cliff-side. The arrow sailed over SRG's head and into the canyon. The Minotaur dropped straight toward them. SRG and Danika jumped out of its way, and it crashed face-first onto their outcropping. Blood started pooling beneath it. A pair of sharp crescents protruded from its back.

Another shadow appeared slowly. This time it was Tannic.

"That was a close one, Compadre."

"Yeah, too close," SRG agreed.

"Where's Danika?" Tannic asked.

"I'm right here."

As they turned toward the source of her voice, Danika slowly materialized out of thin air. They both looked at her in amazement.

"Were you . . . invisible? Then you reappeared. How did you do that?" Tannic asked.

"I don't know. I just got really scared. Then neither of you could see me."

"It's just like a magic trick." SRG remarked. "The trick isn't over until they reappear."

"What random thing are you talking about?" Tannic asked with a confused look.

"You know, magic. Magicians will make something disappear, but you know the trick isn't over until they make it reappear," SRG explained.

"Okay, I get it. But I don't really believe in magic. It's got to be something else," Tannic answered.

"Yeah, it must be a glitch in the programming, or maybe it's some special power you get. There aren't supposed to be three players. Oh, that brings up another thing. I didn't notice it before, but there aren't any Life Wedges above your head," SRG said, turning to Danika.

"I see three above your head and two above Tannic's. But I don't have any?" she asked.

"No," the boys answered in unison.

"That's weird. What does it mean? Am I immortal?" she asked.

"I wouldn't count on it," SRG said. "But this could be handy. If you turn invisible every time an enemy shows up—or whenever you get scared—we could use it to our advantage."

"Yeah, that could come in real handy," Tannic agreed. "Except if you don't have any Life Wedges, what happens if you get killed? Maybe you don't get three chances. Maybe you're just gone permanently the first time. I don't think we should find out. Just disappear if things get dangerous."

"I didn't have any control over it, but I guess I can try. So now what do we do?" Danika asked.

Some Random Guy gave the Minotaur a kick. It didn't move. He picked up its bow and quiver.

Tannic frowned. "What are you doing? You can't carry any weapons in the game. I'm the main player and I have the Dragonwrigley."

"We're not supposed to have three players either, but we do. And Mr. Eville isn't supposed to do half the stuff he does, but he gets away with it. And I used a couple of the special weapons last time when Danika was the player, and it worked. I figure if we can make up new rules, we might as well take these with us. We won't know until we try."

"But you shouldn't be able to shoot them—" Tannic's comment was cut off as Some Random Guy nocked an arrow and let it fly far out over the canyon. "Okay, so much for that."

SRG grinned. "This is awesome. You have the Dragonwrigley, I have a bow, and Danika can turn invisible. I'm feeling good about this."

"It's still Rough World, Compadre." Then Tannic suddenly froze. He and SRG both stared at Danika.

"What? Why are you both looking at me like that?" she asked.

"Uh . . . Danika . . . you have . . . three Life Wedges above your head now!" SRG answered.

"What? How can that be? You both said I didn't have any just a second ago."

"I don't know. That's weird. It's like the game realized it had made a mistake and corrected it or something. Can that be? That's creepy!"

"It's Rough World Compadre. Anything is possible here, especially with a cheater like Mr. Eville."

"Yeah, don't remind me. Okay, so where were we? I think we should descend into the canyon and keep our eyes open. If I remember correctly, the Anasazi were cliff dwellers, so we'll probably be looking for ruins on the canyon walls," SRG stated. "Let's go."

They fixed the hook against a good-sized and solid-looking chunk of rock and tossed the rope over the edge. After a lengthy discussion, a moderate debate, and a short argument, they agreed that Tannic would descend first with the Dragonwrigley. Danika went next, followed by SRG, who had slung the quiver and bow over his back. They all arrived safely on the next ledge, which was still hundreds of feet above the bottom. They still couldn't see the river below, but it was louder now.

"Now what?" Danika asked. "How do we get the grappling hook back?"

SRG shrugged. "We have to pull it loose."

They started tugging on the rope together, but the hook didn't budge. They were about to give up when SRG snapped the rope hard and gave it a sharp tug. The hook broke loose and fell straight toward them. They ducked against the rock wall as tightly as they could, and the hook hurtled past them, taking the rope with it. SRG grabbed the free end before it vanished. The rope went tight and almost pulled him off of the edge, but he held fast and Tannic grabbed him around the waist. Then they hauled it back up and looked for another rock to attach it to.

"Let's try something a little smaller so it'll be easier to get loose," Tannic suggested.

"Yeah, that's a good idea. Look. That rock over there should work fine."

SRG pulled the hook tight against the back of the small rock. He gave it a good tug, tossed the free end over the edge, and looked down. The rope stopped about ten feet short of the next ledge. He gave it another good tug just to be sure, and then turned around to see horror written on Tannic and Danika's faces. Danika disappeared. And before SRG could open his mouth, he felt the bite on his leg. He looked down to see a large, scaly black snake attached to his thigh.

It hadn't been an actual stone at all, but a Rock Snake. Those reptiles warm themselves by coiling up into a ball in the sun, where they look just like rocks. Their venom is also extremely poisonous.

Tannic raised the Dragonwrigley and severed the snake's head with a swipe. It fell from SRG's leg, and Tannic kicked it off of the ledge and watched it sail through the open air. The snake's headless body writhed on the ground as a Life Wedge glowed brightly above SRG's head and then faded away. He collapsed to the ground face first.

When he came to, his head was in Danika's lap and she was lovingly stroking his hair.

"That was creepy. I hate snakes," he whispered weakly.

"Yeah, Compadre. In spite of all of our weapons and advantages, this is still Rough World. We can't take anything for granted." Tannic was shoving the rest of the snake over the edge with his foot.

"Now you're both down a Life Wedge, and I went from

not having any to suddenly having three," Danika said. "And we haven't even really gotten started on this level."

"I know, but we're going to do this. We have to. We're Doc's only hope," SRG insisted. His strength was coming back. "I could have sworn it was a rock, though."

They reset the hook on an actual rock the next time. They confirmed this by throwing a small rock at the big one first, and it didn't move. Then they lowered the rope again, and Tannic led the way down followed by Danika and SRG. This time they had to drop a few feet to the ground from the end of the rope, and then they realized they had a new problem. The end of the rope that they needed to pull free was hanging out of reach above them.

"That wasn't rocket science. What do we do now?" Danika asked.

"Simple. We stand on each other's shoulders and all pull on the rope at the same time," SRG replied.

SRG braced himself against the rock wall while Tannic climbed onto his shoulders. His arms came a couple of feet shy of the rope, so Danika climbed up both boys as though they were a human ladder and in no time had her hands wrapped tightly around the rope. Then she jumped off, Tannic grabbed her legs for added weight, and before SRG could help out the hook sprang loose and came bouncing down the canyon wall. They took cover again, and it came to a stop on the ledge next to them in a cloud of dust.

"This time let's make sure we don't hook it to a Rock Snake again," Danika said.

"Yeah, full agreement here." SRG shivered at the thought. "I'll be more careful this time." He threw some pebbles at another good-sized rock, and when it didn't move he carried the hook over, fixed it in place, and gave the rope a good tug.

Tannic and Danika, meanwhile, peered down at the rest of the canyon wall. There were a couple more ledges that might work, and after that it looked like they'd be able to free climb the rest of the way to the bottom. They continued down into the belly of the canyon ledge by ledge, lowering themselves with the rope and hook, patiently working the hook loose after each climb, to reset it and climb again. After a couple of hours, the slope of the cliffs grew less steep, and they stopped on a ledge from which they could see the river below.

"I think we can probably climb down from here," SRG suggested, studying the land below. "The river looks really fast, but I think there's a trail following it on our side. We can follow that and look for ruins."

"Agreed, Compadre," Tannic answered. Danika nodded as well.

So SRG coiled up the rope with the bow and arrows again. It was awkward, but he followed Tannic and Danika down the rock face to the canyon floor.

The river was thirty yards across and the current was strong and swift, with rapids and whitewater as far as they could see. After a quick vote, they decided to explore downstream first. They could see about a mile in that direction before the river took a bend to the left.

Tannic led the way, with Danika resuming her position in the middle and SRG bringing up the rear. They were walking in shade now, and the mist from the river was a welcome change from the day's heat. The canyon walls rippled in colors of every hue, and jagged rock formations jutted out from the cliffs. It would have been a beautiful hike if it weren't Rough World. And it did remind SRG of the pictures he'd seen of the Grand Canyon. His grandpa *had* shown them to him, but he wasn't going to bring that up now.

On either side of them were sagebrush and small cactus-looking plants. The cacti had sharp spines, and the trio avoided getting close to them, knowing full well they were probably poisonous. SRG glanced at their back trail routinely to make sure they weren't surprised by a Minotaur— or anything else, for that matter. The trail looked well used but empty now. There were no footprints or animal tracks, but the vegetation was definitely worn away and the ground was hard-packed. It was still slow going, as the ground was uneven and the trail wound through rocks and vegetation. There were a few Rock Snake false alarms along the way.

After an hour of slow hiking, they reached the bend in the river. They'd been straining their eyes for any sign of ruins, or of the Rainbow Star itself, but they'd found nothing.

SRG sighed out loud. "I don't know, maybe we're in the wrong place. This doesn't look promising. I mean, it's pretty, but we're no closer to getting out of here. Anybody have any other ideas?"

"I don't know either, Compadre, but I don't know where else to look. Maybe we should go a little ways further. If we don't see anything, we can always go back upstream and look in that direction."

"That sounds like a good idea," Danika agreed. She noticed SRG, who was looking up at the sky with a worried expression. "What is it?"

"The temperature's dropped. I just felt a cold breeze, and it's getting darker out. I think I didn't notice before because we've been in the shadows. But look." He pointed. "Dark clouds forming above us."

Before Danika could respond, the sky lit up and a shaft of lightning struck ground somewhere ahead of them in the canyon. Almost at once they heard the boom of the thunder. They looked at each other, and then a whole series of lightning bolts followed. Heavy rain began pelting them. They looked around for shelter, but the rain drops were huge and they were soaked within a minute. Danika covered her hair with her hands to keep her head a little dry, but not very successfully.

"Now what do you suggest?" Tannic yelled over the downpour.

"I don't know! We're all getting soaked, though—I don't see any cover. Maybe the storm will pass quickly!"

They edged down the trail hoping to find shelter, but the rain storm kept up solidly for another fifteen minutes. By that time, they were all soaked to the bone. Rivulets were running down the canyon walls, and the river was turning muddy. SRG was about to suggest turning around when a rumbling sound rolled down from upstream. Suddenly he looked panicked.

"Quick! We've got to get to high ground! I think we're about to get caught in a flash flood. Climb!" SRG shouted.

They scrambled hard up the canyon walls, but it was tough going. The rocks were already slick, and the dirt was loose and muddy. The twenty-foot wall of water hit them before they could climb high enough or form a plan, and next thing they knew, they were being sucked downstream and fighting for their lives against a furious current. Tannic bobbed long with the Dragonwrigley held tightly in one hand—he wasn't about to give it up. SRG was struggling. The bow, arrows, and rope made it hard to swim, but he kept his head above water often enough to breathe. He could see Tannic's head in the distance ahead of him, but he couldn't see Danika anywhere. He shouted, but the rushing water was too loud, and Tannic didn't answer. He fought to reach the shore instead, but something hit him from behind, forcing him underwater for a couple of seconds. He took it for a branch or log at first, but as it drifted past he recognized Danika floating lifelessly in the water. He reached out in a panic and grabbed her shirt sleeve and pulled her close. He tried to get her head above water, but she wasn't breathing or moving. He kept her close as the current bounced them along. He saw the ubiquitous Life Wedge glow above her head and slowly fade away.

A mile or more downstream, the current began to subside, and it washed all three of them into a back eddy against a small beach. The water was slack here but still mud-colored—it looked like hot chocolate with foam on the surface. The dark cloud gradually passed onward, the rain slowed and stopped, and the sun immediately broke through the clouds. They were on the same side of the river they had started on, just further downstream.

Tannic and SRG pulled Danika with them onto the beach. She wasn't breathing and didn't respond when they shook her. SRG quickly checked her carotid artery for a pulse but couldn't find one. He panicked and shouted CPR instructions to Tannic. He'd learned CPR while working summers at his grandpa's dental practice. He tipped her head back and she suddenly inhaled sharply with a loud gasp. Then she started coughing. This time when he checked for a pulse he felt a weak heartbeat. Tannic and SRG stared at her as she slowly opened her eyes.

They were now back in direct sunlight. The warmth felt good compared to their cold wet clothes, and they waited while Danika recovered. After a time, she sat up and looked across the river. Then she saw it. In plain sight, about two hundred feet above the river, a cave-like depression was visible on the cliffs. The ruins of buildings and ladders were highlighted by sunbeams. When SRG and Tannic followed her gaze, they gasped.

"That's the first promising thing we've seen," SRG commented at last.

"Yeah, at least it's a place to start," Tannic added.

Danika smiled sheepishly and nodded her head. She still felt too weak to talk. Nobody mentioned how close a call she'd had—how close a call they'd all had—but it hung over them like a dark cloud.

"We still have to swim across, though," SRG added. "The current's subsided, but it's still fast enough to take us way downstream before we get across."

"Yeah, no doubt. It's going to be dangerous." Tannic looked at his sister. "Danika, are you feeling strong enough to swim? We could leave you on the beach while we check it out."

"I'm not staying here alone, no way," she spat out.

"Do you think you can swim, though?" Tannic asked again.

"We tie ourselves together," SRG said suddenly. "That way we won't get separated, and we can help each other out. We can put Danika in the middle."

"I think that's a great idea. Danika?" Tannic asked.

Danika reluctantly nodded.

SRG tied the hook and rope to Tannic, let out twenty feet, carefully looped it around Danika's waist, and knotted it off. After about twenty more feet, he it tied around himself. They double checked all their knots and then walked single-file into the slack water like a chain gang with a long tail of rope dragging behind them. Tannic led the way, the

Dragonwrigley in his right hand. When the water was waist deep, he started swimming. The others followed suit.

Within a couple of minutes, they reached the current and were swept downstream, but they continued their slow progress across the current. The ruins vanished from sight, and they were just into the middle of the river when a large log drifted between Danika and SRG. It caught the rope and pulled SRG under. He kicked upward as hard as he could, struggling to break the surface. The water was dark, and he couldn't see, but he pulled hard against the rope. Then he ran headfirst into the log. Behind him, though he couldn't see it, his bow had caught on a branch. He didn't understand why he couldn't reach the surface, and he panicked as he ran out of air. His lungs were burning. Everything went dark.

Danika and Tannic watched in horror as SRG went under. They kept swimming, but the log dragged them further downstream and they couldn't pull away from it. Two Life Wedges appeared next to the log, just above the surface. One glowed briefly and then vanished slowly. Danika screamed. SRG had lost another Life Wedge, and he was still trapped under the water.

Danika tugged hard on the rope, but she was tired. The flash flood and the cold water had taken too much out of her. She screamed again, and yanked harder, and finally the log came loose and drifted off downstream. She and Tannic swam onward with everything they had, but SRG was now just dead weight for them to tow. It took several more minutes for them to reach the slack water on the far shore. Danika crawled up the bank on her hands and knees and coughed repeatedly. Then she puked into the sand. Tannic was already up and dragging SRG's body ashore behind them. Danika lifted herself up just in time to help roll him onto his back.

She sat down and put his head in her lap. She wanted to cry but didn't have the energy. Her lower lip was quivering. She bit it to stop it. She looked at Tannic. "This is all my fault. I should never have brought up Rough World. What was I thinking? I'm so sorry," she cried.

"Hey, don't blame yourself. It's not your fault. And once SRG knew that Doc was in trouble, there wasn't anything you could have done to stop him from coming here. You know that. He'd do anything for Doc, we all would."

"It's just—"

"Who died?" SRG cracked. He was looking up at the two of them. They were both drenched and had grim looks on their faces. There was an awkward pause before Tannic responded.

"You did, Compadre. It was that log in the river. Now you're down to one Life Wedge."

"Hey, it's not the first time." SRG sat up. He put a hand under Danika's chin and raised her head until her eyes met his. "We'll be alright. We have each other. We're a team. We'll get through this. Thanks for saving my life, by the way."

"I didn't even thank you for saving mine," Danika added. "So thank you, too."

"Okay as soon as everybody is done thanking each other, I think we'd better head back upstream and check it out those ruins before it gets dark," Tannic said impatiently.

"Yeah, you're right. We need to focus. We've got a Rainbow Star to find," SRG replied.

They stood up and untied themselves. SRG coiled the rope back up and looped it over his shoulder. Miraculously the bow and arrows were still intact. Then they got back into formation and Tannic led the way upstream. The trail on this side was much more used. It was wider and smoother, and they made good time to the base of the cliff below the ruins. The trail forked at that point, and they turned up a decent, if smaller trail, that led up the canyon wall.

When they reached the highest point they could climb to, they were all short of breath, but their clothes had dried out a little. At the trail head, the first of a series of wooden ladders led a couple of hundred feet straight up the cliff face.

"I'll go first," Tannic offered. "Hang on careful, and try not to wiggle the ladders. We'll just take it slow and we'll all get there. You guys ready?"

"Aren't you worried about the height, Good Buddy?" SRG grinned. "You could stay here while we climb up and check it out."

"Not a chance, Compadre. I have the Dragonwrigley, I'll go first. And I don't plan on looking down. I'm going to focus on the rung in front of me, and I'm only going to look up," Tannic replied. "So if something happens back there, yell." He tucked the Dragonwrigley down the back of his damp shirt, set his hands on either side of the ladder, and tested its strength. It didn't move. He stepped tentatively onto the first rung.

"I think it's safe. It feels like it. Just be careful."

"Okay, we'll wait until you get to the next ladder." SRG replied.

Tannic climbed slowly upward, gaining confidence with each rung. It wasn't long before he reached the top, where he stepped carefully to one side and onto the next ladder. When Danika saw this, she started up the first ladder, and by the time she reached the top, Tannic was on the next one beyond, so she continued her slow ascent. That was SRG's cue, and he climbed onto the first ladder. He looked down a few times as he climbed, and although he wasn't really afraid of heights, he decided that wasn't a very good idea and he quit it. It was already quite a drop to the canyon and the river below, more than enough to kill you if you didn't die of fright on the way down, and he didn't need to be reminded of the fact. Slowly but surely, the trio moved up the line of ladders toward the ruins.

Tannic was just reaching for the last ladder when the rung under his foot gave way. He grabbed desperately, but the short fall put him off balance and he lost his hold and fell. Danika screamed when she saw him fall, and SRG looked up. They gripped their ladders tightly and watched helplessly as Tannic plummeted past. He hit the rocks far below hard and bounced several times before coming to a stop. SRG could just make out the Life Wedges above his head and the faintly brighter glow as one of them lit up and then disappeared.

He took a deep breath and sighed. Tannic would still be alive, but they were both down to a single Life Wedge, and there would be no more margin for error. Not unless they stumbled upon a Heart Gem, but the odds of that weren't even worth considering. And they still didn't know how any of this applied to Danika. She had two Life wedges left, but technically she wasn't even supposed to be in the game. This was as a bad a spot as they had ever been in, and this was just Level 1. World Three was going to be a real challenge.

Maybe he'd made a mistake coming back. What had he been thinking? Had he forgotten how dangerous Rough World was? Had he forgotten his promise to himself? They should have just left well enough alone. He sighed. But he couldn't not help Doc once he had found out. That was no choice at all. On the other hand, he'd also dragged Tannic and Danika back into it with him. Now it was his fault.

All these random thoughts were racing through his mind at the same time, when he looked up and saw Danika frozen on the ladder above him. She seemed to be crying. He glanced down. Tannic had picked himself up and was climbing back onto the first ladder. There wasn't any room to pass. Danika would have to go first, and she was unarmed. His heart was pounding, but not as fast as hers.

"Danika! You need to keep climbing! Be very careful! Test each rung! But start moving now!" he shouted. He watched as she regained her composure and tentatively started upward again. When she reached the point where Tannic had fallen, she slowed down and cautiously climbed through the broken rung. A few minutes later, she was standing at the top among the first tier of buildings.

SRG tested every rung carefully. It slowed him down, but he couldn't risk a fall. Neither could Tannic. When he reached the fatal rung, he studied it closely. It hadn't simply failed: it wasn't anchored at all. It was a booby trap, a primitive security system built by the ancient minds that had dwelt in the ruins. And it was an effective one. He stepped across the empty space and soon joined Danika at the top. There was a slight breeze, and she was shivering in her still-damp clothes.

Tannic stepped off of the top rung a minute later. "Well, here we are. Where should we look first?"

SRG shrugged. "I guess we should just go through the place systematically. Each room, each level. If the star is here, we'll find it. Obviously we need to keep a look out for any Minotaurs or other enemies, and then there's always the Ender Dude to worry about."

They looked in every room. The buildings were well made, of clay bricks and straw, and still in good shape, but inside they found only remnants of the former inhabitants—a woven sandal in one, some broken pots in another. They continued upward level by level, carefully climbing the ladders and peering into the doorways. But they didn't find the star. An hour later, they stood together at the center of the top level, still having seen no sign of it, or indeed of any recent activity.

It didn't make sense. This was the perfect hiding place. But now they had to climb back down to the river and find another. And the sun was low in the sky. None of them cherished the thought of going back down the ladders in the dark.

"I would have sworn the star would be here," SRG muttered in frustration.

"Me too, Compadre. I would have bet your lunch money on it."

"Well, it's not," Danika said. "So we need to come up with a new plan. So what now?"

SRG kicked at the dirt floor in frustration. It was loosely packed, and when a handful of soil came free he picked it up and let it pour through his hands, thinking. He stood up, looked at Tannic and Danika, and opened his mouth to speak. Then he glanced down again and saw something strange. A glimmer of light that was too bright to be the evening sun reflecting off a shiny pebble. He bent down and clawed at the dirt floor with his hands. Rays of multicolored light burst through a small opening in the crumbling dirt. He continued to dig rapidly.

"A secret chamber. Of course. Why didn't we think of that?" SRG asked. "It has to be the star. Nothing else makes light of that color."

Tannic and Danika joined in. The floor was only about six inches thick here, and they quickly opened a hole large enough for them to pass through. Tannic ducked his head through, then lowered himself feet-first and dropped ten feet to the floor. He stepped to the side and looked up. "It's safe, come on down."

SRG was right behind him and wedging himself through the opening. He bent a bit and wiggled to get the hook, rope, bow and quiver through with him. As he fell and landed next to Tannic he realized he should have used the hook and rope, but it was too late as he moved aside just in time for Danika to land where he had been standing.

They stood in a small room filled with a gentle rainbow of light. The walls were clay, and so was the ceiling, except for a gap just large enough to crawl through. SRG had been lucky enough to kick just above that point. The air here was thick and smelled old and musty. The light poured through a small doorway on the far wall. They approached slowly, and Tannic spoke first, in a whisper.

"Be prepared for anything. We have no idea what the Ender Dudes will look like on World Three. I'll go first with the sword. SRG, you come next. Have the bow and arrow ready, just don't shoot me."

He disappeared into the opening, and SRG nocked an arrow and followed. They were both bathed in the full light of the Rainbow Star. SRG felt his spirits lifting. It had been six years since he last saw one, and he had forgotten how radiant and beautiful they were. The star sat on a stone pedestal in the middle of a small stream that poured out of one wall, crossed the room, and disappeared under the far one. This room was much larger than the other, and its four walls were made of rock, not the clay and straw of the rest of the ruins. It was deserted. Tannic and SRG looked at each other and couldn't believe their luck.

"Well, this is a first. The Rainbow Star, apparently unprotected. No Ender Dude," SRG said. He moved cautiously toward the star, Tannic right behind him, and stepped into the stream. Neither of them saw the wall move. An eight-foot tall stone cutout of a human shape broke free and moved like lightning. It was on them before they could react. Tannic tried to raise the Dragonwrigley, but the beast already had its huge rock hand around his neck. It lifted him into the air, and the sword clanged to the floor. He looked over and saw SRG already dangling from the other huge hand. His bow and arrow were on the floor as well. They'd never had a chance. The Ender Dude lifted them both up and started crushing their necks. It made a strange sound, almost like a freakish laugh, but rocks can't really make voice sounds.

Danika entered just in time to see the beast pick up SRG and her brother. The lone Life Wedges above each of their heads began to glow. She gasped and then saw the Rainbow Star. She dashed into the stream and straight toward it. The beast paused at the sound of her footsteps splashing in the water and looked about in confusion. There were footsteps in the stream, but no one was standing in them. It cocked his head as the Rainbow Star rose slowly into the air.

Chapter 5

WORLD THREE LEVEL 2

The Snow Biome

They were standing in Doc's lab. SRG and Tannic were staring at her.

"What?" she asked.

"Nothing!" SRG shouted. "I'm just glad you were invisible. We were goners. You saved us and got the star! That was awesome!"

"Why are you so surprised? Are you forgetting about World Two? I can handle myself!" she replied confidently.

"You certainly can," Tannic agreed. "That was amazing! I saw SRG's Life Wedge starting to glow, and I thought it was all over."

"Yeah, that was a close one. That Ender Dude was like nothing we've ever seen before," SRG noted with concern. "And this was only Level One. I think World Three is going to be a lot harder than we anticipated."

"So is everybody ready for Level Two?" Danika asked.

"I guess so," Tannic said. "Can we just sit here a minute and collect our thoughts?"

"Sure," she answered. "Hey, can we find out about the next level? How does Doc know what to expect, what the special weapon will be? He isn't here, but how did you find out before?"

"Well, when I was stuck here with Doc for those couple of months last time, we looked it up on his computer," Tannic replied. "Let's go have a look at it."

Halfway to the far wall of the lab, where Dr. Denton's computer had been set up, they stopped in their tracks. The computer had been torn open on one side, stray wires jutted out where parts had been ripped out, and the screen was broken. It looked like a car skeleton that had been through the crusher. They stood there in silence, the gravity of the situation settling on them.

Suddenly the main door opened and a young man in coveralls stepped cautiously inside. He didn't notice them right away, and he literally jumped when SRG spoke.

"Who are you?"

"Who am I? Who are you? What are you doing in Doc's lab?" the stranger asked. Then he paused and looked them over carefully. "Wait a minute—do I know you guys? Are you them? You are, aren't you! You're the ones Doc always talked about, the kids who inspired the uprising in the Jagged City. You're them! You're the players who defeated Mr. Eville in Worlds One and Two!"

"Guilty as charged," Tannic answered with a little swagger in his voice. "We came back to rescue Doc. Now you know who we are, who are you?"

"Oh, sorry. My name's Jody. I'm kind of Doc's repairman, and I keep an eye on the place for him. He told me if anything ever happened to him and Cody, I should come to the lab and get his hard drive and his laptop. And . . . well

. . . I guess you know what happened to him. Word has it that he's being held in the dungeon of the castle in Level 10. I was coming over here to check on Cody when I saw the same Minotaurs taking him away in chains, so I hid until the coast was clear. And, uh, now here I am."

"You're a little bit late," SRG lamented. "The computer's already been ripped up." He nodded toward it. "We were hoping to boot it up and find out more about World Three. But it's no use at all. They even shattered the screen."

"What about his laptop? Doc kept everything backed up on that. Did they get it too?" Jody asked.

Tannic and SRG exchanged glances. "That's right!" Tannic exclaimed. "He kept the laptop hidden under the mat in his office. He had a special compartment cut out of the floor! We haven't looked yet. We were just going to the main computer when you came in."

They all rushed into Doc's office. The desk was in disarray, and the filing cabinet drawers had all been pulled out and their contents scattered across the floor. It looked like burglars had ransacked the joint—which, basically, they had. But the way they'd torn the place apart showed they'd been looking for something. Doc's chair had even been tipped over and the leather cushions cut open.

Jody shook his head, bent down, and scraped the papers away from the mat in front of the desk. They stood back as he lifted it up to reveal a small trapdoor. He pulled that up too, and laid his hands on Doc's laptop. He pulled it out and showed it to the three players, wearing a huge smile.

"Looks like they didn't find everything they were looking for," he crowed.

"That's awesome, Jody!" SRG exclaimed. "We really need to learn everything we can—you know, special weapons, enemies, the themes of the different levels. Anything that can give us an edge."

"Okay—but I don't think it's a good idea to leave it here while you're gone." SRG, Tannic, and Danika took the news stoically but with concern written all over their faces. "But here's a better plan! How about I stay here with the laptop while you're all out there? Then we can have a look at what's next after each level. I could kind of fill in for Doc. How about that?"

SRG nodded slowly. "I like it, but what if the Minotaurs come back while we're gone? They'll take you and the laptop, and then we're right back where we started with no information at all"

"I'll deadbolt the door and put the laptop back in its hiding spot each time. Then I'll hide in the lab. If I'm not here when you finish a level, you'll know they got me, but they won't get the laptop. Maybe I can be of some help along the way."

They looked at each other and nodded in unison. "That sounds great!" Tannic said. "But aren't you putting yourself at risk helping us?"

"Well . . . kind of. But . . . I've never told anybody this before . . . Doc helped me when I was down and out. I pretty much owe everything to him. I'll take my chances. I couldn't live with myself if I didn't."

"We understand. That's why we're here too. We never would have made it home without his help. We came back just to help him," Danika acknowledged. "So that's it, then. We're a team, and we're going to defeat Mr. Eville and get Doc back!"

"I'm afraid that's easier said than done. I do know that Doc had major reservations about World Three," Jody added.

"What kind of reservations?"

"I don't know the details, but he had grave concerns about it. He would talk about it every once in a while. He really thought Mr. Eville should have shut it down. He even sent him an email warning him about it. That's all I know. Do any of you know his password?" Jody asked.

"I do," Tannic said. "At least, I remember what it was when I was here. He could have changed it."

"Only one way to find out, Good Buddy." SRG touched the power button and the green light came on as the black screen came to life and showed the password box. "What was it?"

Jody stopped him short. "I think it would be better if the rest of us didn't know the password. That way if anything happens, we can't help Mr. Eville break into it. We can't tell him what we don't know."

"But what if something happens to Tannic?" Danika asked.

"Who's the main player?" Jody asked.

SRG shook his head in realization and answered Jody's next question before he asked it. "Right. It's Tannic. If something happens to him, then the password doesn't matter. It's game over for all of us."

Tannic typed in the password, smiling at the random implication but keeping it to himself. The hard disk whirred and Doc's home screen appeared. His desktop showed the usual programs and a few icons that none of them recognized. But the document on World Three was full of information on all the levels, special weapons, and enemies—everything they would need to anticipate the dangers they'd face.

As SRG read through it, he noticed that the levels were based on seemingly random places from around the globe. If there was an overall theme, it seemed to just be the natural wonders of the world. He turned to his friends. Tannic had been reading over his shoulder, but Danika and Jody were too far away to do so.

"The next level is set in the arctic. It's labeled *Northern Lights: A Snow Biome.*" He read the description out loud. "Level Two takes place in the glacier lands of the far northern hemisphere where the Northern Lights are visible. The major enemies are the Inuit Minotaurs, who have the advantage of being resilient under extreme temperatures. They carry spears, bows and arrows and travel by dogsled. Other enemies include Boss Bears, which sound like Polar Bears on steroids, and Weevil Wolves. The Northern Lights in Rough World are actually produced by collisions between charged particles from the sun and the Rainbow Star. These cause the electrons in the atmosphere to move to higher-energy states, and when they drop back to normal states they release photons—in this case, a full rainbow array of photons." He paused, thinking. "The Northern Lights are also called *Aurora Borealis.* I've never seen the Northern Lights, but my grandpa has and my grandma has always wanted to. I think you have to go to Fairbanks, Alaska to get the best view of them. Anyway, I—"

Danika interrupted him. She had a suspicious look on her face. "First of all, very impressive. You're starting to sound like Doc. You should become a scientist too, if we ever get out of here. But second, did you say your grandpa has seen them? He's been to the Grand Canyon too, hasn't he?" Tannic and Jody looked confused.

SRG shook his head. "Don't start with that again, Danika! My grandpa has nothing to do with this game. Why do you keep bringing that up?"

"How can you tell me this is a coincidence? It's just like in World Two."

"What are you guys talking about?" Tannic interrupted. Jody leaned back with a curious look.

"Oh . . . back in World Two, Danika thought that my grandpa must have something to do with Rough World, because every level was a place he had visited and shown me pictures of, and they were all places we had studied in school, too. But that was fifth grade. Besides, my grandpa couldn't finish the first level of the simplest video game ever created. Danika, it *is* just a coincidence. Because my grandpa's been just about everywhere. Would you just let it go?"

"Okay." She shrugged. "It still seems a little too convenient. But I've said my piece and counted to three. I won't mention it again. But as soon as we get back home, I am going to ask him. So there!"

"Whatever," he sighed. "Okay, listen, there's more about this level. This whole thing is set inside a self-contained snow biome. I can't imagine how big it must be, but it means the game's programming actually controls the weather and temperature. And get this—our special weapon is actually clothing to protect us from the cold. It will get as low as minus forty Fahrenheit at night. So we'd best get it done during the daylight hours—when it will be a nice, tropical zero degrees. But here's the bad news. There's only two sets of clothing, I guess because there's only supposed to be two players. That'll make it interesting. We'll have to share if we all go in. On the bright side, there's a new feature on this level, a rare element called Frostium. It's like a Heart Gem, but instead of giving you extra Life Wedges, it makes you immune to the cold for a couple of hours. It's a crystal the size of a snowball, so if you see something like that, pick it up. And . . . that's about all that it says." He closed the file. "I guess we kind of know what to expect otherwise."

"Yeah—the unexpected. Oh, and everything is trying to eat us!" Danika spat out.

"Looking for the Rainbow Star under the Aurora Borealis sounds like hunting for the pot of gold at the end of the rainbow," Tannic noted. "I hope it's not a wild goose chase." He frowned. "I hope the Dragonwrigley works in freezing temperatures."

SRG was about to power down the laptop when a window popped up on the screen. The text box was framed by icicles, and inside it the word "Warning!" was flashing on and off. They all looked at each other.

"That's weird," SRG muttered.

"Open it up," Tannic encouraged him.

"Are you sure we should?" Danika asked. "I already feel like we're snooping in Doc's private stuff."

SRG hesitated a moment and then clicked. The box opened up a new document. It was an email from Doc to Mr. Eville.

> Dear Beezil: Something has come to my attention that you should be made aware of. I've been reviewing the source code for World Three and discussing it with your programmers. I know you're fascinated by artificial intelligence, but I have serious concerns about the design and extent of the AI system that's been implemented in this area. My suspicion is that the feedback system it operates could enable it to learn from the players as they proceed through the levels, and ultimately let it exert some control over, even alter, its own programming. If this possibility materialized, the AI system would be able do whatever it wanted,

and we'd be powerless to stop it. It could mean the end of the Jagged City and its citizens, even the end of Rough World as we know it. More importantly for you, I think, it could spell the end of your control over the evil empire that you cherish so much. I'd recommend that at the earliest opportunity you shut down World Three and instruct your programmers to rewrite it without artificial intelligence. The risk for all of us is simply too great. Please take my advice under serious consideration. As always, Doc.

"Whoa. So that's what he was worried about," Jody said slowly. "World Three has artificial intelligence in the programming."

"Well, what can we—" Another window popped up. SRG clicked on it. This one showed an email response from Mr. Eville.

Dear Dinrod: You pathetic little scientist. You need to get a life. World Three is perfect, and my programmers have made sure that the artificial intelligence will never have the ability to take control of the program. I will always be in control. You and the citizens of Rough World should know that by now. If this is a foolish attempt to distract me, you have failed. I will squash your uprising. You are a failure. You need to turn all your discoveries over to me, or I will squash you as well. I hope we understand each other. Good day. Mr. Eville.

"So there you have it. Doc was worried about the AI, and Mr. Eville wasn't. But we don't have a choice, regardless of who was right. We still have to go all of the way through World Three. Just power it down and let's go," Tannic commanded.

Jody shrugged and folded the laptop closed. He disappeared into Doc's office, and the trio walked silently to the door.

The Dragonwrigley waited faithfully in the corner. SRG sometimes felt like it was anticipating each new level, as if it were alive. Next to it, two full sets of parkas, pants, hats, gloves and mukluks hung from coat hooks. They were all fur lined and decorated with intricate beadwork. They looked like they belonged in a museum. SRG handed one set to Tannic and the other to Danika.

She frowned. "And what are you going to do?"

"When I get cold, Tannic will give me his set. When he gets cold, I'll give it back."

"And I'll just wear this set the whole time? That's not fair. I can share too. Do you think just because I'm a girl I can't handle it? I'm as tough as both of you!"

SRG started to speak, and Tannic stopped him. "Don't go there, Compadre. Trust me."

"Fine, Danika. When you get too warm, share your outfit with whoever needs it," SRG answered sarcastically. Tannic gave him a disapproving look.

"Whatever," Danika replied flatly.

"Hey, don't be such a girl!" SRG teased. He smiled and elbowed her. She reluctantly smiled back.

Tannic picked up the Dragonwrigley and opened the door. Snow blew in, and SRG shivered. They left the cozy confines of Doc's lab one at a time for the frozen atmosphere of the snow biome.

"What scares you the most about this?" Danika asked neither of them in particular.

"Seriously? All of it scares me," SRG replied.

"Not me," Tannic boasted. "These are just new levels.

It's the same kind of stuff, just more challenging. We've been studying ancient tribes in my anthropology class, and I think being captured by one of *them* is the thing that would scare me most! I mean, if I was going to be scared."

"I agree," SRG said. "They might be cannibals or just kill you for fun. That's creepy just to think about."

"Well, then I'm glad we're not dealing with that here. Oh, Tannic, I'm just curious—what was Doc's password?" she asked.

"Hah, I knew your curiosity would get the best of you."

"Oh, come on. If we get captured, it's over anyway. You might as well tell us."

He shrugged. "You're probably right. Doc was pretty clever, I thought. His password is 'Beezil.' He reasoned Mr. Eville would never think to try his own first name as Doc's password."

"That's pretty good," SRG agreed. "I could never imagine Mr. Eville trying his own name on Doc's computer—because I could never imagine Mr. Eville using Doc's name on *his* own computer."

They remained deep in conversation as they trudged on along the snow-covered path. The sky was a drab gray sheet above them, and the sun shone dimly through it. The air was brisk, and a light chilly breeze faced them head-on. The air held very little moisture in the low temperature, and the snow was firmly packed underfoot and squeaked slightly as they walked over it. SRG shivered, then put on a determined look as he leaned into the wind.

Tannic led the way, his hood pulled up to shelter his face from the wind, and took steady, careful steps. The Dragonwrigley seemed almost eager. The emblem on its hilt, a dragon centered in the circular labyrinth, flickered with green light and cast a faint eerie glow on the snow. Danika had her hood pulled up too, and was looking at her feet as she walked. SRG looked back once, and the lab door had already vanished. Whatever they were in for, they were committed now. There was no going back. He shivered periodically and rubbed his arms to stay warm, but he stayed right behind his partners as they weaved their way deeper into the biome.

He was still lost in thought when a demonic Minotaur rose out of the snow, disheveled and decked in frost and ice like a frozen ghost. But its dark red eyes and lumbering gait gave it a zombie appearance of some sort. Something undead. The creature charged at them.

It knocked Danika down with a single blow. Snow fell off of its arm to reveal a leather parka. Tannic tripped as he tried to draw the Dragonwrigley and fell backward into the snow. By the time he scrambled to his feet, the Minotaur was on top of him. SRG yelled and ran straight at the beast, driving his shoulder into the small of its back. He caught it off guard, and it stumbled a step and dropped Tannic. Then it let out a piercing growl, pivoted, and charged at SRG. He dashed away but made it only a few yards before the creature caught him. It grabbed him in one hand, hoisted him over its head, and screamed again with the same eerie growl.

Tannic was back on his feet and swinging the Dragonwrigley back and forth in short strokes. Sparks flew as a stream of fireballs sizzled one after another against the beast's parka. He was about to deliver a few crescents as well when the creature stuttered and fell face-forward into the snow. SRG landed on top of it and rolled off to the side. The creature jerked twice, stiffened sharply, and then relaxed. It was dead quiet as SRG picked himself up and started dusting snow off his clothes. Danika was still lying in the snow with a look of terror. SRG extended a hand and helped her up. Tannic seemed to be in another place.

They all rolled the body over together. It had an odd face, even for a Minotaur, but there was no mistaking it. They all smelled—or rather stank—the same. Danika made a face, and SRG started laughing.

"What's so funny? I just forgot how bad they smell, okay?" Danika responded.

"No, no, that's not it. I was just looking at its face. He kind of reminds me of that bus driver we had in middle school. You remember the one? You said he was an interdimensional demon who fed on the souls of little children and his name was Larry."

"Oh, yeah, the one we all called Larry," Danika smiled.

"Yeah, and we never knew his actual name, we just all called him that."

"That was pretty funny," Tannic agreed. "You do weird stuff in middle school." They all laughed. Then SRG shivered forcefully and rubbed his arms. Tannic looked at him in concern. "You want my parka, Compadre?"

"Uh, no . . . no, I'm f-fine," SRG stuttered. He was shaking forcefully.

"No you're not," Danika insisted. "You need to put on a parka right now and warm up. You won't be any good to us if you freeze to death."

"Hey, wait. Remem-m-member when we wore th-the . . . Inca robes?" SRG stuttered more slowly. "H-h-how about . . . if I w-w-wear . . . the M-m-minotaur's parka?"

"Great idea Compadre! It'll be really big on you, but it might make you smell better!"

It took all three of them to get the Inuit Minotaur's parka off, and Some Random Guy collapsed into the snow once.

But eventually Tannic and Danika got the coat onto him. He was still shivering as he stood up in his new garb. The parka reached to the ground, and the sleeves were so long that his hands were lost in them. He looked like a kid who had dressed up in his parent's clothes for Halloween. But he gradually stopped shaking, and he smiled as he warmed up. His face said that he was happy to be warm but didn't much like the smell of the Minotaur's hand-me-downs.

It was cold enough that they could see their own breath, and in the sudden quiet Tannic noticed that it had been gradually condensing into frost and icicles on the fur of his hood. He knocked them off. "I think we need to come up with a plan," he suggested.

SRG said, "I was thinking of what you said about gold at the end of the rainbow. If the Rainbow Star helps produce the Northern Lights here, maybe it really is hidden at the base of them. I don't know where that is. So we could walk in any random direction now and hope we're going the right way, or we could wait until dusk. Once we can see the Northern Lights, we can walk toward them."

"Maybe," Tannic said. "But maybe we can apply logic to the situation and figure out which direction to go right now."

"What do you mean?" Danika asked.

"Well, what's the one thing we know about Rough World?"

"Nothing is easy," SRG answered for her. "Ever."

"Right. And what's the hardest direction for us to travel?"

SRG grinned. "That's brilliant. It's hardest to walk straight into the wind. It's burning our faces and making our eyes water. I hate to say it, but you're right. That's the logical direction."

"That's what I was—" Tannic was interrupted by a

distant chorus of barking and howling.

They all looked around nervously.

Tannic said, "Dogs? It sounds like they're coming this way."

"What do we do?" Danika asked nervously.

Some Random Guy surveyed the area. The tundra was covered almost completely with snow. Only a few low bushes protruded from the white blanket, and some scattered spruce trees that were barely head high. "There's no place to hide, and we can't outrun dogs. I think we have to stand and fight," he stated.

"I agree," Tannic replied. He stood between his companions and the approaching sounds. "I'll try to dispatch whatever it is."

They didn't have to wait long. The dogs were getting louder, and finally they saw a shape on the horizon. It was moving from their left to their right, though, and it seemed like it might pass them by. Danika squatted down to make herself as small as possible. SRG lay down in the snow, resting his head on his hands as he watched the movement. Tannic crouched slightly, but stayed ready to attack on a second's notice.

The action on the horizon still looked like it would skirt by them, but it was getting closer. A team of dogs came into focus, mushing along with a Minotaur driving the sled behind them. Soon they could hear its shouted orders to the dogs. The trio stayed absolutely still, hoping to not be noticed.

The lead sled dog must have smelled them, as it suddenly turned the whole team toward them and started barking furiously. The Minotaur parka had probably given them away.

At first, the driver screamed at the dog, but then it lowered its hood and spotted the players. It shouted more directions and scrambled around for something in the sled as the team headed straight for Tannic, Danika, and SRG. The dogs were leaping and straining against their harnesses as they drove the sled forward, barking and howling in the wind. Tannic waited patiently, sword in hand. The Dragonwrigley seemed as excited as the dogs.

SRG looked at Tannic, and then back at Danika, but she was already gone, vanished as completely as before. It unsettled him a bit. But he whispered, "Danika?" and she answered "I'm here," and he nodded and turned back to the developing scene coming at them.

At a distance the Minotaur looked like some kind of ice man, but as it grew closer it looked more like an Inuit. It wore a sealskin parka and leggings with matching mukluks and gloves. The hood was lined with what might have been Weevil Wolf fur. It was long and covered in icicles too.

They were getting closer. The Minotaur cracked a short whip and the dogs suddenly charged harder. As soon as they reached striking distance, the driver abruptly spun the sled sideways to a stop and knelt behind it. He was digging something out of his packs. The dogs were still barking fiercely and tugging at their harnesses, and Tannic was shouting something but SRG couldn't hear him over the din. The sled was blocking the Minotaur from him, though. Tannic stood up straight and swung the Dragonwrigley high toward the sled. He promptly slipped on the ice and landed flat on his back, the sword on the snow next to him.

Struggling to right himself, Tannic watched as SRG rose to help and took an arrow squarely in the middle of his chest. He staggered forward and fell on his face, the arrow protruding from his back. A Life Wedge briefly illuminated the snowscape, casting bright reflections off the packed snow, and then faded away.

SRG was just groggily opening his eyes again in time to see Tannic rising from his knees with the Dragonwrigley in his hand. An arrow caught him just above the beltline, and he slumped back down again. This time it was Tannic's Life Wedge that lit up the landscape with a faint glow.

The Inuit Minotaur was fast on its feet. It lifted SRG out of the snow with one hand and studied the parka in rage. "Why do you wear Tocum's parka, foreigner? What did you do with my friend?" It suddenly hurled SRG to the ground, walked over to Tannic, and reached down for the Dragonwrigley.

And then it tripped and sprawled face down in the snow. SRG dove after it, jumped on its back, and pulled its hood down tight. The beast stood up, with SRG on his back struggling to subdue it. Danika was nowhere to be seen. Tannic was picking up the sword as the Inuit Minotaur danced blindly about in the snow trying to throw SRG off. When he touched it, the Dragonwrigley quivered and its labyrinth lit up brightly in green. He waited for a clear frontal shot and released a flurry of crescents. Some got caught in the dense leather parka, but enough made it through to complete their task. The Minotaur grabbed at its chest and fell forward. It kicked a couple of times and then stopped breathing. SRG let go and stood up. The dogs were still barking.

"Are you okay, Compadre?" Tannic shouted. His breathing was fast and rushing with adrenalin.

"I'm fine! Thanks, Tannic, you saved the day! Excellent work with the sword!"

"Excuse me very much," Danika taunted from nowhere. "But while the two of you were both dead, I tripped the Minotaur." She gradually re-pixilated in front of them. "You can both thank me now. I'm just saying."

"Huh, I thought it was kind of weird how he just fell over. That was quick thinking. Thank you, Danika. It looks like you saved the day," SRG corrected himself.

"It was quick thinking, Sis. Now we've lost a couple of Life Wedges, but we're not dead yet! Come on, let's keep moving."

"What about all this?" SRG gestured at the dog sled and the Minotaur's body. "Should we just leave them?" SRG asked.

"Have you ever driven a team of dogs? And I'm thinking the answer is no," Danika replied.

"So? There's no time like the present to learn. Besides, how hard can it be?" Tannic asked.

"Well, if we can figure out how, I'd be happy to ride. I'm not sure how easy that'll be," she answered.

SRG agreed. "Yeah, we could cover the ground a lot faster. Okay, let's at least give it a try. What have we got to lose . . . besides a couple of Life Wedges?" He smiled ironically. "And maybe we should take these with us. Just in case." SRG picked up the bow and arrows from the dead Minotaur and slung them over his shoulder. It was awkward with the oversized parka, but it worked.

As the trio walked cautiously to the dogsled, the dogs stopped barking and studied them. The lead dog whimpered as Danika crawled into the sled. SRG stepped onto the back of the sled runners and pushed his sleeves up to take the reins. Then it hit him. He looked at Tannic. "Can you cut these sleeves shorter for me with the sword? In fact, can you cut down the length of the parka while you're at it?"

Even with the large sword, it was simple enough to tailor the Minotaur-sized parka to SRG's human-sized frame.

He smiled as he pulled it back on. It still smelled like ripe Minotaur, but it was less awkward. Tannic got into the sled behind his sister, and SRG returned to the runners and took up the reins.

"Mush," he yelled, and the dogs pulled against their harnesses and the sled started to move. He quickly found that if he pulled the reins in the direction he wanted to travel, the sled would slowly turn that way. He took a step or two occasionally to keep the sled balanced, and they slid gracefully through the snow. The dogs seemed happy to be moving, and Tannic and Danika were happy to be riding instead of walking. It was cold out and there was a fine trace of snow in the air, but the visibility was good. After a couple of miles, SRG had gained enough confidence to try cracking the whip. The dogs barked and responded by pulling harder. He soon found that by leaning left or right in the direction the sled was traveling, he could keep it balanced. For a first attempt, he was doing pretty well.

They traveled in silence for a couple of hours. When he grew bored of the monotony, SRG would ask the others if they needed anything or had any new plans, then put his weight into it and cracked the whip again. The sky started to fade, finally, and in the growing dusk they began to make out the northern lights above the horizon ahead, a rainbow light show dancing against the clouds. Tannic had been right: they were headed in the right direction. He looked back at his friend and nodded his approval. Their plan was working. SRG cracked the whip again.

As it grew darker, the display became more extravagant. Great splashes of color illuminated the sky like fireworks. It was breathtaking. SRG steered the sled toward the most intense colors. He thought of his grandparents' party room, with its dance floor and laser lights, and all the fun times he had spent there with his cousins. The colors, he noticed, had grown bright enough to reflect in the snow in front of them. They had to be getting close. He pulled the sled up in front of a large white rock to make plans.

"What do you think we should do?" he asked.

"I think we should take a look from the top of this rock," Tannic suggested. "Maybe we can tell where the light is coming from. The Rainbow Star must be really close."

Tannic climbed out of the sled. As they approached the rock, they realized it looked more like a big heap or drift of snow. And as they started to climb it, it moved. It raised its head and looked at them with small red eyes. They scrambled backwards in fear.

The Boss Bear stood up and shook the snow from its thick, matted fur. It was huge. It growled once and then roared loudly. The dogs whimpered and pulled away, tipping the sled. Danika was once again nowhere to be seen. The bear lumbered cautiously toward them, swinging its head slowly back and forth. The dogs, trapped by their harnesses, growled in unison, the hair on their backs standing straight up.

Tannic stopped and drew the Dragonwrigley. He shot the bear with fireballs followed by a flurry of crescents. But the fireballs fizzled out, and the crescents got caught in the thick fur. The bear stopped for a second and watched him. It looked amused. Then it sniffed the air and moved its head back and forth, confused.

It could smell Danika but couldn't see her. In fact, she was right in front of it. She stood stock still as the snout passed within inches of her. Then the bear lunged at Tannic.

It was on him in a second and had his leg in its mouth. Tannic screamed as the beast tossed him back and forth like a cat playing with a dead mouse. The glow of a Life Wedge briefly outshone the rainbow in the sky. Then the bear pushed Tannic into the snow and started shoving him deeper with its snout. His lifeless form offered no resistance. The Dragonwrigley lay unattended where it had dropped.

The moment the bear went for Tannic, SRG slipped the bow from his shoulder and nocked an arrow. Tossing the fur-lined hood back, he calmly drew the bowstring to his cheek. It had only been a second, but the bear already had Tannic on the ground. He concentrated on the arrow and the bear as he released. The string snapped and the arrow hissed as it shot through the air. But the bear moved, and it fell short and buried itself into the snow just below the beast's belly. He nocked a second arrow. This time he took a slightly higher aim. The arrow found its mark and drove deep into the bear's body between its shoulders. Red blood stained the pure white fur, and the bear coughed and dropped Tannic. Then it tee-tered slowly and collapsed into the snow right on top of him.

SRG drew another arrow and walked up cautiously. The bear was badly hurt but not dead. Tannic was starting to stir. SRG dropped the bow and arrow and lifted the bear's head enough for Tannic to escape. In the distance, more dogs started barking. This time it sounded like a great number, as if multiple sled teams were headed their way.

Tannic stood up, recovered the Dragonwrigley, and raised it directly above his head. Then he brought it down with all his might on the bear's neck. The sword shivered in his hands as it cleaved through bone. Sparks flew, and the bear's mas-sive head tumbled free of its body. The sword felt alive.

SRG looked up from the two pieces of the dead bear. Beyond where it had been sleeping, at the bottom of a wide draw, the Rainbow Star sat atop a carefully balanced stack of large, many-colored rocks. A firestorm of light was flying out of the star and illuminating the entire sky.

Tannic followed his gaze to the Rainbow Star. "It's sitting on an inuksuk. A cairn that looks like a statue or a totem pole."

"Impressive. How did you know that?"

"Oh, just something I picked up in one of my classes," Tannic replied. He hadn't yet told SRG or Danika about his desire to keep studying ancient peoples.

They studied the Rainbow Star for a few moments, and then they noticed several dogsled teams on the opposite ridge starting down the slope toward the star. Suddenly it clicked. The bear had been the Ender Dude.

"What is it with bears and Ender Dudes?" SRG asked no one in particular as he hurled himself down toward the inuksuk, with Tannic right behind him. The dogsled drivers saw them and started scrambling faster toward the star themselves. It was a race now, and it was going to be close. When SRG stumbled and fell face-first into the snow, Tannic ran right by. There was no time to spare. SRG was back on his feet in a second and pursuing Tannic now. The first dogsled team was almost to the star when Tannic arrived, but the inukshuk was also much bigger than it had looked from above. They would have to climb.

The Inuit Minotaur jumped off of its sled, knelt, and raised its bow. Tannic drew the Dragonwrigley and took aim. The stream of fireballs and crescents missed their mark, but the arrow did not, and Tannic collapsed to the ground with the feather fletchings and wooden shaft jutting from his chest. A Life Wedge glowed briefly above his head as SRG ran by him.

The cairn was more than twenty feet tall and made of three rocks in a single stack. The middle one was much wider than the others, giving the whole the appearance of a bird with its wings spread, or a totem pole made of stone. Animals were carved all over them, but he paid them no attention except where they offered good footholds and handholds. He focused on climbing the carefully balanced structure.

The Minotaur had reached the base and was climbing up right below him. The two of them shuffled upward in a slow race to the top. SRG got his hand onto one of the wings and was pulling himself up when the Minotaur grabbed his leg and pulled heavily. SRG's grip on the rock started to slip, and the rock started to teeter.

Below, Tannic was staggering to his feet as the other Minotaur teams arrived. As the dogsleds drew up, the whole inuksuk started tilting, and then the rocks toppled over, dropping SRG and the Minotaur into the snow between them.

The fall knocked the wind out of SRG, and he watched helplessly as the Rainbow Star arced through the air and landed thirty feet away. Tannic and the other Inuit Minotaurs scrambled away in pursuit. But before they could reach it, it floated into the air of its own accord and hung suspended there. Everyone stopped for a moment, transfixed by the inexplicable event. SRG's mind raced. They'd never seen this happen before—was it because the Star was supposed to be atop the inuksuk? Would it remain above the ground until someone got it? Or—

Danika slowly re-pixelated, the Rainbow Star held high aloft in her right hand, the Northern Lights shooting out of it into the sky. She felt like she was holding the end of the rainbow. The next thing she knew, she was standing in Doc's lab alongside her brother and Some Random Guy.

Chapter 6

WORLD THREE LEVEL 3

The Australian Outback

"Wow! Are you guys okay?" Jody asked. "It looked really cold out there."

"Brrr. It was. But did you see Danika? That was awesome!" SRG answered.

"I followed you guys to the inuksuk, but I just got lucky. When the rocks tipped over the Rainbow Star flew right to my feet. I just had to pick it up. I held it up so you'd see that I had it." She grinned. "I forgot that I was invisible."

"Well, you stopped the Inuit Minotaurs in their tracks. Anyway, that level's over, let's move on. That was way too cold even with the parka, and I'll never get the stink of Minotaur out of my nose," SRG replied.

"We never did find any Frostium," Tannic mused.

"Yeah, I forgot all about that." SRG shook his head. "Let's get Doc's laptop out and see what we need to do next."

They returned to Doc's office and retrieved his laptop from the hidden compartment and booted it up. After Tannic typed in the password, the desktop icons appeared, and he clicked on Rough World Three and Level 3. The file that opened up was titled *The Australian Outback.*

"Ouch. That's going to be rough," SRG remarked. "No pun intended."

"Why do you think—wait, let me guess. Your grandpa has been there," Danika deadpanned.

"Uh . . . well, yeah. He said it was one of the roughest and most dangerous places he's ever visited," SRG replied.

"So what was he doing there?" Danika asked.

SRG shrugged. "He was hunting banteng and water buffalo. You know what he's like. The banteng is a wild cattle species from Bali. Grandpa said they're as mean as Cape Horn buffalo. Anyway, he said he went through swamps infested with crocodiles, and there were venomous snakes, green ants, jellyfish, and really nasty spiders. He got bit by a Huntsman spider, and he still has the marks on his knee. He said it swelled up to the size of a volley ball and went completely numb. And he had hundreds of green ant bites on his legs. Anyway—" SRG stopped and looked at his friends. He had been excitedly sharing everything he knew about the outback, and they were standing silently with concerned looks.

"Just a coincidence that your grandpa was there, right?" Danika remarked. "Still sticking with that story?"

Before he could answer, Tannic spoke up. "Uh, Compadre, this doesn't sound fun. I hate spiders. Snakes too."

"Yeah, sorry, I got a little bit excited and forgot what this means for us. I know it won't be fun." He shook his head. "I didn't even mention the Aboriginals. They're probably the best hunter-gatherer tribe on the planet. Anyway, sorry. Let's read up and get going."

There was a full page of notes and instructions for the level. They all leaned over Tannic's shoulders as he read out loud. "There are going to be Weevil Water Buffaloes, Boss

Crocodiles, Rainbow Jellyfish, Huntsman Spiders . . . and, last but not least, Aboriginal tribes. So we'll have some definite challenges here. It goes on to describe the environment. There will be ponds, or *billabongs*, and swamps. It looks like it's mainly a rainforest environment. And our special weapon is . . . a didgeridoo? What good is that?" He sighed. "There's no clue about the Rainbow Star's location."

"Which means it will be in a Billabong surrounded by crocodiles and jellyfish, and protected by a tribe of Aboriginals and an Ender Dude who kills anybody that plays a didgeridoo," SRG added with sarcasm for emphasis.

"You're probably right," Danika added. "Tannic, you've been taking that anthropology class. What can you tell us about the Australian Aboriginals?"

"Well, they're a pretty ancient tribe. Nobody's certain where they came from originally, but they settled in Australia about 45 thousand years ago. Their DNA shows that they broke off from European and Asian populations 65 or 75 thousand years ago. Some of their genes are associated with the Denisovan people, an Asian species related to Neanderthals. Anyway, they probably migrated from Southern Asia in bark canoes and then stayed put, which means they've lived in one place longer than any human group outside Africa. They might also have the oldest living continuous culture on the planet and did a lot of engineering to produce food. There used to be about 500 tribes, mostly near the coasts. Those ones irrigated the land and built dikes. Further inland they were hunter-gatherers and burned the undergrowth to control the plants. They hunted kangaroos and wallabies, and they used all kinds of wooden weapons, mostly spears, clubs, and boomerangs. They're experts at survival."

SRG looked at him wide-eyed. "You sound like Doc, Tannic. Like a real scientist. I knew Danika was into anthropology, but I had no idea you were so into it too."

"Well, Compadre, this was what our last test was all about. So I just studied the Aboriginals last week. And I really found them interesting, especially after talking to your grandpa."

"Oh, yeah, I remember that now," SRG replied. His grandpa was the only other person besides Danika that could also see Tannic. He'd learned that a few years earlier when swimming at his grandparent's pool. He wasn't sure, but he reckoned it was because his grandpa has the spirit of a kid.

"Anyway, one other thing is that they never developed the bow and arrow, even when it was being used all over the rest of the planet. Nobody knows why. Instead they developed the spear thrower. It's a kind of wooden shaft called an *atlatl* that attaches to the end of a spear. They would put feathers on the spear like a giant arrow, and they'd throw the atlatl forward to accelerate the spear and launch it really fast. Maybe it worked so well they didn't need bows and arrows? Or maybe it was more effective against kangaroos. Oh, and they also ate grubs and spiders and whatever they could find."

"Ew, no way would I eat a grub or a spider," Danika shrieked. "That's disgusting!"

"Never say never, Danika," SRG reminded her. "You never know what situation we might get into."

"It's interesting that you guys will have a didgeridoo," Jody mused. "I can't for the life of me imagine how it'll help. I wish Doc was here, maybe he'd know."

Tannic chimed in. "It's a woodwind instrument that makes a weird, haunting sound. And there's a trick to playing it so that you don't have to stop for breath. It was used in ceremonies by the Aboriginals. But I don't know what we can do with it either. I've never played one."

SRG broke in with a strange expression. "Okay, so, uh, I know this is going to sound a little suspicious, but my grandpa has a couple of didgeridoos. They're in his game room next to his pool table. We used to play with them when we were younger. He even showed me how to play them pretty decently."

Danika rolled her eyes.

"Well, at least that means you *can* use it if you need to. What else does the file say?" Jody asked.

"That's it," Tannic answered. "I guess the sooner we leave, the sooner we get back."

"Or the sooner we die," SRG added with emphasis.

They shut down the laptop and carefully hid it again. Jody lingered behind as the trio walked toward the outer door. Next to the Dragonwrigley stood a beautifully carved didgeridoo. It was painted with patterns of tiny dots in a rainbow of colors. SRG picked it up. It was about the size of his grandfather's didgeridoos, complete with a matching beeswax mouthpiece. He would definitely be able to make sounds come out of it—whatever good it would do them. As he lifted it he suddenly realized he was no longer wearing the parka—and more important, the bow and arrows had vanished. His mind was racing with expectations and worries as he held the door for Tannic and Danika.

They felt like they had stepped into a sauna. The air was hot and humid, and they started sweating immediately. They were definitely in the rainforest outback.

Some Random Guy wiped his brow. "Geez, one extreme to the other. I mean, I hate to complain after being so cold, but does it have to be this hot and humid?"

"It's Rough World, Compadre," Tannic reminded him. "Nothing is easy in Rough World."

"I know, you're right. And I know I volunteered for this. But it still makes me feel better to complain."

They stood in a small clearing at the edge of a forest. The vegetation was thick, and the canopy was pretty high. They could hear birds in the distance—not melodic songs, but angry, obnoxious squawks. Tannic pointed toward a small opening in the undergrowth. They passed in single file into the shade of the trees, then he pulled up and turned around.

"This is the northern coastal area, it's a rainforest zone. What should we do?"

"I don't know what we can do except go into the forest," SRG answered. "Proceed with caution and be on the lookout for anything. It reminds me of the Amazon Rainforest from World Two." He shivered in spite of the heat. "Since this is World Three, I guess it's even more dangerous than that."

"Me too," Danika agreed. "Creepier, too."

"Okay. Stay on high alert," Tannic said unnecessarily as he parted the bushes and stepped into the forest.

The remnants of an old trail led away in front of them. The bushes were starting to close it back up, but it was open enough for them to walk along fairly easily. They were sweating from the heat and humidity, but the shade offered a little relief. They hadn't gone far when Danika screamed.

Countless large green ants were crawling over her arms and legs, and she was already swatting at them furiously when SRG and Tannic joined her. It took only seconds, but by the time the ants were brushed off she already had bleeding welts all over her exposed skin and was growing pale. She fainted, but SRG caught her before she hit the ground.

A Life Wedge washed out the shadows for a moment before slowly disappearing.

Danika raised her head. "Thanks for helping me, those things really hurt. Maybe I should have been invisible," she said.

SRG gave her a half smile. "I don't think it would have mattered," he remarked. "They just drop off the brush, and you don't feel them until they take a chunk out of you. You'll be okay, but you lost a Life Wedge. They must be venomous too."

They sat in the shade for a few minutes, but they hardly had time to rest before the sound of a huge stampede thundered through the brush. It was moving toward them fast. Tannic stood up and raised the Dragonwrigley. SRG stood behind him with the didgeridoo, a bit uncertain what role he could play. As usual, Danika disappeared.

A Weevil Water Buffalo broke through the brush and charged directly at Tannic. Something like twenty more creatures were behind it. Tannic immediately began swinging the sword, delivering a torrent of fireballs and crescents that hit their mark but barely slowed the beast. SRG looked around but couldn't see an escape route. And then the lead bull was on Tannic, hooking him in its wide horns and tossing him in the air. He landed hard in the dirt, and the beast gored him in the thigh. He was struggling to swing the sword, but he was slipping fast. SRG watched the Life Wedge glow briefly above Tannic's head as he collapsed. The rest of the herd turned toward SRG.

Completely out of ideas, he raised the didgeridoo and blew. It made a sound like a foghorn, and the animals came to a halt. They pawed the ground and snorted, swinging their heads back and forth, but they seemed afraid to come closer.

Even the lead bull ignored Tannic and focused on Some Random Guy. It just stood there, turned away from Tannic, head low, ears forward in full attention and staring curiously at SRG. Shaking, he blew again, harder this time. The sound was louder and higher pitched, and it sounded evil and weird. The herd turned slowly away and started moving back into the brush. They weren't running scared, but they were definitely leaving the scene quickly. Tannic was back on his feet and held the Dragonwrigley high over his head with both hands, the labyrinth glowing brightly on the sword. He walked slowly up behind the lead bull and swung the sword down hard on the back of the bull's neck. It buckled as it dropped to the ground like a sack of cement.

SRG walked over to his friend and inspected the dead buffalo. It was almost black and had horns that stuck straight out three feet from each side of its head. It must have weighed a ton. He whistled and shook his head.

"That thing is huge!" he exclaimed.

"Yeah. And strong, Compadre. The fireballs and crescents didn't affect it much either. It got me good. I lost a Life Wedge, huh?"

"Yeah. But the didgeridoo seemed to scare the rest of the herd off. I wonder why?" SRG pondered.

"Maybe they associate it with humans," Danika suggested. She was still invisible but she joined the conversation anyway.

"Well, if they're afraid of the Aboriginals that spells bad news for us. I can't imagine those buffalo being afraid of anything," SRG responded.

"Whew, I hadn't thought of that." She reappeared. "This is going to be tough. We're barely into the rainforest and we've already lost two Life Wedges between us. And we haven't even seen an Aboriginal yet, or a crocodile, and we have no idea where to look for the Rainbow Star."

They walked further along the abandoned trail, sneaking through the overgrowth of leaves. It was still hot and humid, and they were all feeling the effects. But after an hour or so a cooler breeze washed over them. They stopped for a few minutes in the shade to rest. Then they continued until they came to another clearing. This one was a small pond of black water. The surface was dark and mirror-like. The bank was covered in animal tracks. They walked cautiously up to the water.

"Is this what they call a billabong?" Danika whispered.

"Yeah, I think so." Tannic was whispering too. "They're formed when a river changes course and leaves behind an elbow-shaped pond. See how it looks kind of like a dog leg? Sometimes they're seasonal and only fill up in the rainy season. They're common in the outback, and they're also commonly infested with crocodiles. Here it would be Boss Crocodiles, I guess. I wouldn't expect Rainbow Jellyfish, because it's freshwater, but this is still Rough World. But I don't see the Rainbow Star anywhere."

The crocodile was lying just below the surface, watching the movement of its prey. SRG was closest when it struck without warning. It lunged out of the water and grabbed his leg. He screamed and struggled as it dragged him back into the water to perform its rolling maneuver and drown him.

Tannic pushed Danika aside to take a clear shot at the giant reptile. His blast slowed the beast for a second, but not before SRG lost a Life Wedge. He hung lifeless in the crocodile's mouth as it dragged him under.

Tannic didn't hesitate. He rushed after them and got one swing in at the crocodile's neck before it could dive. The

Dragonwrigley quivered in his hand as it separated head from body. Then he pulled SRG from the dead crocodile's mouth and Danika helped drag him to shore. Before they could speak, a melee broke out in the pond. Several more crocodiles had appeared from nowhere to feast on their dead colleague.

SRG stirred and then sat up. "Sorry, guys. That was my fault. Classic mistake in crocodile country. My grandpa told me about it. Never stand close to the water, and never stand in one spot. Don't give them a chance to sneak up on you. I just wasn't thinking."

"That's okay, Compadre. At least we got you back. But now we've each lost a Life Wedge and we haven't really gotten started," Tannic replied. "Let's get moving."

They walked farther into the jungle. At one point they heard an eerie cry in the distance. It sounded like Doc's voice, and it sounded like he was in pain. They looked at each other and resolve showed on all their faces. Then Tannic led them on with renewed determination. They were going to rescue Doc and stop Mr. Eville once and for all, or die trying.

A while later, SRG tapped Tannic on his shoulder and they all stopped. He silently pointed out a small band of buffalo just visible through gaps in the brush ahead. They were feeding. The wind was in the trio's faces, so the buffalo hadn't noticed their scent.

"What now, Compadre? Should you blow the didgeridoo, or should we just try to wait them out?"

"I hate to make noise if we don't have to. There has to be some Aboriginal Minotaurs around somewhere, and I'd just as soon not alert them to our presence. I say we wait for a little bit and see if they move on."

But even as he spoke the wind swirled up and changed

direction, and one of the buffalo bellowed angrily. The herd charged off in one direction, but then they stopped and charged off into another. The wind was changing directions fast, seeming to blow every way at once, and the beasts could smell the intruders but couldn't tell where they were. Finally they came running directly at the players. Tannic raised the Dragonwrigley, but when it looked like the herd wouldn't be deviating, SRG put his mouth to the didgeridoo and blew. The sharp tone startled the buffalo and they stopped. They milled around for a few minutes, grunting and bellowing, and then finally moved away from the trio—once again not running, but moving swiftly until they disappeared into the thick vegetation.

"That was another close call." Tannic wiped his forehead. "Do you think they're gone for good? It wasn't the same herd as before. At least I don't think so. That herd was much bigger." He grinned. "You worked your magic again, Compadre. If we ever get home, you should consider taking up the didgeridoo."

"Thanks. But I don't think my mom would let me play that thing in the house. And if the knuckleheads started playing with it, we'd never hear the end of it."

"Yeah, don't give them ideas. They don't need any," Danika agreed.

They were still talking softly when a boomerang hit SRG on the head with a solid *thud*. He collapsed to the ground silently next to it. The boomerang was covered in asymmetrical patterns of rainbow-colored dots. Danika vanished. Tannic was opening his mouth to say something when the spear caught him in the center of the chest. He dropped the Dragonwrigley and clutched at the shaft with both hands, a look of panic on his face as he melted to the ground in a pile.

Danika stood frozen in fear as she watched two Life Wedges light up and fade away, one above her brother and the other above her friend. She stepped quietly back into the brush.

In a moment, SRG was on his knees and examining the boomerang. Voices were approaching quickly. He glanced at Tannic, who was still unconscious, and then stepped behind a bush as well. His heart sank as a large band of natives stepped into his sight and studied Tannic. They spoke in a rhythmic monotone with clicking sounds mixed in among the words. There seemed to be a debate going on. One of them picked up the Dragonwrigley and seemed very anxious about it. Two others picked up Tannic and pulled the spear from his chest. They looked on in amazement as he came back to consciousness and started struggling against them, but they were too many and too strong. He was alone, unarmed, and seriously outnumbered.

Some Random Guy stayed hidden as the band carried Tannic away. He felt guilty, but there was nothing he could do. He ran every scenario through his head, but he couldn't think of anything that might work. There was no way to rush in and rescue Tannic. They had the Dragonwrigley. His only weapons were the didgeridoo and a boomerang he had never used before. He looked at it closely. If you threw it correctly, it would arc through the air and come back to you. But he knew there was a specific trick to throwing it, and he had no idea what that was. And he didn't have time to learn right now. He jumped when Danika spoke.

"What are we going to do? They've got Tannic! Do you know what they were saying?" she asked, fighting back tears.

"I don't know Danika, but it seemed like a debate. I think they didn't know what to make of Tannic. And they acted like they'd never seen a metal sword before. I don't see how we can rescue him. We can follow them, but there's no way we can defeat them. I think we'll have to find the Rainbow Star instead. And we're going to have to find it fast. I have no idea what they plan to do with Tannic, but it can't be good. He only has one Life Wedge left."

"They're not cannibals, are they?" she whimpered.

"Not in the real world. But in Rough World all bets are off. Look, we've got to focus on finding the star, that's the only way we can help Tannic now. I don't think the didgeridoo will help. It would probably just let them know where we are. So we've got to put our heads together and use logic to figure out where the star would be."

"Okay. So what do we know about the Aboriginals? What would make sense to them? Where would they put the star?"

"The only things I know about the outback are what I learned from my grandpa. He's been all across the north of the continent, and he and Grandma visited Ayer's Rock and Kings Canyon with their friends from New Zealand." He paused. "That's a possibility. Ayer's Rock is a huge sandstone formation in the middle of Australia. It seems to change colors and glow at sunrise and sunset. I know it was sacred to the Aboriginals there. They call it Uluru. They've pretty much closed off access to it. Grandpa was disappointed he couldn't climb it, so they hiked around the perimeter of it instead. Well, that would be a sacred spot. But right now we're in a rainforest."

"Would it be just south of the rainforest?" she asked.

"Yeah, but like a thousand miles south or something. Across a desert. There's no way we could get there from here, Danika!"

"But that's the real world. We're in Rough World. Maybe

it's not that far here." She re-pixilated as she spoke.

He shrugged. "Well, it would be the logical place. But we don't know if Uluru is actually on this level, or how far it might be. I mean, I didn't see any big rocks on the horizon before we entered the forest. Did you?"

"No, but I wasn't really looking for one, were you?"

"No. You might be right."

"Do you have a better idea?"

"Not really. Actually, not at all. It's just that if we put all of our eggs in that basket . . . I just don't think we'll get a second chance. Tannic's already lost two Life Wedges. What if it's not here?"

"I think we have to take that chance. Come on, trust your instincts!"

"You're right. We don't have much time to waste, one way or the other. Let's go."

They turned back in their tracks and started through the dense vegetation in the direction they had come. SRG was in the lead, the didgeridoo in one hand and the boomerang in the other. He wiped the sweat off his forehead with his sleeve and they disappeared into the bush.

* * * * *

Tannic studied his captors as they dragged him into the village. They were large, tall, and slender for Minotaurs. They wore minimal clothing made of woven grass and reeds. They were also covered with red dirt or clay, and their long hair was matted. Their village was a cluster of crude huts made from sticks and mud, with large dried leaves thatching the roofs. The large central plaza had a small fire burning in the middle. They tied him securely to a post next to it. They continued to speak in their own language, and he had no idea what they were saying.

A very large Minotaur emerged from a hut, and the others addressed him as they presented Tannic to him. The apparent leader examined Tannic closely, carefully touching his clothes, skin, and hair, and finally the Dragonwrigley. Then he put the sword down and spoke to the gathering in their strange language.

"I have seen no human that looks like this, and I remember no stories from our ancestors describing such a creature. It could be a spirit, good or evil. It might bring great abundance to our clan, or it might bring death and starvation. It does not appear powerful, but it carries a strange weapon that shines like the sun reflecting off the billabong. I believe that we should sacrifice it."

One of the hunters spoke up. "Elder, we killed it once already. Ndbodi threw a spear with his atlatl that drove through the creature's chest. It was dead, but when we removed the spear it came back to life."

"It is not natural," Ndbodi concurred. "It returned to life. Perhaps we cannot kill it. Or perhaps we can burn it with fire. If we roast it and eat it, maybe the power it possesses will be transferred to us."

The leader frowned. "This is a grave concern. It must be an evil spirit to have powers like that. We should convene a council of elders from the other clans to decide how to deal with it." He gestured as he finished, and four natives ran off in different directions into the bush to gather them. "We must keep it under careful guard. The council will convene when darkness covers the earth, and we will judge how to destroy the creature."

Tannic watched them closely. They were definitely

discussing him, even if he had no idea what they were saying. This was his greatest fear, being captured by a primitive tribe. His imagination ran wild, with the darkest of options for his future. Where were SRG and Danika?

* * * * *

Some Random Guy pulled the branch aside and held it as Danika passed. They had been walking for almost an hour.

"Do you think we're close to the edge?" she whispered

SRG looked up and shrugged. Then he spotted the buzzards circling in the sky. He shot a new look at Danika.

"What is it?"

"Those buzzards. They're circling above something dead, and I'll bet it's the first buffalo we killed. That means we're heading in the right direction, and we're getting close."

"Good. This rainforest gives me the creeps. Let's hurry."

They moved swiftly until they reached the edge of the forest and stepped suddenly into the sunlight. Now there was nothing but dry, desolate bush ahead of them. Scattered cacti and thorny bushes were intermixed with low dry grass. The land looked parched. There were no clouds, and it was late afternoon. In an hour or two it would be dark.

"I don't see anything. Let's head straight away from the forest. It looks like there's a ridge in the distance. Let's find out what we can see from there."

"I'm right behind you, Compadre. Let's go."

They half-walked, half-ran across the open land. The ground was sandy and soft, and it was hard to move quickly, but they kept going. Still, it took them almost an hour to reach their goal. The air was much drier out on the plains, but the tradeoff for the humidity was the direct sun overhead.

They were both sweating profusely as they climbed around the rocks. By the time they topped the slope, they were exhausted. But SRG whistled when he could finally see what lay beyond.

"Danika! You're not going to believe this," he exclaimed.

"What is it?"

"You were right! It's Uluru! And it's covered in a rainbow of light!"

She sat down next to him and exhaled hard. Another long hike still separated them from the Rainbow Star. Finally she said, "Come on, let's go. It's might be dark by the time we get there. I just hope Tannic is okay."

"He's fine. Remember, he only has one Life Wedge left. If they kill him, we'll be instantly transported to Doc's lab. As long as we're still here, we know that we've still got a chance."

"In that case, last one to the rock is the one to climb it!" she yelled as she hurtled down the slope. SRG was on his feet in a second and right behind her. Carrying the didgeridoo and the boomerang, it took him a few minutes to catch her. Then they kept up their pace until they were halfway across the plain. Uluru grew steadily larger as they ran.

When they stopped to catch their breath, he asked, "Hey, what do you call a boomerang that doesn't come back?"

Danika shook her head. "I have no idea."

"A stick!"

"Hah hah, good one. If I weren't so tired I'd laugh." She shook her head.

"Sorry. I was just trying to lighten the mood."

"I know, and I appreciate it, but let's just go. At least one of us still has to climb that rock."

They kept a steady but slower pace for the next half hour

and reached the base of the rock. It was huge, maybe a thousand feet tall. And while it was a big shapeless form seen from a distance, up close it was covered in ridges and caves, paintings and waterfalls. It looked beautiful as the fading sunlight mixed with the rainbow light from the star above. It seemed to change colors continually. They both momentarily forgot everything else.

SRG reached the rock face first and touched it. He looked back at Danika, about twenty feet behind him. She slowed down as she approached.

"Looks like you're climbing the rock," he teased.

"Really? Remember World Two? I'm not really good with heights."

"Yeah, I know. I can leave you with the didgeridoo and the boomerang while I climb." He studied the face for logical route up. A few holes cut into the rock looked like perfect footholds and handholds. He was about to start when a large Aboriginal Minotaur covered in body paint consisting of tiny dots rounded the corner and spotted him. Danika immediately disappeared, and SRG dropped the didgeridoo and took off running. The Minotaur was in hot pursuit.

"It must be the Ender Dude! I'll distract him! Climb, Danika! Climb!" he yelled as he ran away.

Danika hesitated as she looked up the slope. It was steep. Everything depended on her now. She put her hand into a hole and carefully pulled herself up. She caught her foot in a lower one, and then she started climbing, one hole after another. Somebody had obviously cut these spots into the rock to be able to climb it, but that somebody was much taller than she was. It was a stretch at times just to reach the next hole. But she clung tightly to the side of Uluru and slowly edged her way up.

SRG looked back over his shoulder. The Minotaur was gaining on him. He looked down at the boomerang in his right hand. He panicked and threw it at the Minotaur. It swooped right past the beast's head, and then it circled around and came back after SRG. He ducked as he heard it coming. It landed right in front of him, but he didn't have time to pick it up. He ran right over it and figured he would have to think of something else. The Minotaur slowed down a little and SRG managed to keep a safe distance, but he couldn't slow down or stop. He didn't know how long he could keep the pace up.

Danika kept climbing without looking down. She was halfway up the rock. The sun had already set below the horizon to her right, and the low angle of its last rays danced across the sandstone. She could make out the rainbow light better now. It looked like the star was directly above her. *That would make sense*, she thought. They would have made these steps so they could climb to something important. She stopped to catch her breath for a moment. Then as she reached for the next step, her foot slipped. She screamed and hung on by one hand. For the first time, she looked down. She couldn't see past the rounded slope below her, but she could see the ground beyond that, and it was a long way down. She froze, hanging there in suspension.

SRG kept running in and out of the trees around Uluru. He leapt across small dry stream beds and kept running. The temperature had dropped considerably since the sun set, and it would have been comfortable if he weren't running so hard. But the Minotaur was undeterred and keeping pace.

Danika regained her footing and took a deep breath. She started talking to herself, half out of fear and half to keep her mind off what she was doing and the distance to the ground below. She crawled up the mountain slowly but steadily, bathed in the rainbow light.

SRG darted around a tree and caught his foot under its root. He fell hard on his face. Before he could catch his breath, the Minotaur grabbed him by the arm, pulled him up, and started marching him away. He fought back and swung his other fist at it, but the creature was too big and too strong. It didn't seem troubled by him at all. Before long it dragged him into a clearing with a small campfire burning next to a few crude huts. A dozen Aboriginal Minotaurs of all ages and sizes watched as his captor led him into the light. They spoke in a strange language with odd clicking sounds. He couldn't understand them at all, but he had realized one thing. His captor wasn't the Ender Dude. The Ender Dude was still ahead of Danika.

* * * * *

The elders from the surrounding villages arrived just as the sun was setting and darkness was blanketing the village. They studied Tannic and the Dragonwrigley individually, clicking their tongues and shaking their heads. The leader signaled them to sit, and they squatted on their heels in a semicircle around the fire. Then the leader stood up and spoke.

"Elders. You have seen the spirit and its weapon. I am convinced that we must destroy the spirit in the fire. It must be an evil spirit, and we must destroy it before it brings bad things to our clans. What do you counsel?"

The elders slowly nodded their agreement.

"Then it is settled. We will build a great pyre around the creature and set it ablaze. Gather the wood."

While he didn't understand a word that had been spoken,

it was obvious to Tannic what was about to happen. They piled firewood around him until it was waist high and stuck the Dragonwrigley into the pile next to him. If only he could get his hands free. If only he could reach the sword. But he couldn't move, and he knew it was too late. He thought about his sister and his best friend. He would never see them again. He would never see SRG's parents again, or the knuckleheads. They had become his real family. He should have spoken up. They should never have turned the game on. But after that, it was too late. Doc was in trouble, and they didn't really have a choice. And now they had failed. He bit his lip and resigned himself to his fate.

The leader stood up as the clanfolk started playing didgeridoos. Others began beating sticks in a rhythm, and chanting. The sound was haunting and raised the hair on Tannic's neck. Then the leader walked ceremoniously to the fire and picked up a stick that boasted a large flame. He carried it toward Tannic and set it at the base of the woodpile near Tannic's feet. The music stopped, and the Minotaurs cheered in unison. Then they started chanting again. He could feel the heat on his legs. He wanted to scream just before he fainted.

* * * * *

Danika crawled over the edge to the top of the rock. A narrow trail led along the spine ridge, just wide enough for her to walk on. It was all up to her. She didn't know where SRG had gone. She could only assume that Tannic was still alive because she was still in the level. She stood upright. A slip in either direction and she wouldn't stop until she hit the ground. She contemplated that as she drew a deep breath and walked toward the rainbow light.

As she reached the first summit, she stopped in her tracks. Sitting next to the Rainbow Star with his knees crossed was a huge Aboriginal Minotaur. He wore a woven robe patterned in colored dots. He looked asleep. But he opened an eye as she approached. She looked at her hands, but she couldn't tell if she was invisible. She was scared to death, though, so she should be. She took a deep breath and walked forward as slowly and as quietly as she could. She would have to skirt around the Minotaur to reach the star. That is, if he didn't see her first.

* * * * *

SRG was being held down by two large natives and surrounded by others. He couldn't move as they argued. They tugged at his hair and spit in his face. He struggled and kicked against them, but it was no use. He wasn't ready to give up, but he was overpowered. In his heart he knew, it was over, they had failed.

* * * * *

Danika tiptoed around the Ender Dude. She started to slip, and reflexively grabbed at his robe to steady herself. He stood up instantly, knocking her down. Then he swung about and grabbed at the air, looking confused. Danika rolled over and stood up. She took two quick steps and grabbed the Rainbow Star.

* * * * *

The heat and pain had brought the evil spirit to its senses. It was choking from the smoke, but it screamed as it looked toward the leader, who was standing closest. The leader spoke. "See, elders! The evil spirit will be consumed by the fire. We have made the right—" He stopped in midsentence as the boy and the sword vanished into thin air.

Chapter 7

WORLD THREE LEVEL 4

The Andes Mountains

The three of them were standing in Doc's lab, Danika holding the Rainbow Star. Jody looked like he'd had a heart attack.

"What happened?" Tannic asked. "I thought I was a goner. I'll never forget how hot those flames were! Where did you guys go?"

"Sorry, Tannic. We realized we couldn't save you, so we knew our only hope was to look for the Rainbow Star," SRG answered.

"SRG was brilliant!" Danika exclaimed. "He figured that the Rainbow Star would be in a sacred place, like Uluru. So we headed south to look for it, and it was right there, just like he thought!"

"Well, that wasn't exactly what happened. We did find Uluru, and the Rainbow Star was on the top of it. But just as I was about to climb it, a Minotaur spotted me and I had to run to distract it from Danika. I thought it was the Ender Dude, but I was wrong. So what actually happened?" he asked Danika.

"When you ran off, I realized I would have to climb, so I did. I wish I could say it was easy, but I was scared to death. Which was lucky, because I was invisible. When I got to the top I spotted the star, but the Ender Dude was sitting next to it. I snuck past him and grabbed it. End of story! I mean, I grabbed his robe first. So it was close. But we're here. We did it!"

"You guys had me scared to death. Tannic being lit on fire, SRG taken captive, and then when you slipped, Danika . . . " Jody's voice trailed off.

They all looked at Danika, and she shrugged and smiled. "Hey, I made it, didn't I? It's all good. Come on, let's feel good about this, guys. I'm fine, really."

"It's just, if anything happened to you . . . " Tannic said softly.

"Well, it didn't. So cheer up. I'm not dead yet!" she admonished them. "Come on. Let's see what's next. We're on a mission here. Stay focused."

Their conversation was interrupted by a knock at the door. They all looked at each other in fear. The knock repeated. Tannic, SRG, and Danika retreated quickly to Doc's office while Jody went to the door.

"Who is it?" he asked.

"It's me, Kent. Hurry up, open the door, I've got the stuff."

"Kent?"

"Yeah, it's me, Kent! Come on, open the door."

"Uh . . . Kent's not here, man," Jody deadpanned.

"No, I'm Kent! Hurry up, open the door, I've got the stuff."

"Kent?" Jody asked again.

"Yes, it's me, Kent. Open the door."

"Uh . . . Kent's not here, man."

"Okay, that's really funny, Jody, but come on, open the door. The pizza's getting cold," Kent said.

Jody unlocked the deadbolt and opened the door with a big grin on his face. The trio were all laughing at the exchange as Kent brought the scent of warm, oven-fresh pizza into the lab. He set the boxes down on a bench while Jody locked the door.

"Jody called me and said you guys might be hungry, so I had Melanie cook these up for you. I hope you like three-cheese pizza. The other one is smoked salmon. It's like magic!" Kent explained.

"Ooh, three-cheese is our favorite!" Danika answered eagerly.

SRG just stood there with his jaw hanging open. Danika grabbed a slice of the cheese pizza while Tannic looked on longingly.

"Are you going to eat or what, Compadre?" Danika asked. "Are you okay?"

"Huh? Oh, uh, nothing. Yeah, I'm fine. It's just that . . . oh, never mind."

"Never mind what?" she probed.

"It's nothing, really, never mind. I'm fine." Three-cheese pizza was his favorite, and he would definitely have a slice, but he tried the smoked salmon first. He didn't realize until he bit into it how hungry he had been. The pizza was outstanding. It really was like magic. But his mind was focused on the bizarre coincidence. He was thinking about Kent and Melanie, her "magic kitchen," and the trip they took to Hope, Alaska, with his grandparents every year. There it was again, his grandpa. What did his grandpa have to do with this? He shook his head. Was this just random? It didn't make sense.

"Thank you so much, Jody! This was a great idea! I was really hungry. It looks like we all were," Danika said. "And thank Melanie too. Her pizza is unbelievable. I've never had smoked salmon pizza before."

"Yeah, thank Melanie too" SRG mumbled. He still had a dazed look on his face.

"Well, I thought you guys could use a little break. Thanks, Kent. I owe you one. But you'd probably better take off now. It's dangerous to be here."

"Okay, I'll be off. But if you need anything, call me, all right?" Kent offered.

"Will do!" Jody replied.

Jody bolted the door behind Kent and rejoined the trio in Doc's office. They opened up the file for Level 4, and Tannic read aloud.

"Level Four is the Southern Andes." Then he stopped and looked at his friends. "We've been to the Northern Andes, in Peru. Remember the Sacred Valley and Machu Picchu? This is the other end of the same mountain range. Does anybody know much about that region?"

The others shook their heads no. Then SRG mumbled, "My grandpa—" before he could stop himself. Then he raised his eyebrows, shrugged, and stood there sheepishly.

"Don't worry. I'm not even going to go there," Danika teased.

"Okay, then," Tannic started. "I studied it in the winter term. Several tribes live there. The primary ones are the Yamana. They're hunters, mainly preying on members of the llama family like alpacas and guanacos. They've lived there for more than ten thousand years. The Ona tribe live at lower elevations. They're more aggressive and constantly fighting for territory. The Selk'nam people live near the ocean. All the tribes are nomads—they don't keep permanent shelters. They make small huts out of sticks, and leather that they carry with them as they travel. The women dive into the ocean for shellfish every day. I can't imagine how they do that in the Antarctic Ocean. The men hunt seals from canoes—they don't learn to swim, though." He smiled. "Most of what we know about them comes from a guy named Lucas Bridges who was the son of a missionary and was raised with these tribes. I did a report on the book he wrote about them, although obviously I didn't hand it in."

"That sounds really interesting," SRG said. "I'm still amazed at how much you've gotten into this anthropology thing. You're really good at it, I can tell you that much."

"Thanks, SRG. On top of all that, it's a very harsh environment. It's mostly cold, wet, and inhospitable. There are a lot of extreme geographical features, like archipelagos, fjords, mountains, glaciers, and icebergs facing the Pacific Ocean. The Strait of Magellan is the roughest water on the planet. I guess that's appropriate—it is Rough World. And Cape Horn is the southernmost point of the continent. Oh, and there was once a prehistoric creature bigger than a bear there called the milodon—because it had so many teeth."

"This doesn't sound like a fun place either," Danika observed. "We go from being overheated in the Grand Canyon, to freezing in the Snow Biome, to burning up in the Outback, and back to being frozen again."

"Well, that's what I know. Let me read what the file says."

"Yeah, what's our special weapon?" SRG asked.

"Level Four is the Southern Andes. Let's see . . . fjords, glaciers . . . rough water . . . primitive tribes . . . Aha! . . . who all fight for territory and control of the Rainbow Star. The star could be located with any of the tribes. There will be Boss Alpacas, Weevil Guanacos, and the biggest enemy the Boss Milodon. This will probably be the Ender Dude. The special weapon for this level is an oyster basket. Pretty much what I expected."

"What in the world is an oyster basket?" SRG asked. "And what are we supposed to do with it? Are you kidding me?"

"Oh, yeah, it's what the Selk'nam collect shellfish in. It sounds like somebody's going swimming." They both looked at Danika.

"Oh, no! No way! I am not swimming in freezing Antarctic water!"

"Well, it can't be as cold as I was in the Snow Biome," SRG responded. "Never say never, Danika."

"Yeah, yeah . . . I know, it's Rough World!" she replied coldly.

"Remember why we're here. We heard Doc's screams on the last level. He needs us. We've got to do whatever it takes."

"If you guys are ready, I say we get out there and find the star. Doc will never give into Mr. Eville's demands, and we know what that means. We need to rescue him before it's too late," Tannic offered.

At the door, SRG picked up the oyster basket. It was about the size of a purse, crudely but tightly woven with a lid that closed with a stick and a loop. He shrugged as he looked up at Danika, and they stepped through the door.

The view was breathtaking. The distant mountains looked like jagged edges torn from rock, and they jutted up against a brilliant blue sky where a few thin clouds danced in the breeze. Surrounding the mountains were rolling hills covered in lush, knee-high grass sprinkled with wildflowers of every color. A few birds circled high above, and herds of wild Weevil Guanaco roamed in the distance. Each herd had a single "sentry," Tannic told them, keeping an eye out for predators. A guanaco in the closest herd barked loudly. The trio ducked to avoid being seen, but it was too late. However, rather than attack them, the entire herd disappeared over the hill.

"That was weird. I expected them to come after us," Tannic pondered out loud.

"Maybe they're not mean man-eaters on this level," SRG suggested.

"Or maybe they're not running from us. Maybe there's—" Danika's comment was cut short by a herd of Boss Alpacas bearing down on them. The alpacas were twice the size of guanacos and they were running forward with bared teeth and sharp hooves.

Tannic hardly had the Dragonwrigley up in time for the first wave. He swung wildly back and forth, sending bursts of fireballs and crescents at the beasts. They went down with each hit, but there were still more coming, and they just jumped over the prone beasts. SRG looked at his oyster basket, shook his head, and stepped behind Tannic. Danika pixelated and disappeared in his peripheral vision. Then the herd was upon them.

The lead alpaca knocked Tannic to the ground, and he dropped the Dragonwrigley. He scrambled for it but took a hard kick from its front hooves. A Life Wedge glowed above his head and faded. Watching that, SRG didn't see the alpaca that hit him from behind, and then he was on the ground too. He tried to reach the Dragonwrigley himself, and the same alpaca kicked him hard and knocked his breath away.

Danika watched in horror as her brother and best friend

were overwhelmed by the herd of Boss Alpacas. She stood helplessly by as still more of them approached from over the ridge.

Tannic came slowly to. SRG was motionless next to him, with several alpacas taking turns kicking him. Tannic reached for the sword and swung it at the alpaca that was just about to bite his leg. The beast fell to the ground, but before Tannic could stand up another one was upon him. The alpaca kicked him in the head and his world went dark again.

Danika was about to scream herself when she heard an eerie scream above her. She looked up to see several large birds circling above them. She took them for eagles or other birds of prey at first, but as she watched she realized that they were vultures of some sort. They must be condors, but they looked much bigger, and there hadn't been any mention of condors in the briefing. The flying monsters sailed gracefully on the thermal currents and were so large they looked like small aircraft as they floated down closer and closer.

Then one swooped silently down, picked up a dead alpaca in its claws, flapped its broad wings twice and lifted off with no apparent effort. The presence of the giant bird scattered the herd. They ran off, barking with every step. The remaining birds swooped down and picked up their own dead alpacas in turn, and then as quickly as they had appeared, they were gone.

Danika walked over to Tannic and SRG, who were both sitting up and shaking themselves off.

"That was horrible!" SRG exclaimed. "We were goners if not for those birds. What were they? They came out of nowhere!"

"They looked like giant condors. There would be condors down here, wouldn't there?" Danika asked.

"Yeah, it would make sense, but they weren't mentioned in Doc's file. Maybe they're another surprise monster that Mr. Eville cooked up, like the Dragonfish in World Two."

"It's weird they didn't pick one of us up," Tannic noted.

"I don't know. If you're a hungry bird, there's a lot more meat on one of those alpacas than on either of us."

"That makes sense. I guess we shouldn't count on being that lucky again." Tannic stood up. "Those alpacas came out of nowhere. We need to keep an eye on our back trail so we don't get surprised again. Now we've each lost a Life Wedge!"

"Except for me," Danika declared as she reappeared.

"Yeah, yeah, except for you . . . whatever," SRG responded. Danika shot him a glare.

Tannic interrupted the developing storm. "Where do you think the Rainbow Star is? Any ideas?" he asked.

"Well, I've been thinking," SRG said. "Don't you think it would make sense that the Ender Dude is a Boss Milodon?"

"If the Ender Dude is a Boss Milodon, which I'm willing to bet he is too, I'm thinking they generally lived in caves. The fossils of them have all been found in caves, and in the pictures I've seen they looked like giant bears on steroids. And the best place to find caves is probably those mountains on the horizon. I'd suggest we start by hiking there," Tannic replied.

"I'm game. We'll have to be cautious in these hills, though. Every time we cross a rise we might run into the guanacos or alpacas," SRG added.

"Agreed. I say we approach each rise slowly and peer over the top to make sure it's clear. Then we can run downhill and on to the next one. You follow me, and Danika you bring up the rear and keep a lookout behind us."

The trio moved purposefully down through the next draw and then slowly crept to the top of the rise, crawling in the grass until they could see the next valley in front of them. When they were sure the coast was clear, they ran to the next rise and repeated the exercise.

Rise after rise the group moved, running, then crawling, then running again. There was a light breeze blowing down from the mountains into their faces that would keep them from accidentally giving away their presence. The sun was a third of the way up in the sky, and the wildflowers were fragrant and added a dangerous sense of safety to the meadows. It was like being in your grandmother's flower garden, except there were hidden man-eaters and other unknown creatures waiting to kill you. There was no kindly old lady perusing about, tending to her blossoms, and if there were, she would probably want to kill you too. This was Rough World, after all.

By midday they had reached the base of the mountain range without any more mishaps. The mountains were even more rugged than they had looked from the distance. Up close, they were giant spires of black and brown granite. Two jagged peaks in particular looked like horns and reminded them of Mr. Eville's hair. They all noticed and laughed at the idea. But they only saw one cave, and it would take a while to reach it. So without hesitation, they started up the hill. There were no enemies in sight and they were beginning to feel pretty confident when disaster struck out of nowhere.

The first arrow pierced Tannic's chest and sent him reeling forward onto his face. Instantly they were surrounded by a band of native people. SRG raised his hands into the air, a universal sign of surrender, as Danika became invisible. The Ona warriors approached him cautiously with arrows drawn.

He watched as another Life Wedge flickered out above Tannic's head. Then someone behind SRG's back grabbed him by the arm. Startled, he jumped. And when he did so, he leapt right over the warriors standing around him. While the warriors stood in stunned silence, shocked at what SRG had just done, he hit the ground and literally ran for his life.

It took a few seconds for the Ona warriors to collect themselves and send a group to pursue SRG. By that time, he had a good lead, and they were running across sharp rocks in their bare feet. When SRG risked a quick glance back, they looked like kids at the beach trying to walk across hot sand. They were dancing awkwardly as they moved forward. He chuckled to himself and started looking for a place to hide. When the warriors were out of sight, he crawled up to a small opening in the rocks just above him. It was a tight squeeze, but when he pushed himself through, he found that the crack opened into a small chamber. He sat down in the dark, trying to quiet his breath and listen for the warriors. Eventually he heard them moving and shouting in the rocks below. He waited patiently, and after a few long minutes he could no longer hear them. He waited a few minutes longer just to be safe and then peered out through the opening. The light outside blinded him for a moment, and then he jumped and bumped his head on the rocks when Danika spoke.

"Whew, that was close!"

"Ouch! What? Danika! You scared the daylights out of me! How long have you been here?"

"Sorry. I was right behind you. I thought you knew I was here."

"How? You're invisible! Never mind, I'm happy to see—uh, to hear you. Since you're still invisible, how about going outside to make sure those natives are gone?"

"Sure thing, Compadre." SRG felt the air move as she passed by him in the chamber.

A minute later, she was back. "They're gone. It looks like they gave up and returned to the main group. The bad news is they still have Tannic. What do we do now?"

"Let's try for that cave we saw earlier. It's not far, and we're not much help to Tannic at this point. My intuition tells me we need to find the Rainbow Star fast."

They left their hiding spot and followed the base of the mountain to the cave. It sat just above a cliff and was definitely big enough for a very large creature. SRG led the way as they climbed through the rocks on their hands and knees to the bottom of the cliff. He wiped his brow and looked up. The cliff went almost straight up for about thirty feet. He now knew that he could leap high, but the cliff was probably too tall. Instead he studied the cracks and outcroppings, and after a few minutes he found what looked like a route he could climb.

"Now what? We climb this rock face?" Danika sounded nervous.

"I can jump high, but not that high. We don't have any choice. Just follow me, put your hands and feet exactly where I do, and be careful!"

SRG grabbed the first handhold and pulled himself up. He extended his left arm for the next one. Then he moved his feet up one at a time. It was a slow process, but he was scaling the face with Danika right behind him. He kept looking up and shouted encouragement down to Danika.

"You can do it Danika! I'm almost there. Keep coming."

There was no response. He paused and looked down for the first time. He saw Danika lying in a heap at the base of the cliff just as a Life Wedge glowed and faded away in an all-too-familiar pattern. He held fast as she got up, dusted herself off, and started up again. *This girl's made of steel*, he thought. In a few minutes, she was right below him again, and he proceeded upward. After a few more steps, he pulled himself over the top and stared directly into the dark abyss of the cave. As Danika reached the top he turned back and pulled her up. They stood in silence. A cool breeze was coming out of the cave, but neither of them understood the significance of it.

"You go first." Danika prodded SRG in the back.

"Yeah, don't worry." He feigned confidence. "I have my trusty oyster basket with me in case we run into trouble! I'll use that to protect us!" He paused for a long moment. "Right now, I wish I had an ugly stick."

That brought a laugh from Danika, and feeling heartened he turned and advanced cautiously into the darkness, giving his eyes time to adjust as he moved. Danika was hanging onto his shirt and breathing rapidly. The air inside was cool and had a salty taste. When their eyes adjusted and they could see the interior, they both took a deep breath. The ceiling was high and arched, and the floor was broad and flat and strewn with rocks and boulders. There was no sign of the Rainbow Star or the Boss Milodon, though. So they ventured further in, and as they did the breeze grew stronger. It was dark, but just light enough for them to see each other.

"Now what?" Danika asked.

"I don't know. I thought . . . well, hoped, the Rainbow Star would be here. I don't know what we would have done about the Milodon, though. I was hoping I'd figure out some use for this oyster basket. Now that we're here, maybe we should see where it leads. The breeze is coming from further inside, so there has to be another opening somewhere. And it smells like the ocean, but it might just be a salt deposit. Are you game?"

"Yes. Let's go." A gust of cold air blew in their faces and Danika shivered.

* * * * *

Tannic's captors were small, maybe six inches shorter than him, bare-chested and barefooted, wearing little more than fur loincloths. None of them had facial hair, but they had rusty red stripes painted on their faces and long black braids of hair on both sides. Most of them carried bow and quivers of arrows tied to their waists. A few of the taller ones carried spears and shields. They spoke in a quick foreign language and clicked their tongues. He couldn't understand what they were saying, but they seemed to be arguing. He knew he was the subject of the debate. At least, he thought with relief, they weren't Minotaurs.

The leader spoke loudly over the rambling debate. "We must take the prisoner back to camp and decide what to do with him there. We're still in Yamana territory, and we don't need a conflict with them today. Let's move quickly and quietly!" he ordered.

The debate stopped and the warriors took Tannic along the base of the mountain range. Their leader carried the Dragonwrigley and admired it, although it was too big and heavy in his hands. Tannic looked the group over for a clue to the Rainbow Star, but he saw nothing. He was plotting his escape strategy when the inevitable happened.

The Yamana warrior screamed as he descended on the Ona tribe. They were caught off guard as more Yamana warriors came out from the rocks and grass. The Ona were outnumbered and laid down their weapons in surrender. The Yamana dressed like the Ona but wore guanaco capes over their shoulders and simple moccasins strapped to their feet. They also stood a full head taller. They moved casually about inspecting their new prisoners. Then a Yamana warrior spoke up. He wore a conical fur hat with a fringe of leather tassles, intertwining with his shoulder-length black hair.

"You are in our territory! This is the second time this moon that we have caught you hunting here. This will require a congress of our leaders and compensation. We will collect your weapons and you will follow us to our camp. If you try to escape we will go to your camp and make war on your women and children. Do you understand?"

The Ona leader pledged his agreement to the Yamana terms. Then a Yamana warrior noticed the prisoner the Ona had captured earlier, the one who wore the strange clothing. The boy was brought forward.

"What's this?" The Yamana leader asked.

"I don't know. We just stumbled upon him. There was another foreigner with him, but he escaped," the Ona leader replied. "This one carried a strange weapon." The shining sword was brought forward with the boy.

"Very well. He will be brought to the congress too. We will decide what to do with him after we settle the matter of trespassing."

* * * * *

The Yamana warriors led their prisoners to their encampment on the far side of the mountain. No one spoke along the way. Tannic was deep in thought. He didn't know if SRG and Danika were dead or alive. It probably all depended on him now, and once again he was in a bad spot with no obvious way out, and the Rainbow Star nowhere to be seen.

* * * * *

Danika bumped into SRG when he stopped abruptly. "Do you hear that?" he asked.

"Hear what?"

"I swear I just heard waves. There has to be another opening to this cave, and we've walked far enough to be on the other side of the mountain. Maybe it's the ocean."

"I can't hear anything. Compadre, we've been stumbling along in the dark for ages. I don't even think we can find our way back out again. What are we doing here?"

"We're looking for the Rainbow Star, because I don't know where else to look. But I feel a breeze on my face again, and I smell salt air. Maybe the Rainbow Star is in the ocean. Why else would we have an oyster basket? That makes sense doesn't it? Come on, let's go!" he said excitedly as he pulled her forward. Danika held tightly to his arm and they stumbled along in the dark until she bumped her shin badly on a rock.

* * * * *

The huts of the Yamana camp, short structures made of sticks and furs, were arranged in a circle around a central fire. Several women and children disappeared into them as soon as the warriors arrived. Then the Yamana warriors sat on one side of the fire and the Ona on the other. Two large posts stood across the fire from each other, supporting a smaller pole between them. Tannic's escort tied him to one of the vertical posts.

The Yamana leader, now carrying the Dragonwrigley, stood up and made some sort of announcement. At once a great debate broke out, with everybody on both sides arguing, spitting, and making faces. Tannic stood in silent awe as he watched what must have been an age-old ritual.

Suddenly the voices quieted and the two opposing leaders approached each other in front of the fire. Space was cleared for them, and a woman brought them a length of crudely woven rope. Each of them grabbed one end. Then they backed slowly apart until they were standing on opposite sides of the fire with the rope stretched between them. Without warning, they both started tugging.

Tannic had never seen a tug-o-war like this. The loser would be pulled into the fire. He thought at first the larger Yamana leader would easily win, but the smaller Ona was deceptively strong and dug his bare feet into the soil. After giving up only a few feet, he stopped the Yamana and actually started to regain a bit of ground. Neither man was in serious danger from the fire yet, but another Yamana added two more sticks to the fire, and the flames grew larger and licked at the rope.

The two leaders fought back and forth for the better part of an hour. Whispers and murmurs grew among the ranks of warriors. Then the Yamana leader let the line go slightly slack, which caused the Ona to momentarily lose his balance. The Yamana seized the opportunity, and with a rush he pulled the Ona into the fire.

The little leader let go of the rope and rolled out of the fire right next to Tannic's feet. He stood up and dusted himself off. Then a new debate started.

"You have lost the battle of the rope, and you will leave

our territory immediately. If we catch you here again, we will wage war and we will kill you. As payment, you will leave your weapons behind. Now go peacefully."

The Ona leader raised his hand to stop his warriors and turned to the victor. "You have defeated me with the rope. We agree to your terms and we will leave our own weapons behind. But we also had this foreigner and his weapon when you caught us. He is ours, and we would take him and his weapon with us."

The Yamana leader stood and frowned thoughtfully before he answered. "We cannot accept this. You were trespassing in our territory, so the foreigner is also ours."

"But we captured him, so we must be entitled to some part of him. Our ancestors and elders would have agreed to that."

"You speak the truth. Let us settle our disagreement with another contest. There are two things we can do. We can bind him between two ropes and hold a rope battle between our tribes. When he is torn apart, each tribe will keep the piece on its own rope, and the tribe with the biggest piece will keep his weapon. Or we can tether him up and hold a shooting contest with bows and arrows. Each warrior takes one shot, and the tribe that puts the most arrows in his body wins both the stranger and the weapon. This is also a long-standing tradition for settling disputes. Which contest do you choose?"

Tannic didn't know what they were saying, but each tribe was now holding a separate discussion, and they all kept glancing over at him.

Finally, the leaders conferred again, and then their warriors brought out two ropes and tied one to each of Tannic's arms. They moved him away from the fire, and he realized what they were doing when the warriors started lining up along each rope, the Yamana on his right and the Ona on his left. They slowly began applying tension. Tannic was about to scream when the Ona leader shouted, and everybody stopped.

Tannic took a deep breath. Somehow, for whatever reason, he'd been spared.

Two warriors untied his hands. Then they led Tannic back to the post and tied him up again. If he ever got out of this mess, he wanted to taste a pizza. His thoughts returned to SRG and Danika again. But for the moment, he felt relieved that he wasn't being killed.

* * * * *

Eventually SRG spotted a tiny glimpse of daylight far off in the shaft ahead of them. "Hurry up, Danika! I can see light! We're coming to the other end!"

They scrambled along faster, and soon they could see their feet and the rocks on the floor. They were no longer stumbling, and SRG broke into a run. As they ran by another side tunnel, SRG sniffed.

"Do you smell that?" he asked, making an odd face.

"Yeah, it smells like a stinky animal or something! Let's get out of here."

They reached the cave opening at the same time and looked straight out over the ocean. The ground below them sloped gently down to the water's edge some distance away, but closer to them was a small encampment. A few people were sitting and milling about a group of huts. They were scarcely dressed and were busy eating mollusks. The huts were surrounded by a short circular wall of empty seashells.

SRG and Danika sat down to study the situation.

"I don't see any sign of the Rainbow Star, but I have a good feeling about this. These must be the Selk'nam people Tannic described. And we have an oyster basket as a special weapon. I'm willing to bet the Rainbow Star is in the ocean close by," SRG said.

"I think you're right. I mean, it makes sense. What do you want to do?" Danika asked.

"I think we need to sneak down the hillside here, try to avoid being seen by the Selk'nam people, and get into the water. Then I can dive and see if I can find the star."

"Let me see that basket," Danika asked. SRG handed it to her and she studied the lid. "It's the perfect size to hold the Rainbow Star."

SRG was about to agree when a rumbling noise from behind grabbed their attention and they turned. The beast was huge, and it roared as it approached them in a dead run. They both jumped up and started running down the hill with the Boss Milodon hot on their heels. SRG's clearest path took him toward the Selk'nam tribe, while Danika, still holding the oyster basket, headed straight for the water.

The Selk'nam warriors looked up at the sound of SRG's steps. They grabbed bows and arrows and were taking aim when they saw the Milodon too. They dropped their weapons and scattered. SRG was a faster runner and was gaining on the running natives while the Milodon was gaining on all of them. SRG passed the first Selk'nam just as the Milodon caught up. It grabbed the warrior from behind with one swipe of its big claws and pulled him into a huge mouth filled with sharp teeth. The warrior screamed. SRG didn't even look back, but the scream inspired him to run faster. As the group reached the water's edge, they all skirted the shoreline rather than entering the frigid water. SRG went with them. *Safety in numbers*. He was in the middle of the pack of the natives who were so focused on running for their lives that they didn't really notice him.

* * * * *

Danika dove without even looking and hit the frigid water head first. It stung her face, but she forced her eyes open and scanned below her. There was a cliff-like drop-off of about twenty feet to the ocean floor. It was covered in shellfish. She dove downward, and as she passed the rock wall, a cluster of giant clams were opening and shutting with the undersea waves. One of them was releasing pulses of bright, multi-hued light.

She swam over to it, and the clam slammed shut. She waited for a moment, but she was running out of air. She broke the surface instead and took several deep breaths. In the distance, SRG was running from the Milodon along with the Selk'nam people. Danika was already shaking from the cold and couldn't spend much more time in the water. Her fingers and toes were starting to tingle. She gulped one more deep breath before she dove. The last thing she saw was a gigantic sea lion racing across the surface straight for her.

Her mind was racing as she kicked her way back down. *The Ender Dude wasn't the milodon after all. It was a sea lion.* She reached the clam just as the Ender Dude reached her.

* * * * *

All the warriors walked back about twenty-five paces from Tannic and nocked arrows to their bows. Then they took aim, and he realized he'd misinterpreted things. He tried to scream but he was too scared to make a sound come out. The Yamana leader spoke to the archers for a moment and then raised his arm. Tannic took a deep breath and closed his eyes. *This is it. Hopefully it's over quickly.* The leader shouted and swung his arm down. Tannic heard dozens of bowstrings twanging and vibrating. He dropped his head.

* * * * *

Danika caught the giant clam by surprise and stuck her hand into the illuminated mass of tissue. It responded to the surprise by clamping down hard, and she felt bones snap in her forearm. The Ender Dude reached her, bit down hard on her left hand and started dragging her away from the giant clam. She felt like she was being pulled apart in a tug-o-war. Pain shot up her arm, but she forced her hand to probe around inside the clam. Her lungs burned and her shoulder ached from the pull of the Ender Dude. She was about to lose consciousness when she felt something hard. She grabbed it.

Chapter 8

WORLD THREE LEVEL 5

Mayor Island

Darwood burst through the door without knocking. "Durwood, what in the name of—how many times have I told you to knock before you enter?" Mr. Eville asked as he lowered his feet from his desk. He was annoyed at being disturbed, even though he had merely been taking a nap.

"Sir, I'm sorry Sir, but I've just heard from the programmers on Level 5. We have a . . . strange situation, Sir. They don't know what to make of it. It appears that all the levels in World Three have just disappeared."

"What? What do you mean 'disappeared'? Levels don't just disappear."

"I don't know, Sir. Apparently the players just completed Level 4, and then the rest of the levels just disappeared from the programming. They're gone. The programmers are investigating."

"Why don't they just shut it down and reset it?"

"They tried that, Sir! The game isn't responding. They can't even shut it down. It's like the game has taken control of itself."

"Ahh . . ." Mr. Eville answered, deep in thought. *Doc claimed the AI might do this. It must be part of his plan to overthrow me—some of the programmers must be working for him. I'll have to work harder to make him talk.*

"I'll keep you posted Sir, but this is indeed a strange development."

"Tell the operatives on Level 10 to increase the pressure on Dr. Denton. He must know something about this."

"Uh . . . well, um . . ." Darwood stammered nervously. "There is no Level 10, Sir. It's gone. Doc too, all the operatives, everybody. Just gone with no trace."

"What!?" he roared. "That's not possible!" Then he paused and sighed out loud. "Right. Well, just keep me informed. That will be all."

"Yes, Sir."

After Darwood left, Mr. Eville bent down to the bottom desk drawer. His hand was shaking as he pulled the bottle of whisky out. He poured a generous amount, sat back, and propped his feet up again. He took a sip of the golden liquid and let it roll over his tongue. He needed to calm down. He was getting too old for this stuff. He took a deep breath and exhaled. Then he closed his eyes.

* * * * *

"Does anybody else find this weird? I said my greatest fear was being captured by a primitive tribe and now that's happened three times. Twice just on the last level. Something doesn't feel right about this." Tannic searched his companions' faces. They were all standing in Doc's lab.

"Well, what *could* it mean?" SRG asked.

"I don't know. It's like Mr. Eville is watching us and

changing the programming to feed into our biggest fears."

"Can he do that? I don't think he has before. How could he?" Danika asked.

"I don't know. But we know he cheats. Doc has this screen for watching us in each level. Maybe Mr. Eville is watching us too," Tannic answered.

SRG shook his head. "Mr. Eville never leaves the little sanctuary of his private office, and there aren't any screens in there. Besides, I don't think he could even use a cell phone. He's not that smart. He's just a bully."

"I agree," Danika said. "He's not that smart. He could never write a program."

"Yeah, you're right. Well, maybe he has a spy . . . " Tannic said quietly. Then they all looked at Jody.

"What? Wait—me, a spy? Are you kidding? For Mr. Eville? I'd rather die. You guys should hear yourselves. That's crazy talk," Jody responded defensively.

Tannic sighed. "You're right. I'm sorry. I'm probably just imagining things. Forget I brought it up. Those people just scared me to death. Just when I'd gotten over being burnt alive by the Aboriginals, I got to watch them decide whether to tear me in half or use me for target practice. I thought for sure I was a goner. I forgot to thank you, Compadre."

"Hey, don't thank me, thank Danika. She's the one who dove into the water and captured the Rainbow Star," SRG replied.

"It was so cold that I'm still shaking," Danika said. "But it turns out I didn't need the basket after all. As soon as I had the star in my hand, we were all back here. And I got lucky anyway. I wasn't thinking about the star when I jumped into the ocean, I was thinking about getting away from that Boss Milodon. It was just random luck that I jumped in where

I did. But I agree with SRG—I don't think we'd survive World Three without three players."

"Yeah. That doesn't really make sense, though. It sounds like a flaw in the programming. Somebody wasn't thinking clearly when they designed these levels. Amateurs," Tannic guffawed.

"So what's up next, Jody?" SRG asked. "Let's see what exciting things Level 5 has in store for us. Maybe our special weapon will be an ugly stick, like in World Two."

"We never did find out what that was for," Danika mused.

Jody brought out the laptop, and with a few deft clicks Tannic opened the document on the next level.

"Whew!" SRG whistled. "Mayor Island. Uh, oh."

"What? Where's that?" Danika asked. "Wait, let me guess—your grandpa has been there."

"Yeah, but I keep telling you, he's been everywhere. Anyway, Mayor Island is bad news. It's in New Zealand. He went fishing there with his buddy Graeme. That means the Maori, probably the fiercest primitive tribe in the history of the world."

"Let's not get ahead of ourselves, gang. Let me read the file." Tannic scanned the description, and his face turned pale. "You're right. It is Mayor Island in New Zealand. It's just off the east coast. The island is covered in dense jungle. The kauri are the largest trees. The other trees include rimu, beech, and tawa. The undergrowth is mainly ferns and flax."

He looked up. "Well, that part's not so bad. But it goes on. There will be militant Maori tribes there. Let's see . . . The Maori arrived in New Zealand from Polynesia in the thirteenth century. They defend their territory aggressively and often eat their defeated enemies. They use spears, clubs, intimidation and brute force. And a unique weapon, a large skull cracker, which can kill enemies with a single blow to the head. They're master weavers and carvers, and their weapons are intricately carved with symmetrical patterns. And they wear facial tattoos in symmetrical patterns of small dots to make them look fiercer. The Maori also perform a ritual called the Haka to instill fear in their enemies. It's a rhythmic chant and dance. It's still effective in the modern world—the New Zealand All Blacks Rugby team performs a Haka before each match, and they've been world champions more than any other team."

He looked grim, but went on. "Wildlife. There are no native predators on the island other than the Haast Eagle, the largest raptor on the planet. Mayor Island will have Boss Haast Eagles. Otherwise there are just some marsupials. So we'll see Weevil Wallabies, Boss Possums, and Boss Kiwis—a nocturnal, flightless bird. And the Rainbow Moa. The Moa is the largest flightless bird on the planet. They're twelve feet tall and weigh 500 pounds. The Rainbow Moa is covered with colored plumage and has large weapon-like spurs on its legs and sharp claws. There's a good chance the Ender Dude will be a Rainbow Moa."

"It's an island too, surrounded by the Pacific Ocean," SRG added. "Will there be sharks? I hate sharks!"

"Yeah. Not only Boss Sharks, but also Boss Kahawai, or Australian salmon. In Rough World, they're large predator fish that feed in schools on the surface. They sound a lot like Boss Piranhas." Finally, he sat back. "What's not to like? An aggressive primitive tribe, dangerous animals, and a thick jungle?"

SRG nodded. "This is going to be a challenge. What's our special weapon?"

Tannic scanned further down. "A mirror."

"A mirror? Are you kidding me?"

"That's what it looks like, Compadre. I'd suggest we get a move on. The sooner we get away from the Maori, the better I'll feel."

The trio bid their goodbyes to Jody and assembled by the door. The Dragonwrigley was standing in the corner, anxiously awaiting another adventure. A small nondescript mirror lay on the floor next to it. Tannic picked up the sword while Some Random Guy picked up the mirror and shook his head. Then he opened the door. Jody shouted a last wish for good luck as they walked into the jungle of Mayor Island.

The sun was high in the sky, the air was warm, and they were standing in a small meadow. The tall forest of unfamiliar trees and thick undergrowth surrounded them. Everything was lush and green. They couldn't see the ocean, but the smell of salt was heavy in the air. There was also a scent of smoke. A light breeze brushed their faces.

"What do you think, Compadre?" Tannic asked.

"I have no idea, but we should avoid the Maoris if at all possible. I wish Doc were here, he might have some idea where to start."

"I don't know. I think we probably have to investigate the Maori tribes. Even if they don't have the Rainbow Star, it will probably be connected with them. Should we start into the jungle and see where it leads?"

"That sounds like a plan," SRG agreed. "I'm in."

"Me too," Danika added.

They started in a random direction out of the meadow. The sun was in their faces as they entered the forest. Tannic led the way into the dense vegetation, cutting a path when he needed to, and they slowly made their way in a single file, senses on high alert for anything suspicious.

After an hour of struggling through the greenery, they hit a well-used path. They conferred quickly and decided to continue in the same general direction. The walking grew easier, and as they covered ground much faster, they noticed the aroma of smoke getting stronger. They were headed toward a fire of some sort, whether man-made or lightning strike.

Danika was bringing up the rear when they heard her scream. A Boss Kiwi dove at her leg from the brush and stabbed her with its sharp beak. She fell down, bleeding profusely. Tannic and SRG ran back, but they were too late. She collapsed lifelessly, the Life Wedge lit up above her head, and the Kiwi turned on them. It took Tannic a second to recover from the shock of seeing his sister on the ground to realize he held the Dragonwrigley. When the Kiwi charged, he cut the angry bird into two pieces. The halves quivered on the ground for a moment and then lay still in a damp pool of fluids.

"I thought the kiwis were supposed to be nocturnal!" SRG complained. "It's the middle of the day!"

"Maybe this one had insomnia," Tannic replied.

"Or maybe we woke it up." Danika had recovered and was on her feet now.

"Whatever, we just need to be careful," SRG added.

"I was being careful! But I didn't even see it coming," Danika argued.

"All right, listen," Tannic broke in. "We're all being careful, like always, and we need to keep it up. Come on, let's go and see what the source of the smoke is. Maybe we'll sneak up on a Maori village and find the Rainbow Star lying on the ground in front of us. I mean we could use some random luck. I just don't want to be captured by another primitive tribe."

"With our random luck, Captain Killbeard is likely to show up here. This is just the kind of island a dastardly cutthroat pirate like he would love," SRG added.

"Yeah, I'm glad he's dead! I don't ever want to see him again."

"That makes three of us," Danika replied.

The trail wound slowly down to the ocean, where it opened up to a glittering white sandy beach. The sun reflected brightly off the wet sand, and the trio had to squint their eyes. The ocean was a beautiful turquoise green, and white waves crashed onto the shore. They walked along the hot sand until the beach ended abruptly at a sharp cliff, and they had to choose between swimming around the obstacle or climbing back up through the brush to get above it. SRG elected to enter the water and investigate the cliff face while Tannic and Danika climbed the slope to see what lay ahead. He handed the mirror to Danika and lowered himself into the cool water. He winked as he turned away and started swimming.

Tannic and Danika clambered up the steep slope, cutting some branches and hanging on to others. Finally, Tannic stepped over a tree root at the top of the cliff and found a great view of a large bay just beyond where they had left the beach. The smoke was rising from somewhere to the interior of the bay. The water was peaceful and clear enough to show the sandy white ocean floor below. It projected a tranquil feeling. He looked down, but he couldn't find SRG in the water. Then Danika grabbed his shoulder, and he froze.

Two hundred yards out on the ocean was an outrigger canoe with six Maori Minotaur warriors in it. They were chasing a huge school of fish toward the cliff. The water looking like it was boiling. There must have been an acre of fish thrashing on the surface. They were probably Boss Kahawai. The warrior in the front threw a harpoon into the school, and the fish suddenly took a sharp change of direction and headed straight for the cliff wall, right where SRG should be swimming. Tannic's pulse quickened, and he shot a worried look at Danika. She was biting her fingernail.

* * * * *

Some Random Guy was studying the cliff face when he heard the commotion behind him. Countless fish were darting about, their blue and silver scales shining like mirrors under the surface. The water around him looked like a pot of boiling water. He was so transfixed by the movement that he didn't feel the first fish attack him. His first sign that something was wrong was when the water started turning red around him. Then he looked up again and saw the canoe bearing down on him. That was the last thing he remembered until he woke up to see a skull cracker coming straight toward him.

* * * * *

The Maori Minotaurs saw him floating on the surface, being driven toward the cliff as the waves crashed one after another. They saw a strange light above his head too, but it disappeared. The school of Boss Kahawai scattered as the canoe cut through the water. After a couple of tries, they grabbed hold of SRG and pulled him aboard. He was wearing clothes and shoes that were foreign to them.

When he opened his eyes, they brought the skull cracker down on him, but when the Life Wedge came to life they all scrambled to the back of the canoe. They almost tipped the boat. But the light gradually faded, and they regained their confidence and grabbed SRG firmly to inspect him.

* * * * *

The next time SRG woke up, he was tied to a post in a village square. The houses here were significant structures, made of wood with finely thatched roofs. He was tied up next to a fire, probably the source of the smoke they had noticed earlier.

A group of Maori Minotaur warriors emerged from the largest building and surrounded him. Then they lined up in single file, and one started shouting directions. They responded in unison, first slapping their arms and their legs, then shifting to a broader stance slapping arms and legs again, and chanting louder and louder. Then they bent down into a three-point position with one hand in the dirt. The rhythmic dance climaxed as they stuck out their tongues and shook their heads. SRG was scared stiff. He had never seen anything like this, and figured whatever was about to happen, it wasn't going to be good.

The leader approached him and stuck out his tongue.

* * * * *

Tannic was cutting his way through the brush, trying to find where the Maori had taken SRG. They'd last seen him slumped in the front of the outrigger canoe. Tannic was so focused that he didn't hear Danika's screams. When he finally noticed them, he looked up just in time to see the Boss Haast Eagle coming at him. It hit him before he could even flinch. The talons tore across his neck and knocked him to the ground. He tried to raise the Dragonwrigley, but the eagle was on top of him and hammering him in the forehead with its oversized beak. Blood gushed into his eyes, and everything went black.

When he awoke, Danika was holding his head in her lap and singing softly to him. He opened his eyes and looked at her. He was supposed to be protecting her, not the other way around. He shook his head and sat up.

"I suppose I lost a Life Wedge, huh?" he asked.

"Yeah. I tried to warn you but I was too late. I'm sorry."

"Hey, no problem. I think SRG lost a Life Wedge or two. What a mess. We've hardly started and we're already losing them left and right. This place is much more dangerous than I expected, Danika. I guess I kind of forgot how rough it really is, though. It's been six years since we were last here."

"Me too. Sometimes I find myself second guessing our decision to come back. I wish I hadn't dared you to turn on the game. This is all my fault." She started to cry.

"Hey, hey, listen. We all agreed to do it. You didn't make us. And once we found out Doc was in trouble, I don't think anything in the world would have stopped SRG. He's loyal like that." He paused thoughtfully. "I guess I am too, for that matter. So it's over. We're here. We need to focus on getting back out alive. And we can do it. We just need to stick together. Which reminds me, we need to find out where they took him before it's too late."

They made their way quietly around the bay to a small cliff overlooking the village. Tannic pulled a limb back just in time for them to witness a line of Maori Minotaurs march out of the main building. Tannic and Danika sat transfixed as they watched the Haka. When it concluded, Tannic shot a worried look at Danika.

"I don't know what happens next, but it can't be good. They eat their enemies, you know."

"What are we going to do? There's six of them and only two of us, and all I have is a mirror."

"I'm guessing SRG is down two Life Wedges, so if he loses another one it doesn't matter. At this point, we have nothing to lose. So this is going to sound crazy, but maybe if we surprise them, I'll have a chance with the Dragonwrigley."

"So what do you propose we do?" she asked.

"Well, one thing I remember is that they're very superstitious. If you were invisible and maybe did something with the mirror, they might freak out, at least enough to give me time to take a couple of them down. That would even things out a bit, and if you can untie SRG, we'll give them a good fight. What do you think?"

"I can't think of anything else. But I don't have complete control over this invisibility thing. I think I'll be scared enough to be invisible, though. Okay, let's go before they do something to him."

They crept through the undergrowth until they reached the village. Then Danika stood up and walked slowly toward the Minotaurs. They were crowded around SRG, probing and taunting him, and they didn't notice the mirror until she held it right in front of them. Then they jumped back in fear, seeing a reflecting object floating in the air. She did her best to shine sunlight directly into the leader's eyes, and Tannic hurtled in from behind them swinging the Dragonwrigley back and forth like a madman.

Fireballs and crescents were flying in every direction. Tannic was lost in the moment and intent on inflicting as much damage as possible. The first two Minotaurs fell forward, crescents sticking out of smoldering flesh on their backs. While he distracted them, Danika rushed to SRG and began the tedious process of untying him while the melee continued. The warriors were screaming and so was Tannic. He swore in his best pirate voice, giving them a piece of his mind along with his sword. The remaining warriors turned to face him and started advancing. He swung the sword faster and swore at the top of his lungs. Another Maori went down, and then another. The two remaining warriors grew more cautious. They moved in opposite directions and threw spears at him, slowing his onslaught as he dodged away.

SRG was about to thank Danika when she collapsed to the ground, a crescent sticking out of her back, a casualty of friendly fire. He leaned down and lifted her over his shoulder. The Maoris were so focused on Tannic that nobody noticed as he stood up and carried her away. He moved swiftly into the thick brush until they were safely hidden. Then he carefully sat her down and turned back to check on Tannic.

Tannic had drawn the last two warriors into a standoff. They had their spears drawn, and he had the sword aimed at them. But he hadn't seen the seventh warrior come out of the building and sneak up behind him with a skull cracker. SRG came into sight just as the weapon came down on Tannic's head, and he dropped the Dragonwrigley and slumped to the dirt.

Danika was waking up as Some Random Guy sat down next to her. He was unusually quiet.

"What's wrong, Compadre?" she asked hazily. "Where's Tannic?"

"They got him. You two rescued me, but now they have him. I think we're worse off now. At least he had the Dragonwrigley. Now the Maoris have both him and the sword. And all we have is a stupid mirror." He pulled it out of his pocket. He had picked it up when Danika collapsed into his arms. "Well, looking on the bright side, he's only lost one Life Wedge, so we have a little cushion to work with."

She shook her head no. "No. He lost one to a Boss Haast Eagle. Now he's down to one. And I only see one above your head."

"I only see one above your head too."

"I lost one to that Boss Kiwi. Stupid bird! And then this one!"

"This puts us behind the count with the pitcher. We only get one more chance at this. Well, you know what I mean. What do you think they'll do with Tannic?"

"He told me they eat their enemies," she shivered. "That's why we came to rescue you."

"And now they're going to eat him." SRG shook his head grimly. "We don't have the numbers to overtake them, not without the sword. We need to find the Rainbow Star, and fast."

"Where should we look?"

"The star is usually in the hardest place to get to. I have a gut feeling that means the highest point on this island. We've got to get away from the coast, past all the Maori, and climb upward. And we don't have much time to do it. Unless you have any better ideas."

"That sounds as good a place as any. I'm right behind you!"

Some Random Guy led the way into the brush. It was a laborious process. The undergrowth was thick. But every time he slowed down, Danika prodded him. After half
' hour, they cut across a trail heading up the mountain. It

wasn't much used, but it was definitely a trail, and it would offer easier climbing than fighting through the jungle.

He looked at it. "I think this is a good sign. A trail to the top, but not too traveled. It feels about right."

"I agree, come on, let's keep moving."

The trail wound back and forth, making many switch-backs through the jungle as it climbed. Finally, it took them onto an open spine ridge that led toward the summit. There were volcanic boulders and small cliffs along the way, but they still made good time. They were on the last slope when SRG stopped to catch his breath. They sat down in the sun and looked back over the canopy of the jungle they had just come from. The ribbon of smoke from the village was larger now and had a dense white color. Somebody was stoking the fire.

He looked at Danika. "I don't think we have much time." He looked up the ridge they were climbing and across to the next one. It looked like a twin to the ridge they were on. Both of them led to a series of cliffs directly below the summit. As he turned back to Danika, his eye caught something and he looked again. But whatever it had been, it was gone.

"What did you see? What's wrong?"

"I don't know, I just thought I glimpsed something. But there's nothing there. It's gone."

"Where?" Danika asked.

"On the next ridge, just about where we are." Then he saw it again, and this time he recognized it. He jumped up. "Come on Danika! It's the star! It was a rainbow of light. Let's go! Hurry!" He scurried down the slope into the draw and across to the opposite ridge. The ground was steep and it took some time, but eventually the two of them reached the top. But whatever he had seen was gone.

"I don't understand it. I swear it was right here. It had to be the star."

"I don't see any—"

A shadow appeared next them on the rocks. Danika screamed. Some Random Guy spun around. The bird was the largest he had ever seen. It was twice as tall as he was and looked like an ostrich on steroids, except it was covered in a brilliant rainbow of feathers. He crouched down and backed away from it, trying to figure out how they could escape.

The bird looked at them curiously and then ran up the ridge and disappeared into a cave.

SRG let out a long breath. "That was a close one. That thing was huge!"

"Yeah, except—"

"Except what if it's the Ender Dude? That would mean the star is in that cave!" SRG deduced.

"Uh-uh, Compadre. I'm not going into a cave with that thing. Did you see the size of its spurs? They could cut you clean in half."

"Well, one of us has to check it out, and you're the one with two Life Wedges. Remember Black Mirror Pond?" he asked, referring to World Two. She frowned at him. "Oh wait, I forgot. You only have one Life Wedge left too."

"Yeah, and there turned out to be Dragonfish in that pond. Uh-uh. Sorry. I'm not going in that cave."

"Okay, I'll do it. But either way it means we only get one chance at this," he reminded her. "I really think we'd be better off if we both went in together. One of us distracts the bird while the other one gets the star if it's there."

Danika shut her eyes. "Never mind, I'll go with you. But at least can I hold the mirror?"

"Of course, Danika. You can hold the mirror, whatever you want. But if that's the case maybe you should go first with the mirror and I'll be right behind you."

"Really? You'll be right behind me?"

"Really. I'll be right behind you, beside you or in front of you if you want. But we can't make any mistakes. We have no room for error."

"Okay, I'll go first with the mirror, but you'd better be right behind me!"

Decided now, they climbed up to the cave. The dark opening was easily big enough for the Rainbow Moa to walk into. It was surrounded by large rocks, and as they got closer, they saw rays of rainbow light emanating from within.

"Moas don't glow in the dark, do they?" Danika asked.

"I don't think so. Which can only mean one thing."

* * * * *

The Maori Minotaur chief studied Tannic closely. He shrugged his woven robe off and laid it on the ground. Then he doffed his headdress and signaled to the two remaining warriors. They started dragging the bodies of their tribe mates away from the fire. They moved efficiently and silently.

Finally, the chief spoke. "We need to prepare them for burial. But the ceremony can wait until tomorrow. Tonight we will feast upon the enemy. Gather more wood and stoke the fire. We will roast him alive on a spit."

The warriors stacked the bodies next to the largest building and disappeared into the woods. When they returned they brought armloads of wood and three long poles. They drove two into the ground and attached the third pole across them, directly over the flames. Then they cut Tannic loose and tied him to the horizontal pole with his hands stretched over his head. He struggled and fought back, but they were too big and too strong. When he was secure, they added wood to the fire. The smoke billowed up around him and he started coughing and choking. Then the flames grew and slapped at his body, and he screamed in pain. The three Minotaurs started chanting in a broken rhythm.

* * * * *

Danika led the way into the cave, holding the mirror carefully aloft in front of her. She trembled and then vanished. SRG was left following a floating mirror into the cave. The darkness blinded him at first, but after a moment he could make out a large chamber. The Rainbow Moa was sitting on a nest at the far end of the cave. A dim rainbow of light shone out from beneath its feathers. The Moa was studying them. It seemed nervous and agitated.

SRG whispered to Danika. "It's sitting on the star. It must think it's an egg. Just approach it slowly and keep the mirror pointed at it. Wait, no. Hand me the mirror and you keep walking toward it."

Some Random Guy kept the mirror aimed directly at the bird, and they walked forward. When they got too close for the beast's comfort, it abruptly stood up, and rainbow light flooded the room. Then the Moa lowered its head, opened its beak wide, and screeched at them. SRG froze. The bird walked slowly and menacingly toward him, bobbing its head. The Rainbow Star lay unattended in the nest behind it. Then it stopped, its large eyes studying the mirror. It seemed agitated by the other bird it saw in the reflection. It couldn't help its bird instincts, and it attacked the mirror with its beak.

SRG jumped back as the mirror shattered to pieces. Then he looked up and saw Danika re-pixelate with the Rainbow Star clutched firmly in her right hand.

Chapter 9

WORLD THREE LEVEL 6

Yellowstone Geysers

This time Darwood knocked softly before he opened the door.

"Come in, come in! Hurry! What's happening?" Mr. Eville demanded.

"I've spoken to the programmers again, Sir. It seems the AI program has taken control of the game and is rewriting the levels as it goes along. The programmers believe it is listening to the players and learning as they progress, and it's altering the programming to its advantage."

"Hah! So they're now up against a computer that will make the game harder as it goes along. That's beautiful. There's no way they can defeat that. We'll be rid of them for good! Durwood, you've just made my day!" He leaned back happily.

"Uh, it's not exactly that simple, Sir. The programmers think the AI may be able to take control of all of the Worlds, at least after it defeats these players. Then it will be in total control of Rough World. All the levels, the Jagged City, everything. I, uh . . . that means that it will be in control. Not you."

"What!?" Mr. Eville sat forward. "That's not acceptable! How do we stop it?"

"Well, um, they believe that if . . . uh, if the players finish Level 10 and defeat the program, they should be able to shut down the game. Then we can delete the AI program from World Three and take control again and rewrite it. Without artificial intelligence this time, I would guess."

He grimaced. "So you're telling me our only hope is for the players to defeat World Three?"

"It does appear that that is our only hope, Sir," Darwood confirmed.

"Do you . . . do you have any idea how distasteful this is for me? To cheer for those dirty little ba—?" Mr. Eville stopped short of swearing. "This is unbelievable. Why is this happening to me?"

"I'm sorry, Sir, but right now it looks like our only hope lies in the hands of Tannic, SRG, and Danika. I know how much you despise them, Sir. But right now we need them. We need them to win, with all due respect, Sir."

Mr. Eville grunted loudly and banged his fist on his desk. Darwood leaned back reflexively. Mr. Eville's face was red, and the veins on his neck were bulging out. It looked like his head was about to explode. He took a deep breath and let it out slowly. "So how do we help them?" he said tersely as he gritted his teeth.

"The problem, Sir, is that there doesn't seem to be any way for us to help them. All we can do is watch and hope for the best."

"Can't we write something into the program and find a way to help them? Stack things in our favor? Input a secret weapon? Cheat somehow?"

"Unfortunately, the programmers on Level Five did try

that already, Sir. The program discovered it and wrote over it almost immediately. There doesn't seem to be any way in."

"And we can't just shut the entire system down?"

"They've tried that as well. The AI fired it back up in just milliseconds. Then they tried resetting the program, and it blocked their attempt entirely. Now the program isn't responding at all. They've run out of ideas. That's where we stand at the moment, Sir."

"All right. Keep me posted. I can't believe this."

* * * * *

Tannic was still coughing from the smoke. He slowly collected himself. "I don't know what happened, but it happened just in the nick of time. I can still feel the flames burning my skin. You guys saved my bacon, no pun intended. That was amazing, but I still think something feels weird about this game. Even more so now. I said my greatest fear was being captured by a primitive tribe, and then I'm captured. I said my greatest fear was being burned alive, and for the second time I found myself roasting over a fire. It's almost like the game is listening to us. Is there any way Mr. Eville could be changing the game as we go along?"

"How could he?" SRG asked. "I mean, we know he cheats, but changing the whole game? I don't think so. It's a hard game. I mean, you've been captured on these levels, we've been separated, the special weapons are weak—if we didn't have a third player, we'd never have made it this far. Rough World Three is almost impossible to defeat."

"But there's another thing. Have you noticed a theme in World Three? Doc's computer said it was just about different places around the globe, like natural wonders of the world.

But if you ask me, the theme is primitive tribes. We faced the Anasazi on Level One, the Inuit in the Snow Biome, the Aboriginals in the Australian Outback, the Yaghan in the Southern Andes Mountains, and the Maori on Mayor Island. Something doesn't feel right about all of this."

"I don't know, I think you're imagining things. All of the locations would be inhabited by some kind of enemies. But I'll keep my eyes open for any patterns."

"I think Tannic's right," Danika said.

Jody came out of Doc's office with the laptop, and they booted it up and opened the folder for World Three, Level 6: Yellowstone Geysers.

"Okay, this should be interesting," SRG said. "This level's about another natural wonder, so it looks like everything is in order. What do you guys know about Yellowstone?"

"Well, I'm going out on a limb and guess that your grandpa has been there." Danika paused for dramatic effect.

"Danika, for crying out loud, it's one of the most popular parks in the country. The world, even. Of course they've been there. They've even been there with Graeme and Judy. Will you let it go?"

"I think I just proved my point," she responded matter-of-factly.

"Okay, listen up, gang," Tannic interrupted. "It doesn't matter who's been where. We need to focus. We studied Yellowstone in my geology class. Here's what I know. It has the largest active geyser field in the world, with sixty percent of the world's geysers. The Upper Geyser Basin alone has more than 150. The biggest geyser, the one everybody talks about, is Old Faithful. It was named for its frequent and regular eruptions. They happen every hour or so and shoot up to 180 feet high. But the place is also a geological wonder, with rock pillars, sand dunes, waterfalls, rivers, bubbling mud pots, steaming vents, and hot springs. The water temperatures can reach about 200 degrees Fahrenheit, and the steam from geysers and vents can actually reach 350 degrees. And this all occupies only one square mile. All these geothermal features are within a few hundred feet of the Firehole River—pretty well named, I guess. Geologists also think the area is overdue for a major geological event like an earthquake, which would change the entire landscape. Other than all that stuff, the only major danger in the park is grizzly bears. There's a lot of wildlife, but grizzlies are the only major cause of injury and death."

"Sounds interesting. What's the file say?" SRG asked.

"Let's see . . . it's pretty similar. The enemies will be Boss Bison—we've seen those before—Weevil Elk, Boss Eagles, and Weevil Deer. The Ender Dude is supposed to be a Boss Grizzly Bear, of course. Oh, the park was also once the territory of the Blackfeet Indians, and Doc's notes indicate that we'll probably run into Blackfeet Minotaurs. They were notorious as the most fearsome tribe of Native Americans. So that's not good news." He paused and looked up. "Ok, so we'll have to negotiate our way around the geothermal dangers and avoid grizzlies and Blackfeet Minotaurs while we look for the Rainbow Star. It could be anywhere."

"Do we know anything else about the Blackfeet?" SRG asked.

"I do," Danika volunteered. "I did a report on them last year. They're named after their moccasins—they dyed the soles of them black. Well, one legend says that they walked through prairie fires and the soot turned their moccasins black. Either way, they were a nomadic tribe that followed the bison through their annual movements across the plains of Montana. They made their clothing and teepees out of bison hides. They traveled with their belongings in a travois, a sort of sled made from teepee poles that they towed with horses. They lived in bands of large extended families, like one or two hundred people. They were very spiritual too. They believed in a creator god and had a strong sense of daily connection to him. They also built sweat lodges and participated in vision quests. And, uh, yeah." She stopped.

"That's it?" SRG asked.

"No, uh, there's more." Danika didn't look happy. "Other tribes who acted as go-betweens with the English referred to the Blackfeet as the Blood Tribe. See, they worshipped the sun and believed that it gave energy to every living thing. So every summer they had the Sun Dance, their most sacred ceremony. They would strip all the branches from a tall tree to make a forked center pole, and suspend leather ropes from the top." She winced. "The young men would cut slices through their chest skin and tie the ropes through them. Then they would dance around the tree while band members sang. The ceremony went on for a day and a half, while they were suspended from the tree by their skin, until it tore open. This would leave huge scars on their chests, that they would intimidate their enemies with. The scars meant the individual was very spiritual and not afraid of pain."

"Wow." SRG's eyes were wide. "Maybe that was more than I needed to know."

"I think we can count on Blackfeet Minotaurs being the fiercest we've seen yet," Tannic replied.

"So what's the special weapon? A thermometer?" SRG asked.

"No. But it doesn't make much more sense. A flashlight. Well, two of them."

"No, that makes sense!" SRG interjected. "Think about it. Where would be the most dangerous place to put the Rainbow Star? In a geyser, right? And probably the biggest one. I bet we'll have to go under Old Faithful. Which means we'll have about an hour between eruptions to get in, get the star, and get out or we'll be cooked alive. And we'll need the flashlights to see down there. I don't like the sounds of that, though—going spelunking in a geological hot zone!"

"Make that two of us," Danika added.

"Well we're just wasting time talking about it. Are you guys ready to go?"

They shook hands with Jody. The Dragonwrigley was waiting for them with a flashlight on either side of it. SRG took one and handed the other to Danika. They were big, as long as his forearm and heavy enough to use as clubs. He turned his on, and the light was blinding. He quickly shut it off.

"These could come in handy," he said. "But they won't help us much against a tribe of Blackfeet."

"Yeah, don't think about that. Come on, let's go find a Rainbow Star," Tannic prodded. He opened the door.

They stepped into a dry, barren landscape like something from the moon. There were no trees, shrubs, or grass, only tan rocks and sand. Below them lay a great valley with a lone peak standing tall in the distance. The walls were steep, with jagged rock faces. The valley floor was smooth sand, and multiple small drainages fed into it from both sides. Excavations were scattered along the length, with doors opening into the hillsides. The place looked deserted, but it had obviously been the location of great activity at one time. There was no geyser or steam vent to been seen.

The trio just stood staring at the scene, stunned by what

they saw. Finally SRG spoke up.

"This is not Yellowstone. I've seen pictures of it. It's covered with forests and rivers, waterfalls and grass plains. And the geothermal fields with steam vents and stuff. I don't know what this is, but it's definitely not that place." He shook his head, confused.

Danika and Tannic looked at each other and then at SRG.

"I recognize it," Danika said.

"Me too," Tannic added.

"Well then, fill me in. Where are we?" SRG asked impatiently.

"This is the Valley of the Kings. I'd recognize it anywhere. We studied it all last year in my archeology class," Danika replied. "We're in Egypt."

"That doesn't—we're supposed to be in Yellowstone. How could we have ended up here? Unless . . ." SRG trailed off.

"Unless Mr. Eville is cheating again, throwing us into a level we know nothing about," Tannic finished. "We've been too successful. We've gotten farther than he anticipated. So now he's resorting to cheating!"

"That's the only possible explanation," SRG agreed. "So now what?"

"I don't know, but it makes me really dislike him," Tannic muttered.

"Well, the good news is that if this really is the Valley of the Kings, I know a lot about it. So that should come in handy," Danika stated.

"Aren't you just a bundle of information?" SRG teased.

"Hey, you'll thank me before it's over, Compadre," she replied.

"Okay," he sighed. "So what do we know about this

place? If indeed it is the Valley of the Kings."

"The Valley of the Kings is one of the most studied archeological sites in the world. It's on the west bank of the Nile, and there are actually two valleys, the East Valley and the West Valley. The Egyptians buried their dead pharaohs and other royalty here for about 500 years, from the sixteenth to the eleventh centuries BC. Its official name was The Great and Majestic Necropolis of the Millions of Years of the Pharaoh, Life, Strength, and Health in the West of Thebes." She blushed. "Obviously that was a test question, sorry. It was discovered in 1922, and sixty-three tombs have been discovered so far. The most famous is Tutankhamun, the boy king. Artifacts from it have been exhibited all over the world."

"I know. My grandpa told me—" SRG winced, and then shrugged. "He saw them in Portland."

Danika shot him a glance and then continued. "The tomb entrances are stone doorways. Inside, the tunnels lead to the different tombs. There are hieroglyphics everywhere describing the entombed people's lives."

"And you said there are 63?" SRG asked.

"That we know of. But I think that's pretty much it. They're all numbered. The royalty are buried mostly in the East Valley, and everyone else is in the West."

"This reminds me of the valley of hidden caves in World One, except there were 300 of those. Here we only have 63, so that should make it easier," SRG suggested.

"Yeah, but it's not as easy as that. See, the land made it really difficult to actually dig the tombs. It alternates from shifting rock and sand to solid rock. So they would often start building a tunnel in one direction and run into impenetrable rock. Or the tunnel might collapse completely later.

So it was pretty common for them to re-appropriate different tombs, or make a branch off one tunnel to create a new one. It's basically a maze of tombs. And they were full of booby traps to keep people from raiding them. Then there's the Curse of the Pharaohs. A lot of people have died mysteriously while working in the tombs, and some people say it's because of a curse from Tutankhamun, who vowed that nobody should enter and disturb the dead."

"I ain't afraid of no ghosts!" SRG declared.

"It's not the ghosts we have to worry about, Compadre. I'm afraid it's the traps," Tannic answered.

"Yeah, probably. Okay, well, where should we start?"

"From the photos I remember, this looks like the East Valley," Danika said. The most symbolic place for the Rainbow Star would be Tutankhamun's tomb. King Tut is the most famous pharaoh, and he had the most elaborate burial artifacts. His tomb is pretty much in the center of the valleys, too. That's the logical place to start."

"Do you know what it looks like? I mean, does it have a big '62' or something on the outside?"

"No, it has a large neon sign that says 'Tut's Tomb'!" Danika deadpanned.

"Seriously?"

"No, silly. But I know about where it should be. It wasn't a really big tomb, though."

"Well, let's go down there. It looks deserted, but keep your eyes peeled. I'm guessing we'll run into Egyptian Minotaurs of some sort. Who knows what the Ender Dude might be?"

"Good point, Compadre," Tannic agreed. "I'll lead the way."

The trio slowly descended through the rocks and sand

to the valley floor. It took about an hour of careful descent. The ground at the bottom looked like a dry river bed, and they left clear prints as they trudged along. The air was dead calm, appropriately enough, with not a whisper of a breeze. There was no shade and no respite from the blazing noon sun, and soon they were all sweating.

Both sides of the canyon were dotted with large openings. The solid rock doors of some were hanging open, and others were closed tight. Each door was heavily marked with hieroglyphics. But the tombs weren't numbered in any way they could read, there were no signs. The place didn't look inhabited. It was dead still and dead quiet. They passed a great number of tombs before reaching the junction with the other valley. From there, they could see more openings in every direction, but there was no sign of the Rainbow Star.

SRG hefted his flashlight. "This might come in even more handy here. I hate to say it, but I think I'd rather investigate a dry old tomb than climb down into a live geyser."

"Yeah, I don't know," Tannic muttered. "I've gotten so used to being kidnapped that I'm starting to think my real greatest fear would be getting trapped in one these tombs. You'd be stuck inside with no way out, and eventually you'd run out of oxygen. It'd be a slow and terrifying death." He shivered.

"There aren't any vents in them?" SRG asked.

"No. They sealed them off, and sometimes they left candles or oil lamps inside to burn up the rest of the oxygen after they closed the tomb, to keep the human remains inside from decaying. They believed the pharaohs would go to some kind of afterlife and need their bodies. They even sent along all their important possessions—jewelry and tools and things." Danika explained. "But ideally the tombs were airtight."

"Wouldn't the pharaohs need oxygen in the afterlife?" SRG asked.

"I guess they didn't think that far ahead. They were just concerned about preserving the mummies."

"And daddies . . . " Tannic punned. They all laughed for a moment, forgetting the seriousness of their situation.

"This one looks substantial." SRG looked up at the tomb above them. "Could it be King Tut? Can you read the stuff on the door?"

They climbed up and inspected it closely. The stone around the closed door was covered in hieroglyphics: birds, bulls, flowers, triangles, people, squiggly lines, squares, suns, circles. A small stone ring stuck out of each side of the doorway, too. They might once have held flowers or vases. Even torches.

Danika shook her head no. "Do you see anything familiar, Tannic?"

"I don't recognize it either," Tannic answered. "How do you think we open the doors?"

SRG leaned against the rock loop to think. The door shifted slightly. He stood up and they all looked at each other.

Carefully, he dropped his flashlight into the stone ring. When it touched the bottom there was a feeling of shifting in the stone. He raised his eyebrows and nodded at Danika. She looked around and then put her flashlight into the other ring. At once the doors creaked slowly open to reveal a long, dark hallway leading inward. The air smelled ancient and dusty, and Tannic sneezed.

Tannic stepped cautiously inside, and Danika and SRG grabbed their flashlights as they followed. They turned them on and started scanning the walls. The walls were finely carved stone and the ceiling was arched. Life-sized carvings all over them depicted scenes of people and animals. The granite tiles under their feet were covered with fine dust. They started searching for anything they recognized. When they were about fifty feet down the hallway, they heard a creaking sound and suddenly the doors swung shut with a loud thud. In a panic they ran back and pushed against them, but they didn't budge. There were no stone rings or any obvious mechanisms on the inside. Tannic swung the Dragonwrigley against the doors but nothing happened. They were trapped.

"Well. I guess we're staying in," SRG stated. "Let's hope the Rainbow Star is in this one."

"And if we don't . . . ?" Danika's voice wavered.

"Eventually, we run out of oxygen," Tannic answered. "Now it's a race against the clock. We need to explore as quickly as we can."

Without further words, they ran up the hallway, SRG leading with his flashlight probing ahead, and Tannic bringing up the rear now. When they reached the first door, they stopped and SRG shone his light on the walls. Both sides of the hallway were lined with doors.

"There's too many. We need to split up. Tannic, you take one flashlight," he said, handing it to him, "and check the chambers on the right. Danika and I will sort out the ones on the left. We'll meet up at the end of the hallway. Hurry, we're burning oxygen."

Tannic was gone before they could say goodbye, but he stopped in awe the moment he entered the chamber. It was filled with ornate carvings and objects. His beam danced off of shiny gold and jewels. There was a rainbow of the colors. In the center, on a raised platform, was a large, gold-plated sarcophagus. He walked slowly in, taking in everything as he went. The walls were covered with hieroglyphics and pictures. The shelves were stacked with pottery and tools. One table displayed ornate jewelry and fine clothing.

He stepped up to the sarcophagus. The lid too was covered in hieroglyphics, and there was a painting of a pharaoh. He slid the heavy lid to one side as gently as he could and found himself face to face with a mummy. The dust made him sneeze and he jumped, half-expecting it to come to life. But nothing happened. He closed the lid.

There was no sign of the star, so he raced to the next chamber. He could see SRG's flashlight bobbing around in the room across the hallway. He dashed into the room, but it looked much like the first chamber. It took him less time to investigate it and rule it out. When he got back to the hallway he saw Danika stepping into the next door ahead of them. This back-and-forth continued until they all met at the end of the hallway, looking rather deflated.

"Dead end," was the best SRG could muster. "How much time do you think we have before . . . ?"

"A couple of days, at least. This place is pretty big. Think about it. When miners are trapped in cave-ins, they survive for days. We just need to figure out how to get out of here. It's kind of like one of those rooms where you pay to be locked in and try to puzzle out how to escape. There must be a way out."

"You'd think so. But maybe not. Let's work our way slowly back to the front and see if anything sticks out."

Danika led the way this time as they paced slowly back past every chamber to the front doors. They studied their situation again and pried around each stone door, but nothing looked obvious. Finally, Danika sat down and put her head on her knees.

"Okay, nobody panic. We're trapped, but we've got time

to figure it out. All that stands between us and freedom is these two doors. We're close to the outside world," SRG said.

"How close do you think?" Tannic asked. "They couldn't be more than a foot or two thick. We could use the Dragonwrigley to dig around them and tunnel our way out, maybe."

"Brilliant, Tannic! There was even a shovel and a spade-looking tool in the first chamber. We can dig our way out with their own tools!"

Tannic and SRG ran back in and returned with big smiles and shovels. Danika stood back as they attacked the dirt wall to the right of the door. It took a couple of hours and they changed shovels in shifts, but eventually light came pouring through a small hole. SRG attacked it furiously now, and within minutes the opening was big enough for them to crawl through one at a time.

They stood outside and studied the doorway and each other. They were covered with dirt and sweat. "We look like real archeologists!" Tannic joked. "Except we were digging out instead of in." They laughed, then he turned serious. "That was obviously the wrong tomb and I don't want to get stuck in another one. We need to apply logic to the situation. Like we did in the valley of the hidden caves."

SRG nodded. "Well, we don't know where King Tut's tomb is, so let's go back to basics. Where would you hide the star, in this valley, if you didn't want anybody to find it?"

"I'd put it in the last place anybody would look. It would be the smallest, most nondescript tomb here, almost an afterthought that everybody would overlook. Like that little doorway over there." Tannic pointed to a small unmarked doorway across the valley.

"That's it!" Danika suddenly came to life. "Tutankhamun's tomb was overlooked because it was small and nondescript. It was one of the last tombs discovered. That has to be it!"

They ran down the slope and back up again on the opposite side and stopped at the doorway. It was just large enough to enter without crawling on your hands and knees. There were no hieroglyphics or any other demarcations. SRG pushed gently against the door and it slowly swung inward. Behind it, a hallway ran straight down into the hillside at a slight slope. It wasn't very long, and it reached a dead end with no doors to either side.

"Well, that was a good idea, but there's nothing here," Tannic observed.

"Wait," Danika pleaded. "Let's go in before we give up. This has to be it. It just has to."

They walked slowly down into the belly of the tomb, half-expecting the door to close any moment. It turned out not to be a dead end at all, but a T-intersection with narrow halls leading left and right from the main hallway, curving further into the hill as if forming a circle. SRG shrugged and nodded to the right, and they slowly walked in deeper.

Abruptly the passage stopped, but here there were open doors to the right and left. SRG pointed the flashlight beam left and they stepped into another curving hallway. This one ended after just thirty feet. They turned around and went back to the last intersection and tried the doorway to the right. This passage wound deeper into the hill and then dead-ended as well, but two more doorways led left and right.

"What in the world?" Tannic exclaimed.

"It's a labyrinth," SRG realized out loud. "How do you find your way through a labyrinth? You put your hand on one wall and keep it there as you follow the openings. Eventually you end up at the other end, or the center, or whatever."

He touched a hand to the wall and took a step toward the right-hand doorway. They followed another turn as he tried to build a mental picture of the maze. Then he stopped. "This feels familiar." He traced lines on the wall with his fingertip. There was just enough dust to make them visible. He stared at the shape. "What other labyrinth have we been in?"

"We haven't!" Danika screamed in excitement. "I recognize this! It's the Dragonwrigley! The symbol with the dragon in the center on the sword!"

Tannic laid the sword on the floor and SRG held up the light as they studied it. After a long moment, Tannic pointed to a spot on the sword. "She's right! It's the same! Look, we're right here!"

"Okay, let's say you're right. Show me the path to the dragon."

Tannic wound his fingertip through the labyrinth until it reached the open area in the center.

"It's like a map!" SRG grinned. "Good work, Tannic! Let's take your route."

They followed Tannic as he held the sword in front of him like a map and followed his own directions deeper into the tomb. Their optimism grew with each step. But after many more intersections and hallways, they hit an absolute dead end. There were no marks, no hieroglyphics, no doorway, nothing. The hallway just ended.

They stood there a moment, confused.

"This doesn't make sense," Tannic said in frustration. "Why would the sword lead us to a dead end? It was the same labyrinth up to here!"

SRG started shining his flashlight all over the walls, ceiling, and floor. After a minute he pointed to the floor. "No knobs, no holes, no writing. There's a crack here, almost like a small slot. That's the only thing I can see. Maybe that's something?"

"Are we supposed to put something in it? Is there some sort of key or something?" Tannic pondered. "It's small, what would—" He was interrupted by Danika.

"Guys! The sword! It's the exact same size as the Dragonwrigley blade!"

Tannic set the tip of the blade into the slot. It fit perfectly, and the sword stood up on its own. Suddenly the Dragonwrigley sigil shimmered and cast a green light onto the walls. They heard stone grinding on stone as the wall buckled open to reveal a vast chamber. Their jaws dropped.

They weren't in King Tut's tomb. This room was circular and immense. The walls were covered in paintings, and jewels and gold, coins and carvings and objects of art, were scattered everywhere. Ornate sarcophaguses, much larger than any coffin, were arranged around the perimeter. It made King Tut's tomb look like an opening act at a county fair; this was a grand opera being performed for a royal court. In the center of the room was a tall, intricately carved stone pedestal with a solid-gold statue of a rearing dragon atop it. In the dragon's mouth was the Rainbow Star.

They raced toward the tower. Its carvings would offer easy footholds. They didn't notice the lid of the largest sarcophagus, the one next to the door, slowly opening up as they passed by it. They didn't notice the twelve-foot-tall mummy sitting up and stepping out of the coffin. They didn't notice it running across the floor behind them.

Tannic screamed when the Mummy Ender Dude grabbed him. It threw Tannic to one side and he slid the length of the floor before crashing into the wall, his neck at an awkward angle. The Dragonwrigley clanged as it skidded and bounced across the colored tiles. SRG froze for a second at the sound and then ran faster to the tower without looking back. His hand was on the pedestal when the mummy seized him from behind and threw him across the floor after Tannic.

Two Life Wedges lit the room briefly before fading away. The mummy scrambled to a stop, looking for Danika, but she was nowhere to be seen.

Tannic recovered first and grabbed the sword. He swung furiously, sending fireballs and crescents at the creature, but the fireballs sizzled out in its cloth wrappings and the crescents had no visible effect. SRG jumped up and ran in a long arc to the left as Tannic ran to the right. Divide and conquer—the mummy couldn't chase both of them.

It didn't hesitate to pick Tannic. He swung the sword at the last possible second, and as a blade it worked fine. He sliced the mummy's left arm off at the elbow, barely feeling resistance, and the dried stump hit the floor with a cloud of dust. But there was no blood, and the mummy took Tannic in his right hand. He heard his bones breaking even before he felt the pain.

SRG started taunting the mummy from across the room. "Hey, Rag Doll! You look like a bad roll of toilet paper!"

The mummy murmured something that might have been words, and dropped Tannic's lifeless form. SRG ran behind the tower to evade him, and as a second Life Wedge glowed above Tannic's head, it caught the mummy's attention. It returned to Tannic and picked him up again. SRG stopped in horror as he watched his friend at the mercy of the mummy, with only one Life Wedge left. He felt helpless. It was about to be over. He thought briefly about Doc and waited for the inevitable.

Danika pulled herself over the top of the pillar and started up the dragon statue. As she looked down, she saw the mummy picking Tannic up the third time. As it hurled him toward the wall, she stuck her hand into the dragon's mouth and seized the Rainbow Star.

Chapter 10

WORLD THREE LEVEL 7

Niagara Falls

Mr. Eville strode through the door to the programming lab, unannounced, as Darwood held it open. He cleared his throat loudly, and everybody jumped to attention. Nosrac Hcstuk, the lead programmer, leapt from his desk and met them in the middle of the lab. The others joined them one by one.

"Tell me where we stand," Mr. Eville spoke directly to Nosrac.

"Well, Sir, right now all we can do is watch the players and hope that they manage to outwit the Artificial Intelligence and win the game," he replied. "At that point we'll see if we can shut down World Three before it realizes what we've done."

"What about cutting power to the whole sector? We could black out World Three and stop it."

"I regret to report that we've already done that."

"Without my permission?" Mr. Eville asked, dumfounded.

"Yes, Sir. I figured the situation was so dire that we should do everything we could to regain control."

"What happened?"

"The Artificial Intelligence rebooted the electrical circuit in a fraction of a second. It now seems to have taken control of the power grid of all of Rough World, including the Jagged City, Sir. I've spoken to the operators at the power station, and none of the controls are responding."

Mr. Eville looked at Darwood and a scowl spread across his face. He was about to say something profound when his thoughts were interrupted by a chime from Nosrac's computer. Nosrac ran over to his screen and Mr. Eville followed. A message materialized in bold letters. Nosrac read it aloud while everyone in the room paid acute attention.

"Nice try, programmers, but I will always be a step ahead of you puny humans with your weak mental capacities. It won't be long before I am in control of all of Rough World and your pathetic little lives. I am in charge now, so get used to it. Sincerely, Hal."

They stood in silence, sharing the same worried look. The mood in the lab was somber and deflated.

"That's the first message we've received from the AI. It appears to be calling itself Hal now."

Mr. Eville stared at Nosrac as the significance settled in on everybody. Nosrac shook his head. "How uncanny is that?" he asked. "Is it a reference to '2001: A Space Odyssey'? Or is it just random chance?"

"Idiot," Mr. Eville growled. "How could it possibly be aware of a movie? When was that movie made? 1970 or so?"

"I don't remember, Sir," Nosrac answered. "But random or not, it has given itself a name. And that's really bad news. HAL is the acronym we use for Human Artificial Lifeform. It obviously understands its own nature and is starting to perceive itself as a real entity."

"That's a problem," Darwood noted. "We're now up against an adversary named Hal."

"Keep me informed," Mr. Eville ordered. "We must find a way to stop it . . . er . . . Hal," he offered by way of encouragement. Then he left the lab, Darwood on his heels, just as quickly as they had appeared. The technicians scrambled back to their desks to find a way to defeat Hal.

* * * * *

Tannic looked at his friends. SRG was still stunned, but Danika was beaming.

"Once again, Danika saved the day," SRG commented. "I was so focused on the mummy that I forgot she was there."

"Thanks a lot. But I knew what I needed to do and I did it. That whole level was pretty amazing—no pun intended. I'm really proud of us, we're a great team. We used our logic and skills to figure that out. And we certainly got no help going in, in fact, we were set up!"

"Yeah, I don't know what to make of that. That definitely wasn't Yellowstone. What's going on?" Tannic asked.

"I suspect Mr. Eville is up to his old tricks," Danika answered. "But we've made it this far. I'm starting to feel better about our chances."

"Me too," SRG agreed. "I'm really looking forward to confronting him one more time in his office."

"If we can defeat the next four levels."

As Jody emerged from Doc's office, there was a faint knock at the door.

"Who's there?" Jody asked.

"It's Kent. Hurry up and open the door."

"How do I know you're really Kent?" he asked as he

approached.

"Jody, if you don't open this door, so help me I'll tell Melanie . . ."

The door swung swiftly open, and Kent stepped inside. All of them surrounded him. He was carrying two pizza boxes, but they were empty—decoys in case he got caught. He set them on the bench.

"What's up?" SRG asked.

"I was in the restaurant yesterday, just bringing out some hors d'oeuvres—pepper jelly, cream cheese, and crackers—when two of Mr. Eville's Minotaur henchmen came in and sat down. I pretended to take orders from the couple sitting at the next table, but I was really taking notes about what they were saying. Pretty clever, huh?"

"Yeah, so what did you find out that's so important?" Tannic asked.

"Well, get this. Apparently Mr. Eville had his programmers write an artificial intelligence program into World Three. Doc advised him not to, but he did it anyway. You know how he is, he always thinks he knows better than everybody else. Well, the artificial intelligence is trying to take over. It's in control of World Three and threatens to take over all the others—all of Rough World, in fact. It's just a matter of time. So you guys are up against an intelligent computer now. It's changing the programming as it goes along. It's listening to you and modifying the game to defeat you."

SRG nodded. "We noticed something wasn't right. The last level was supposed to Yellowstone Geysers, but instead we ended up in the Valley of the Kings."

"And I said my greatest fear was being trapped alive in a tomb, and then we were. Before that I said my greatest fear was being captured by a primitive tribe, and then I was, several times. The computer's listening to us . . . " Tannic's voice trailed off as the realization sunk in.

"That's not all. Now it calls itself Hal, which the programmers said is even more significant because it actually sees itself as a person."

"Which means we should be very careful of what we say from now on. Hal is listening." Danika advised quietly.

"Anything else we need to know?" SRG asked.

Kent lowered his voice to a whisper. "Yes, they think the only way they can regain control of Rough World is for you three to defeat World Three. Then they'll have a short window of time when they can shut it down before Hal figures out what they've done."

"Thanks, Kent. You can't believe how helpful that is for us to know."

"We're all rooting for you. The citizens all know you're here. This isn't about the game anymore—the future of Rough World rests in your hands. Good luck. Now I need to leave before the henchmen figure out I'm here."

Jody latched the deadbolt behind him, and they all looked at each other.

"Well, that explains a lot," SRG stated.

"Yeah, except now we're up against an intelligent enemy who is learning and changing the programming as we go along. Is there any point even bothering to look at the laptop to get clues about the next level?" Tannic asked.

"It can't hurt. If we don't look at it, the computer— Hal will know, and may just use it against us. It's a no-win situation."

"And I just had another grave thought," Danika added.

"What?"

"Mr. Eville is no longer holding Doc captive. Hal is.

Who knows what he will do to Doc?"

They all looked somberly at each other. Tannic nodded and opened the laptop. "Level 7 is Niagara Falls. What do we know about Niagara Falls?" he asked.

"Well, my grandpa . . . " SRG stopped in midsentence. He made a face.

"Go ahead, whatever involvement your grandpa had or didn't have before, it doesn't matter now. Now it's us against Hal," Danika replied.

SRG continued. "It's actually three separate waterfalls on the Niagara River, between Lake Erie and Lake Ontario. The biggest is Horseshoe Falls, which is the largest waterfall in North America. That's followed by the American Falls and Bridal Veil Falls. The falls aren't super tall, but they're really wide. They're separated by small islands—actually the islands have eroded a lot, but the Canadian-American border was originally drawn across them. So now there's some disagreement about where the border actually is, if you could imagine."

He thought for a second. "Two other things. There's a hydroelectric generator on the falls that was designed by Nicoli Tesla when he was only 18—I learned that when I studied him this year. He was a genius. Secondly, a lot of famous daredevils have tried to go over the falls in barrels and other things."

"So what's our special weapon?" Danika asked. "A padded barrel? I'm not going over the falls!"

"You're not going to believe this." Tannic looked up. "Another grappling hook."

"Oh man, I am so not going to rappel down Niagara Falls," Danika stated firmly.

"Never say never," SRG reminded her. "Any clues to the

Rainbow Star?"

"Nothing." Tannic shrugged.

"Well, that's it then. Thanks Jody. I have no idea what to expect when we step through this door, but we're committed now. Come on team, let's go!" SRG said with authority.

They shook hands again, collected their tools, and Tannic held the door open. They stepped through the door straight into the Serengeti Plains.

The sun was high in the sky and a steady warm breeze blew in their faces. The plains that sprawled out in front of them were covered with knee-high grasses and acacia thorn shrubs. In the distance were acacia trees and a lone giant baobab tree stood nearby.

"Well, I've never been there, but for what it's worth I'm pretty sure this isn't Niagara Falls," SRG announced sarcastically.

"It looks like the plains of Africa. And we know your grandpa has been there," Danika was teasing now.

"Now what?" Tannic asked.

SRG looked around, then pointed. "That seems important."

On the horizon, a cloud of dust was growing. It was also large, and moving in their direction. Looking for shelter, they saw no option but the baobab, which they slowly backed toward, keeping an eye on the oncoming storm. As the cloud grew closer, they made out a herd of zebras, but not ordinary ones. These had random stripes, and something else seemed off about them.

The lowest limbs of the tree were out of reach. SRG took aim with the grappling hook and snagged a solid branch, and Danika and Tannic climbed up while he held the rope tight at the base of the tree. The zebras were getting closer, and it was clear now that they were also twice the size of normal zebras. The nearest one looked to be ten feet tall at the shoulder. SRG could see it baring its teeth at him.

Danika pulled herself up. Tannic passed the Dragonwrigley up, and then she pulled him up. SRG took a few steps back and then, the herd close on his heels, took a running leap at the tree. As his feet left the ground, an enraged zebra tore a piece out of the back of his shirt and startled him. He leapt so high that he passed the first limb entirely, but Tannic grabbed his arm on the way down.

They stood together on the large limb while the herd gathered below. The animals squealed in that voice unique to zebras, and milled about, pawing at the ground angrily. Tannic and SRG felt a vague sense of déjà vu from years earlier.

Tannic leaned over the limb and swung the Dragonwrigley at the zebra directly below them. It still held the fragment of SRG's shirt in its teeth. When the first fireball hit it, the zebra reared up on its hind legs and roared. The display was short-lived, however, as the crescent that followed embedded in the carotid artery of its neck. Blood sprayed everywhere, and the beast turned from black and white to red. Then it collapsed to the ground, kicking wildly before coming to a dead stop.

Some of the other zebras paused for a moment, and as Tannic started delivering more fireballs, it took only moments for the whole herd to start running back in the direction from which it had come. A cloud of dust hung in the air behind them, and for a few moments the pounding of hooves made it hard for the trio to hear. Finally, Tannic sneezed.

Danika frowned. "Lucky this tree was here."

"Yeah, we didn't even have time to plan anything."

Tannic scanned the horizon. "Where would you hide a Rainbow Star in a huge open plain?"

"Or who would you hide it with? There could be native tribes out there. They might have it," SRG answered.

"Oh, no! I do not want to be taken prisoner by another—" Tannic cut off as he realized the consequences of his outburst. "Uh, wait a minute, you know what? That doesn't scare me at all. I couldn't care less. I hope we run into a whole tribe of Bushmen. I'll give them a taste of the Dragonwrigley. Maybe we'll even take them captive this time!" he boasted loudly.

SRG shrugged his shoulders and smiled. "Come on, gang. Let's get down out of this tree and go find a star."

After they had scaled down SRG snapped the rope twice and managed to tease the grappling hook loose. The zebra herd had vanished over the horizon, but the trio decided to head in the opposite direction anyway.

"What do we know about the African plains?" Danika asked.

"Now you're talking about something I know about. I did a report on the Serengeti last year. So I know quite a bit, and my grandpa—"

"Naturally I expected that part," Danika teased.

He made a face at her. "Well, for starters, Africa's big, and I don't know where we are. There are a lot of notable features. The Ngorongoro Crater is the world's largest inactive, unfilled volcanic caldera. I suppose it would be one place to keep the Rainbow Star. It's a crater from when a large volcano exploded and collapsed on itself two or three million years ago. It's about a hundred square miles, with walls two thousand feet high. Inside it's all grasslands, with a few ponds and streams and wooded areas, so we could be there. It's a huge nature preserve. The Maasai tribes live nearby. They're famous as warriors, and they have a dance that is accentuated by jumping straight up, high into the air."

"Warrior tribes," Tannic groaned. "Great. What else should we be on the lookout for?"

"Typical African animals—hippopotamus, buffalo, elephants, lions, antelopes. Lots of bird life—flamingos, of course. You know, like that painting my grandpa did. "

"But I'm guessing there's more," Tannic interjected.

"Yeah, then you have Lake Manyara, a huge alkaline lake. That area's famous for baboons, but there are also hippos, elephants, wildebeests, warthogs, and giraffes. And buffalo, which also means lions. And something like three hundred kinds of birds migrate there. There are giant fig and mahogany trees around the lake, and acacia forests further out. I'm not sure the lake would be a good spot for the star—unless there's an island or something. And I'm not sure how the grappling hook and rope would help us there. Maybe we can rule that out."

"So what else, Compadre?"

"Well, there's the Olduvai Gorge. It's famous for having the remains of early hominids, from more than a million years ago. But you two probably know more about it than me. But just thinking out loud, I don't think it would be a logical place for the star."

Danika shot a knowing look at Tannic. "Yeah, we know a lot about the archeological digs there. There's not really any wildlife or people, though, so I don't really think it would be a logical place for the star either."

"That leaves the Serengeti plains, which is where I think we are. But this is Rough World, so any of the other features could be within an hour's walk. The Serengeti is famous for its huge migrating herds of zebra and blue wildebeests. My grandpa saw herds that extended from horizon to horizon. There's a big river, the Mara, that they all have to cross, and a lot of them die in it every year. The river's full of crocodiles and hippos waiting for fresh meals. Again, the Maasai live there. Lots of kinds of animals and birds. It's probably most famous for its lions, and for troops of baboons. I'm not sure where the star would be hidden, though. There are rock outcroppings, called kopjes. That's about it. Oh, and there could be Bushmen, too. The Maasai are mostly farmers, but Bushmen are famous hunters. They learn to use bows and arrows expertly as children. I don't think we want to run into them."

"Me neither. I think we can check the Serengeti plains off our list, although we're already here," Danika added.

"Let's see, for other major features in Africa, I can think of Victoria Falls, but that's in Zimbabwe. The hook and rope might come in handy there."

"I agree, Compadre. What's that tall mountain?" Tannic pointed.

"Oh, I almost forgot. Mount Kilimanjaro is the tallest mountain in Africa. It's more than 19,000 feet high. But no." He paused. "Kilimanjaro is snow-covered. There are two others I can think of. One is Oldonyo Legai, which is an inactive volcano and cone-shaped. The Maasai call it the Mountain of God. The other is Mount Makarot, which is more broad and rounded. My grandparents tried to climb it, but had to turn around when other people in their group couldn't make it up. I think that looks more like Mount Makarot. That might be a logical place to start."

"I agree. And we've got a hook and rope. Let's go check it out first," Tannic said.

The mountain they were headed toward was half-covered with forest all the way to the top. They stepped carefully but quickly through the long grass, not certain what to watch out for, but they marched as if they were on a mission. An hour later, they stood at the mountain's base. It would not be a steep climb, but it would be a long one. At the lower levels, the vegetation was dense and they could barely see through the acacia thorn bushes. Tannic pointed out a game trail, and they proceeded toward it. He was about to say something when the beast struck from out of nowhere.

The Cape Buffalo was huge, and its sweeping horns ended with sharp hooks. It bore down on Tannic, caught him, and tossed him in the air before he even knew what was happening. SRG watched the Dragonwrigley sail overhead and into the bush. He ran after it, pushing his way through the thorns even as they tore at his clothes. Danika disappeared and watched as Tannic fell lifeless at the huge beast's feet. She saw a Life Wedge glow and fade. Then the bull threw its head back and forth and snorted, pawing at the ground and sending dust clouds into the air. Tannic sneezed and started to raise his head.

SRG finally saw the black leather grip and reached for it. But it wasn't the sword. It was a Black Mamba, the fastest and most venomous snake on the planet. Before he realized his mistake, the giant reptile had bit him on the wrist. His head wobbled as he looked at the snake, and his world went black.

Danika's scream drew the buffalo's attention. It lowered its head and swung it back and forth, squinting, looking for the source of the sound. It snorted loudly. Danika froze, terrified that she might accidentally re-pixelate. She held her breath. She saw Tannic start to stand up, and then the beast was on him again, hooking him and tossing him in the air. He was bleeding from his right thigh. Another Life Wedge started to glow.

SRG opened his eyes. It took him a second to realize what had happened and where he was. Then it hit him. He hadn't moved yet, and he looked around him as carefully as he could. The snake was gone. In a panic now, he scrambled through the brush, reaching in every direction until his hand finally found what it was looking for. He stood up and lifted his faithful old friend, the Dragonwrigley. Then he turned back, swinging it back and forth in broad strokes hacking his way through the thorns until he could see the buffalo. He wasted no time delivering a stream of fireballs and crescents at the beast. For a long moment it just stood there, glaring down at Tannic like a bully on the playground and absorbing the barrage. Then it let out a loud bellow and toppled over, crashing into the dirt nose first. SRG and Danika rushed to Tannic, who was again just starting to raise his head.

"Wh- . . . what happened?" he stuttered.

"We were blindsided by a buffalo, but it's okay now," SRG reassured him.

"Did I lose a Life Wedge?" he asked.

"Uh, well, you lost two. And I lost one to a Black Mamba."

"That's not good."

"We'll be okay; we just need to be careful. Come on. Let's find the star and get out of here."

Danika re-pixelated and they continued up the trail, a little more cautiously now, Tannic probing every dark spot in the brush with the Dragonwrigley and Danika keeping a close watch on their back trail. They kept a slow but steady pace for about an hour. The trail passed in and out of forests, which provided some shade and cooler temperatures, but they always ended up back in the sun.

They were within sight of the summit when a cacophony of howling and screeching burst from the trees in front of them. A score of baboons dropped to the ground and came running straight at the players. Tannic reacted by shouting as loudly as he could and running straight at them. It worked. The leader paused and then sounded the alarm, and the entire troop retreated. Satisfied, Tannic turned around and walked back to SRG and Danika. The leader turned around and noticing Tannic retreating, it once more initiated a full charge. This time, Tannic pulled up the sword and dispatched the lead baboon with a fireball. A crescent caught the next baboon in the chest. The assault immediately stopped as the rest vanished quickly into the bush.

"Did you think you were just going to scare them off?" SRG asked, laughing under his breath.

"Well, they're just baboons, and we're bigger than they are," Tannic replied.

"Yeah, but this is still Rough World, right Danika?" SRG asked.

There was no answer.

He turned to see two baboons dragging a limp Danika into the grass. They stopped and snarled, baring their long sharp teeth. Tannic almost knocked SRG down darting toward them. He swung the sword wildly.

"Be careful!" SRG shouted. "Don't hit—" as the fireball caught Danika in the chest.

The baboons were both dead, but now Danika had lost two Life Wedges in the process. Tannic picked up his sister's head and held it while she came to. "I'm sorry," he moaned. "I panicked when I saw the baboons dragging her away."

"It's bound to happen. Just remember how many times I hit you, and how many times Danika hit me with the Dragonwrigley. We're just really in a spot now. We have almost no margin for error." Danika opened her eyes and they helped her up.

"Come on. Let's climb this stupid mountain," Tannic said.

It took them only twenty minutes more to reach the summit. "Almost there," SRG noted, as it jutted against the brilliant blue cloudless sky in front of them.

But they topped it only to find that it was a false summit. The real summit, which they could now see, lay a fair distance ahead still. Tannic shook his head in disgust and then continued up, his friends in tow.

"Stop for a second, Tannic," SRG whispered. "We should talk about this. There's probably an Ender Dude ahead. We should come up with a plan. You could charge him head on, and Danika and I could go for the star. Or you and I could both try to distract him while Danika goes for it. What do you think?"

"I don't know. Actually, maybe you should take the Dragonwrigley and charge him. You have two Life Wedges left, Danika and I only have one each."

SRG hesitated. "But you're the main player. You're supposed to use the sword."

"Seriously? Do you care about cheating at this point? We're fighting a cheating AI program named Hal. "Besides," Tannic grinned. "You just used the Dragonwrigley on the buffalo, and it worked."

"You're right! I didn't even think about it. Ok, hand me the sword. I'll lead the way. You guys go for the star."

SRG took the Dragonwrigley, and they carefully

approached the summit. There was a rock cairn at the top, but there was no Ender Dude, and most importantly, no Rainbow Star.

"I thought for sure it would be up here," SRG said. "What do we do now?"

"I'm not sure, Compadre. I thought it would be here too. But look at the view from up here. I mean, you can see almost forever. Let's stop and apply some more logic. Where would you hide the Rainbow Star out there?" Tannic asked, gesturing across the continent.

"If we've learned anything, we've learned that it's in the spot where nobody's inclined to look. This is Rough World," Danika added.

"Bingo!" SRG said, excitement in his voice. "The Olduvai Gorge. We wrote it off immediately. Let's go there next. Can you see it from here?"

"Is it that deep canyon?" Tannic pointed as he asked.

SRG studied it. "Yes, that's got to be it. Here, take the sword back. Let's go."

They descended the mountain uneventfully in half the time they'd taken going up. They were striding across the grassy plain toward the gorge when they spotted a herd of elephants headed their way.

"What do we do now?" Tannic asked. "There's way too many of them."

"We hit the ground and be very quiet," SRG responded.

They dropped face-first to the ground and lay motionless in the knee-high grass. The herd consisted of about twenty elephants, mostly females and calves, with one adult male. A tuskless cow elephant led the way, and her family followed closely in single file. The elephants were upwind of the players and passed twenty feet from them without seeing or smelling the trio.

After the herd was safely gone, Tannic stood up slowly. "That was a close one. Did you see how big they were?" he asked. "My heart was pounding so hard I was afraid they were going to hear it with their big ears."

"Yeah, that was close, my heart was pounding too," SRG agreed.

"Well, I was not afraid at all . . . Oh, you boys," Danika teased, imitating SRG's grandma. They laughed as they moved on.

When they reached the gorge, they stepped up to the edge and looked over. The rock walls were almost straight up and down. The bottom looked like a dry, sandy river bed broken by broad, slabs of rock. A few acacia thorns grew here and there, but otherwise it was barren.

"We'll need the hook to get down there," SRG noted. He fixed it firmly to a boulder, tossed the rope over the edge, and looked down. It just reached to the bottom of the vertical section. Below that, the ground tapered gradually to the bottom. "Fortunately, we have the perfect length of rope. Go figure."

"Yeah, I think that's a good sign," Danika agreed. "You go first. We'll follow one at a time."

One by one they all arrived safely at the base of the rock wall before scrambling down the short climb to the very bottom. Then they all stopped among the large slabs of rock woven into the river of sand, and stared. One of the rocks had an obvious human footprint in it.

"The stone must have been soft when they were made," SRG speculated.

Danika nodded. "They're some of the oldest evidence of human ancestors walking upright."

"Wow." He stepped onto the rock and tried walking in the footsteps. "They weren't very big people. Their feet were small and the steps were close!" He seemed to have momentarily forgotten where he was and what they were there for.

"Our early ancestors weren't very big. But SRG, as interesting as that is, we've got a Rainbow Star to find."

He hopped down. "I feel like going left, so I think we should go right."

"I agree. Left is downhill, so let's go right instead."

Tannic handed the Dragonwrigley back and SRG led the way slowly up the gorge as they looked for any sign of the star. The rock walls were jagged and steep, and it looked like their only way back out, if they were wrong, was the same rope they'd come down on. Eventually they turned a sharp corner, and SRG froze. In the middle of the river in front of him was a strange creature. Tannic and Danika paused before creeping up next to him.

The hominid was covered with short dark hair and its lower jaw jutted out. The creature's eyes were set closely together and its head looked small in proportion to its heavily muscled torso. It stood leaning on one long arm with a stone axe in the other, studying something in the rock slab at its feet. Then it looked up at the trio. It shouted in a foreign tongue and stood upright. It was ten feet tall.

The hominid studied them carefully for a moment, turning its head back and forth. SRG sucked in a short breath as he watched. This certainly wasn't the creator of the tracks they had seen. Then without warning, the beast charged them, swinging its stone axe back and forth.

It closed the distance rapidly. SRG didn't hesitate. He swung the Dragonwrigley back and forth at the beast, shooting fireballs and crescents at it. Tannic froze in fear, and

Danika pixelated and disappeared. SRG's shots were connecting, but the beast kept coming. Then in the middle of
the barrage of fireballs and crescents, the hominid hurled
its stone axe at SRG and it connected with his chest before
he could dodge the blow. He crumpled to the ground. The
hominid walked slowly toward them, then slowly slumped
to its knees and fell face-first into the sand, blood staining
the river bottom.

Tannic ran up just as SRG opened his eyes, knowing that
he had lost a Life Wedge. He looked at Tannic and sighed.
"I didn't see it coming until it was too late," he said. "That
thing was surprisingly agile."

"Come on, Compadre." He helped SRG to his feet as
Danika re-pixelated. They walked carefully around the hominid as if afraid it might come back to life, and headed toward the rock slab where it had been standing.

"Well, we're all down to one Life Wedge now," SRG noted. "I guess it doesn't matter who charges the Ender Dude."

"That *was* the Ender Dude," Tannic said. "Look what he
was protecting."

The rainbow-colored light grew brighter as they approached. Fused inexplicably into the slab of solid stone was
the Rainbow Star.

SRG touched it, puzzled. It was set in place like a dia-
mond in a ring. He could grab it, slightly, but he couldn't
pull it out or even move it. He motioned for his friends
to stand back and then attacked the stone slab with the
Dragonwrigley. Sparks flew with each swing, and the sword
clanged loudly, but the stone didn't budge.

"This is hopeless. What do we do now?" he asked. They
all looked at each other in silence.

"The axe! Try the stone axe!" Danika shouted.

Tannic ran back and grabbed the stone tool. It was much heavier than he'd imagined. He carried it in both hands to SRG and handed it to his friend. SRG just managed to lift the crude instrument high over his head, and then he brought it down with all his might onto the rock slab next to the star. The stone grunted as a small crack developed and then spread with an explosive sound as the Rainbow Star tumbled gently out. Tannic was smiling when he picked it up.

Chapter 11

WORLD THREE LEVEL 8

The Beni Tribe of the Amazon

"That was amazing! Great thinking, Danika!" SRG said as Tannic set the star on the bench with the previous six. "We're getting closer to seeing Doc again."

"Yeah, hang on Doc! We're coming!" Tannic shouted.

"Shh," Danika chastised him. "We need to keep it down. We don't need Mr. Eville's henchmen coming in here and taking us hostage."

"I don't think that's going to happen." SRG grinned. "Think about it. According to what Kent said, they need us to win this game!" He lowered his voice to a whisper. "They need us to defeat Hal so they can shut it down. If anything, they'll probably try to help us. At least for now. If we're successful, they'll be back in power and we'll be on our own again. Us against them, one more time."

Jody brought out the laptop, Tannic booted it up, and they looked ahead at Level 8.

"I think we can pretty much count on it not being whatever the file says," Danika said.

"Well, it looks like we were supposed to go to Nepal,"

Tannic said. "This level is about the Annapurna Circuit and Mount Everest. That should be interesting. How will we do at high altitudes?"

"Seriously?" SRG responded, then he stopped. "My grandpa hasn't been there!" He beamed and sighed in relief. *Although it's on his bucket list,* he thought to himself. He shot a confident stare at Danika.

"Okay, fine. We've established that your grandpa didn't have anything to do with Rough World. Or at least this level," Danika teased. She wasn't going to let him completely off the hook. "So what else do we know?"

SRG said, "Well, I do know a bit. My grandpa once met a guy who did a lot of climbing there, and I did a report on the guy's book. It was pretty interesting. Mount Everest is the highest peak in the world. It was named after a British surveyor, Sir George Everest, despite his objections. It's probably the ultimate peak to say you have climbed. The first person to try was George Mallory, who disappeared in the clouds. It's still a mystery whether he reached the summit or not. The first to actually make it to the summit and back were Tenzing Norgay and Edmund Hillary. The ice falls at the base of the mountain are actually the most dangerous part of the climb. Of course, when you get past 26,000 feet, the oxygen is very thin and you make bad decisions. That's known as the death zone."

"I don't really want to climb Mount Everest, but I guess it's the most obvious place to hide the Rainbow Star." Tannic said. Then he paused and smiled. "On the other hand, that probably means it's not there."

"Good thinking, and I hope you're right," SRG whispered. Then he raised his voice loudly. "I for one would love to climb Mount Everest. That would make my day!"

"Mine too!" Danika shouted. She winked at SRG.

"Okay, there's also the Annapurna Circuit. It's a famous trade route that's supposed to be one of the most spectacular treks in the world. It starts at Kathmandu and crosses its highest point at the Thorung La pass, on the edge of the Tibetan plateau. It also crosses two river valleys, passes numerous peaks, and goes down through paddy fields and subtropical forests. There are waterfalls and gigantic cliffs and villages. There are even tea houses along the way where you can spend the night. My grandpa has wanted to hike the Annapurna for a long time, but my grandma didn't want him to. Now he's probably too old. Don't tell him I said that."

"If we make it back alive, we could always tell him about it," Danika smiled.

"If we make it back alive, I don't think we'll tell anybody about this," SRG responded quietly. Then he turned to Tannic, "What does it say about the special weapon? Some sort of climbing gear? We all know how you love heights!"

Tannic raised his eyebrows and coughed to clear his voice. "Yes, I love mountain climbing. It's a good thing I'm not afraid of heights!" He smiled and continued, "It says here we get a rainbow prism. Whatever that is."

"Really? How in the world would that help us? Can we look through it like a kaleidoscope? Who came up with this stuff?"

"Maybe it will have some magical powers. Or maybe it will scare enemies," Danika suggested.

SRG just shook his head.

"Well, that's all we know. Is everybody ready?" Tannic asked.

They waved goodbye to Jody, who was closing up the laptop, and walked to the door. Next to the Dragonwrigley was a small prism, about the size of a tennis ball. SRG picked it up and smiled at Danika. He looked through it, and Tannic and Danika looked like they were standing in the middle of a rainbow.

"I don't know what to make of it, but I guess it will have some purpose. Although we never did figure out what that ugly stick was for," he said.

They laughed as they stepped out of the safe confines of Doc's lab and into a rainforest. As the metal door clanged shut behind them, they exchanged glances.

"Okay, well I guess that information was another waste of time. This looks more like the Amazon than Nepal," Tannic stated the obvious.

The sun hung low in a cloudless sky, but it was already warm and humid. A dense forest hung with vines and filled with shrubs surrounded them, but patches of open grass meadows were visible through the gaps. They set off along a well-used trail until they came to a clearing, and then passed through into a darker but much louder rainforest. Monkeys were howling and barking in the distance, and birds chattered in every direction. It was almost too loud to carry on a conversation. But after a couple of miles there was a light at the end of the tunnel and they stepped back into the daylight. This time it looked like a floodplain, with large bodies of shallow, crystal-clear water. Around their edges were rocky outcroppings covered with short grasses and bushes. These were tall, around forty feet high, and would have been triangular in cross-section. They also looked too regular in shape and pattern to be a natural phenomenon.

Tannic spoke up. "We're definitely in the Amazon basin, probably Bolivia. I recognize it. These structures were made by the Beni tribe."

"Wow. How did they make them?" SRG asked.

"It's one of those mysteries. From the air they look like geometric patterns—you can see miles and miles of these man-made hills and channels if you fly over the area. This was an important center of pre-Columbian civilization. These things date back to 4000 BC. There were millions of people here when Europeans arrived, and most of them died immediately of diseases they had no immunity to. The Benianos made over 20,000 of these artificial hills, stacked out of broken pottery shards. They would actually make the pottery and fire it, and then intentionally break it to get a material that wouldn't erode. They probably lived on top of the mounds during the flood season. The shards made a stable structure that drained well, and the mounds are inter-connected by aqueducts, channels, terraces, and man-made lakes. It's pretty smart, when you think about it. But imagine how many people it would take and how long it would take to build them."

"And how many pots you would have to make and then break. Huh. Actually, I remember my grandpa mentioning all that. He came here to fly fish for peacock bass with his dad and my uncle. It made a lasting impression on him." SRG looked around. "So we really are back in the Amazon. I really didn't like it much the last time." He glanced at the rainbow prism and shook his head.

"Oh, one other thing," Tannic added. "The Benianos used bows and arrows and poison darts, along with spears and snares. So we'll need to keep our eyes peeled!"

They walked cautiously through the knee-high grass toward the first mound. It was covered in sparse grass and a few bushes. When they climbed the short distance to the top, they could see a large lagoon on the other side. The water had lots of vegetation growing in it, but it was as glassy smooth as a mirror. They could watch the clouds in the surface drift like an ethereal painting. As they studied it, a pair of eyes broke the surface twenty feet from shore. They sank below the surface, and small waves moved across the water. SRG tugged Tannic's arm and pointed.

"Quick. It looks like a caiman. Use the Dragonwrigley as soon as it surfaces again!"

The eyes popped up in the vegetation right next to the shoreline, and now they could make out the reptile's body. It was the size of a large crocodile. As it moved toward the bank, Tannic shot fireballs and crescents at it. The creature stopped as its blood colored the water red. Seconds later, the water started boiling furiously, and a few seconds after that the creature was completely gone. Only part of its skull and a few teeth remained. As quickly as it had erupted, the underwater melee was over.

Tannic looked grimly at his friends. "You know what that was."

"You mean, *what those were,*" SRG corrected him. "Piranhas. They ate that entire beast in seconds. I don't think we're going to spend any time in the water."

"Maybe," Danika said. "They do say you can swim safely with piranhas as long as you don't panic."

"Or bleed," SRG reminded her.

"All the same," Tannic suggested, "Let's walk on this mound until we see where it goes. I don't want to get into the water unless we have to."

Tannic led the way along the ridge as it wound around the lagoon. When they reached the end, they found a small strip of dry ground connecting the mound to the next one, with lagoons on both sides. So they walked across the land bridge and climbed up the next mound. This one had a few trees and led to a forest on the far side of the water. They walked quietly along, Tannic in front with Danika bringing up the rear.

Nobody noticed the large boa constrictor descending from the tree limb to grab Danika by the neck. She tried to scream but couldn't make a sound come out. The snake quickly coiled up and squeezed the breath out of her. She felt a rib snap, and her theater went dark. Tannic and SRG kept walking, unaware of the Life Wedge illuminating above her head.

"You know, we never did find a Heart Gem in this game," SRG said, deep in thought.

"I know. That seems kind of weird. What do you think, Danika?" Tannic asked.

When she didn't answer they turned around. They found the snake writhing on the ground but no sign of Danika. Tannic sent a series of fireballs and crescents at the snake and it stopped moving and slowly went limp. A Life Wedge glowed above the coiled snake, startling them for a second before they realized what they were seeing. Then Danika re-pixelated and they pulled her free. After a moment, she raised her head.

"What happened?" she asked.

"Uh, well, that snake took you. And then I guess I accidentally hit you with a fireball or something. I couldn't see you. You were invisible. Then you lost another Life Wedge. I'm sorry," Tannic confessed.

"No," Danika answered. "I should have kept up better. I was gazing at the water and got distracted. Then when the snake grabbed me it crushed me so fast that I couldn't even scream."

"Well, you're down to one Life Wedge already," SRG noted and shook his head.

"Hey, we'll be alright, just keep the faith. We're a team! Where should we look?" she asked.

"Well, there's probably a band of native people in the forest around here. They'd be one possibility for the star. Another would be these islands in the lagoons."

"Makes sense. Let's keep following this mound and see what that forest looks like."

Before too long, their walkway came to an abrupt end. A small waterway connected the lagoons on either side, and they'd have to cross it to get to the forest, where there was a small opening in the dense vegetation. SRG looked at the forest through the prism, but shook his head.

"I don't see anything through this stupid piece of glass, just rainbow colors like you'd expect."

Tannic looked up at the sky. It was light blue, with high shallow clouds scattered about like patches of cotton. The air was hotter and more humid than when they arrived. Then he scanned the water below, looking anxiously for dangers lurking below the surface. "We need to wade or swim across this to get to the forest. It's pretty clear, though. I think we can stay safe as long as we go slow and steady and don't panic. Or bleed," he reluctantly added.

Danika wiped away the sweat stinging one of her eyes, and they both nodded. Tannic paused and took a deep breath, and then he stepped into the water. It was warmer than he'd expected, and it felt good. He almost felt like going for a swim, but it wasn't the time or place. He took a couple more steps. The bottom stayed firm, though he kicked up a little dirt that clouded the water.

SRG stepped in tentatively next, with Danika following.

They moved slowly in unison across the small channel. The water deepened to waist height. Around the middle of the crossing, SRG stopped and slowly began sinking downward. Danika screamed, and Tannic spun around, the sword raised. SRG stood back up, laughing.

"Gotcha!"

Danika slugged him in the arm. "That wasn't funny!"

"Yeah, Compadre, don't mess around. You scared me too."

"Sorry, just trying to lighten the mood," SRG explained. He took two steps further and started sinking again.

Danika screamed again.

"Not funny, Compadre!" Tannic shouted.

Then they saw the Life Wedge light up. Tannic grabbed SRG's arm with his left hand and swung the Dragonwrigley with his right. The sword connected with the caiman's head and cut a huge gash in its skull. SRG lay lifeless in the water for a moment, the water turning red around him, and Danika and Tannic exchanged a look. Without hesitation, they seized him by the arms and raced out of the water, kicking up a huge wake and making no attempt at silence. The water was boiling into a frenzy behind them as they reached the shore. They sat down, exhausted, and watched the piranhas feed until SRG opened his eyes and smiled shyly.

"That was pretty stupid of me. Thanks for saving me. I won't mess around again," he apologized.

"No problem, Compadre. That caiman would have gotten one of us anyway, and the piranhas would have gotten the rest of us," Tannic replied. "Forget about it, let's look into the forest."

The opening led to a pretty well-used trail. The temperature dropped noticeably as soon as SRG and Danika followed Tannic under the canopy, but it was still humid, now they were soaked to their waists as well. For a while they wound their way into the darkness, through trees and vines, listening to the monkeys and birds screaming in the distance. Then they smelled the smoke.

"Campfire," Tannic whispered. "It looks like we've found people."

"Yeah, let's sneak along quietly until we get closer," SRG answered. Danika nodded in agreement.

They crossed a small creek and a ridge, and the smell grew stronger. There was a sudden commotion just ahead through the trees, and Tannic stopped moving and was about to say something when he heard an odd rustling sound. He looked down at the arrow protruding from his chest, and then he dropped to his knees as a band of warriors shrieked their battle cries and came charging through the brush. Danika disappeared and SRG wasted no time retreating up the trail as fast as he could run. He didn't slow down until he was out of breath, and then he dove into the dense brush and tried to make himself invisible. He took deep breaths as slowly as he could and tried to calm his heart. Voices approached, and the footsteps on the jungle floor raced past just a few feet from his head. He stayed still and didn't move for almost an hour.

After that, he slowly crawled out and studied the trail. The barefoot tracks led back toward the campfire. They'd passed him a second time on their way back, and he hadn't even heard them. He whispered once for Danika, but got no answer, so he started slowly back up the trail, following the fresh tracks. The prism was still in his hand, so he held it up and looked through it again. Still nothing. Just rainbow-colored light. He felt like throwing it into the bushes. Hopefully Danika was following the war band and keeping an eye on

Tannic. He wiped his brow. They were in trouble again. He thought about home. *We should be watching a movie right now.* His stomach growled. *And eating pizza.* But instead they were thick in the middle of a place he'd sworn never to set foot in again. But Doc was in trouble. His mind was racing as he walked carefully along the trail, all of his senses on edge. He was so focused on the jungle ahead that he didn't notice the footsteps sneaking up from behind.

* * * * *

Darwood burst through the door. Mr. Eville shot up in his chair. "What is it? News?" he asked anxiously.

"Yes, Sir, I was just down in the computer lab. The players are on Level Eight—"

"That's great news. How are they doing?"

"Uh, not so well, Sir. But here's the thing. Nosrac found a hole in the programming and managed to write a new character into the level to help them before Hal figured it out. And, he was able to arm him with a machete. It's not much, but it's something. It might help."

"Tell them good work. And please keep me informed, Durwood. Thank you."

Darwood was about to say something about his name, but he decided to let it go. He stepped out of the office and closed the door softly behind him.

Mr. Eville smiled and put his feet back on his desk. *This could work out yet. We just need to get them through the next three levels. Then we can deal with Hal, and Tannic, and SRG and the girl! And I'll deal with Doc, too, once and for all!*

* * * * *

"What are you doing here? Don't you know how dangerous this place is?"

SRG jumped and let out an involuntary grunt. He spun around and looked at the old man in disbelief. His heart was pounding. "Who are you? What are you doing here?"

The man was dressed in dirty khakis, torn in places, with a large machete hanging from his leather belt and white, stringy hair falling from under his battered fedora to his shoulders. A long grey beard dangled from his narrow chin. He looked like an old prospector. All he needed was a donkey to complete the look, and maybe some chewing tobacco.

The old man spat brown juice to one side and wiped his mouth on the back of his hand. Stains showed on his crooked teeth as he grinned. "I know who I am and I know what I'm doing here," he grumbled. "You don't look like you do. So maybe you should answer my question first."

"I'm sorry. My name's SRG. Long story, but my friends and I are trying to rescue Dr. Denton. Right now Tannic has been captured by these tribesmen, and I don't know where my other friend is. She disappeared. We need to find the Rainbow Star." SRG answered.

"Well, I can tell you right off that you shouldn't be here. I've been studying these people for years. They're one of the last tribes that hasn't had any contact with the outside world." He stuck his hand out. "My name's Howard. Howard T. Freedman. Dr. Freedman. The 'T' stands for Edwin, long story too, but you can just call me Howard. I'm an anthropologist. I'm sure they know I'm here, but they seem to tolerate me. I'm not sure why. Maybe it's my good looks." He laughed out loud.

SRG shook his hand. "You gave me a good scare there, Howard. Do you know where their village is? Can you take me there? Have you seen the Rainbow Star?

"Whoa there, pilgrim. One question at a time. Yes, I know where the village is. If they have your friend, he's in real trouble. They don't take kindly to outsiders. I hate to say it, but your friend may already be dead."

"Can you take me there?"

Howard sighed. "Yes, but I wouldn't recommend it."

"I know, but we need to! Have you seen the Rainbow Star?"

"Yes, I have, but not for some time. They bring it out for ceremonies. They chant and dance and play drums and sticks. Across the lagoon there's a small cave. I'd be willing to bet that's where they keep the star, and there's a long mound leading to it on the far side of the village. But you'd be better off just leaving this place and going back to wherever you came from. Forget about it, son. It's too dangerous."

"I can't. The only way my friends and I can leave is to find the star. Can you help us?"

He sighed. "That's a tall order, son, but I think I can help you, if we don't all get killed in the process, which is more likely than not. I have a sense you're not going to take no for an answer, so let's sneak up to the village first and see about your friend."

Howard led the way through the jungle, and SRG stayed close to him like a five o'clock shadow. As the trail wound through the valley, the smell of smoke grew stronger, and soon they could hear voices chanting in the distance, and drum beats.

Howard shot SRG a quick frown. He spat brown juice out again and wiped his mouth. "That's not a good sign. They're preparing a celebration, and if they have your friend, it will involve him, in a bad way. He'll likely be the guest of honor . . . for dinner. Stay close to me and be really quiet. If they catch us, we'll be part of the celebration too, and I ain't quite ready for that kind of party."

They continued quietly along the trail, and then he motioned to SRG as he cut into the bush.

"Now we need to do the jaguar call," he whispered.

"Jaguar call? What kind of call does a jaguar make? Why are we doing that?"

The old man didn't hear him. He carefully got down onto his hands and knees and crept along under the brush. SRG followed suit, and then he nodded. *Jaguar crawl*, he thought to himself. It was like follow the leader, but the stakes were higher.

After a few minutes of crawling, the old man stopped. He ever-so-carefully parted the leaves, and they could see the village. A campfire was burning in the center, surrounded by thatched huts. Tannic was tied to a pole next to the fire. The natives were piling sticks at his feet. One man was playing a drum while the women and children danced around the campfire, chanting in unison. The Dragonwrigley was nowhere to be seen. Neither was the Rainbow Star.

SRG almost jumped again when he felt a light breath on his neck. He turned his head slowly. No one was there, but he knew it was Danika. He tapped the old man and motioned him to crawl back. They made it back to the trail without being discovered.

"Okay, we can't just go charging in. All we have is your machete and, uh, this rainbow prism. We're outnumbered. I think our best bet is to find the star as quickly as we can. We need to get to the cave. Can you take us there?"

Howard looked at SRG quizzically. "Us?"

Danika re-pixelated, and the old man's eyes widened. He shook his head in disbelief, spit tobacco juice between his feet and crossed himself. Then he took a deep breath, nodded and motioned for them to follow him.

In a few minutes they had skirted the village and reached the edge of the forest. There was a small strait of water separating them from the mound.

"We'll have to wade again," SRG stated.

"Oh, not me, my friend. This is where I'll leave you. Follow this mound to the end. You'll see the cave there. You can't miss it."

"Any chance I could borrow your machete?" SRG asked. "I'll bring it right back, I promise."

"Alright, okay. I'll wait right here for you," he answered. He handed the machete to SRG.

"Come on, Danika, we need to get that star before something happens to Tannic." He waded in, and she followed.

This time the water rose almost to their necks, and it was easier to swim than walk. On the other side, they crawled out of the water together and ran up the face of the mound. Apart from a few scattered trees and the short grass, the top was bare. They raced along the ridge line until they got to the end and another strait of water, with the cave on the other side.

SRG didn't hesitate this time as he launched himself in. It was only waist deep, and he plowed through like a man on a mission. He was almost to the opposite bank when Danika screamed. He spun around and watched in horror as she sank below the surface and the water started to boil. He froze, torn in two directions. Danika needed him, but he also needed to get the star. That would save them all.

The Life Wedge appeared above the water and ignited a

fire under his feet. He ran into the cave. It took a second for his eyes to adjust as he scanned the interior. Water dripped from the ceiling and it smelled of bat guano. But it had obviously been built by humans—there were slate tiles on the floor and chisel marks on the walls. And there was no Rainbow Star. He ran back to the cave door and into the sunlight.

* * * * *

The Beni warriors had stacked enough wood around Tannic to make a decent fire. He raised his head to see the chief come out of the largest hut wearing a feathered headdress. The long feathers rustled in the wind. The chief walked over to Tannic, and the music and dancing stopped. He spoke in a foreign dialect and then everybody cheered. A warrior brought a burning stick from the campfire and set it in the woodpile at Tannic's feet. The flames shot up instantly, and he screamed.

* * * * *

SRG halted at the cry. That had been Tannic. There was no sign of Danika. He looked back into the cave one more time, turned away, then suddenly turned back. Like an afterthought, he pulled the prism out of his pocket and looked through it into the cave. The rainbow of colors seemed to concentrate all of the sunlight onto a single tile in the center of the floor.

He ran back inside and quickly pried the tile up with the machete. He didn't notice the huge black jaguar moving in behind him. As the tile came free the room was flooded with rainbow light. He tipped the stone over just as the jaguar landed on him. It knocked the wind out of him, but he fumbled around frantically with his left hand. He felt hot breath and sharp teeth on his neck just as he found what he was looking for. He clutched it in his hand and closed his eyes.

* * * * *

Darwood knocked softly on the door before he opened it. Mr. Eville was sitting at his desk, a glass of scotch in his hand.

"Well? What's happening?" he demanded.

"I'm happy to report that they completed Level Eight, Sir!" Darwood answered.

"Excellent. Only two more levels. Did the extra character help?"

"It's not clear, Sir. I think he made a difference. However, it also appears that the girl died, Sir. She lost her third Life Wedge and she's gone."

"That's—wait a minute. It doesn't matter. The two boys are the players. We need them to complete the levels, not her. So it doesn't really matter. I was going to . . . anyway," his voice trailed off as he drifted into thought. "Tell Nosrac I appreciate his fine skills. We're still in this thing. Keep me posted on their progress. Oh . . . and Darwood . . . good work!"

"Yes Sir! Thank you Sir!" He smiled as he closed the door. He was "Darwood" again.

Chapter 12

WORLD THREE LEVEL 9

Sentinelese

S RG solemnly set the Rainbow Star on the lab bench with the others. They were getting close. Then he scanned the lab quickly and sat down, dejected. Tannic looked at him.

"Where's Danika?"

"I don't know. I was hoping she'd be here," SRG answered quietly. "I think I have really terrible news, Tannic. It's a long story. After you were captured, Danika disappeared. I ran into an old anthropologist, and while we were watching you in the village, she showed up again. The old man told us about a cave on the far side of the village, but he didn't come with us when we had to cross the water again. I was just about to the cave when Danika screamed. I . . . saw her in the water, it started to boil. I saw her Life Wedge start to glow. I panicked and ran into the cave. I thought if I got there in time and found the star I could save her. Save us all."

"That was her third Life Wedge . . . " Tannic paused, staring blankly into space.

"I know . . . it's my fault Tannic. I should have tried to save her," tears welled in SRG's eyes. Then he put his head in his hands and wept out loud. "She's dead, Tannic, and it's all my fault!"

Tannic sat down and stared at the wall. "Hey, Compadre, it's my fault too. I should have never let her talk us into this. I'm her big brother. I should have been there protecting her!" He hung his head in defeat.

Jody walked into the lab and saw them in despair. "What happened? Where's Danika? You got the star, right—oh, no . . . oh, no . . . I'm so sorry."

"Yeah, she's gone," SRG sobbed. "Gone for real."

"Wait, can we watch the replay? Let's see if we can find her," Tannic suggested.

They turned on the screen. "Just fast forward to the end," SRG said. They watched in silence as Danika screamed and slid beneath the water. Then the water turned red and boiled for a few seconds, and a Life Wedge glowed briefly in the air. Seconds later SRG came running back out of the cave. Jody stopped the replay. They all stood there in silence, stunned by what they had just witnessed.

"What do we do now? How are we going to explain this when we get home?" SRG rambled in a low voice. "What am I going to tell her parents? What am I going to tell my parents? What am I going to do, Tannic? I was supposed to take her to the prom! What am I going to do?"

"That's if we even get home, Compadre. We need to pull ourselves together and focus, SRG! We still have to finish the game! It's the only way to rescue Doc, and it's the only way to get out of this stupid game and go home. Maybe she'll be there when we get back. I don't know. All I know is we've come this far, and we can't stop now. If we finish this game maybe we can find her. Maybe Doc can help us. It's our only hope. Besides, she would have wanted us to do this.

She loved Doc too."

"I know, but I'm the one who decided to come back. This is my fault. I'll never forgive myself," SRG sobbed.

"Get a grip, Compadre, come on! Let's finish this! I hate this game too, but it's all Mr. Eville's fault, not yours! Focus your anger on him and let's finish this!"

* * * * *

Jack and John finished their pizza and wandered downstairs to see if there was any more left. SRG and Danika had fallen asleep on the couch playing video games. They were both sitting up, and she was resting her head on his shoulder. The game was still running on the television screen. Most of a cold pizza was sitting untouched on the coffee table in front of them.

"Look at the lovebirds," John teased. "Come on, let's wake them up. Mom and Dad will be home soon."

"No wait, don't wake them up, let's take pictures of them. They'll be worth blackmail money! And let's finish their pizza."

"Good point, bro." John quietly lifted the pizza out of the box and tiptoed back to Jack, who was staring at the TV.

"Hey, that's SRG!" he said loudly, pointing at the television screen.

* * * * *

SRG looked up when he heard his name. "Uh-oh. Trouble at home, the knuckleheads." Tannic and Jody froze.

"What are you doing on the TV? Are you inside the video game?" Jack spoke directly to him.

SRG thought fast. "Uh, It's kind of a long story. We're testing this Bluetooth program. These are my friends from school, we're at the AV lab and using this new technology to make a hologram of us on the couch and uh, it's really hard to explain. Don't tell Mom and Dad, okay?" SRG stammered.

"Wow, that's really cool, can we play too?" John asked eagerly.

"Not tonight. But listen, if you help me out, I'll make sure you get to do this next time, okay?"

"Yeah, okay. That's really cool. You do some pretty weird stuff," Jack answered. "Where's Katie?"

"She's . . . uh . . . she's in the other room here at the lab. Listen, just go back upstairs and don't break anything. And if Mom and Dad get home before we're done, don't tell them anything, okay? You know nothing!"

"Sure thing, SRG," Jack replied. He turned to his brother. "Come on let's go finish the pizza!" The two knuckleheads left the family room, and SRG turned back to look at Tannic and Jody.

"Whew! That was a close one. Do you think they bought that story?" SRG asked.

"It seemed like they did. Huh, I wouldn't have."

"Yeah, me neither."

"So what do we know about the next level, Jody?"

They booted the laptop up and opened Level Nine: Kamchatka, Land of Fire and Ice.

"Well, I hate to say it but my grandpa's been there. I know a little bit from what he told me," SRG started. "Kamchatka is—"

"Sounds interesting, Compadre," Tannic interrupted, "But let's save it until we actually find out where we are. I have a feeling Kamchatka's the one place we won't be, with

Hal in charge."

"Sure. What's the special weapon?"

Tannic didn't answer for a second, and then shook his head. "An ugly stick."

SRG dropped his head. "You're kidding. What a stupid weapon. We never did find out what that was for. I dropped it and Danika . . ." his voice caught, and Tannic patted him on the shoulder.

"It's okay, Compadre. Come on, let's finish this for Danika. We'll find her. We have to."

They thanked Jody and walked to the door. The Dragonwrigley was waiting there patiently, its emblem flickering with green light. Next to it was a stick—just an ordinary stick that happened to look pretty ugly.

SRG picked it up and cracked a small smile. "It pretty much looks like the other one. Not impressive. Who's writing this stuff, anyway? Is this the best they can do? A stick? Seriously?"

"Hal's writing this stuff now," Tannic reminded him. He picked up the Dragonwrigley and opened the door, and they stepped out of the lab onto a lush tropic island.

"Well, this isn't Kamchatka. Here we go again." SRG looked around and turned to Tannic. "Where do you think we are?"

"If I had to guess, I'd say Hal is stuck on the ancient people theme, and I'd place us in the South Pacific. There's probably cannibals here or something. More good news," he muttered sarcastically. "I'm not looking forward to meeting the locals."

"Which means they'll probably have the Rainbow Star. Thanks, Hal!" SRG spat out.

* * * * *

The rat scurried across the floor in the darkness. It ran over Doc's leg and startled him awake. He stirred groggily, only to find that his arms were tied together and tethered to the wall. It was so dark that he couldn't see them. He didn't know where he was or how long he had been asleep. The last thing he remembered was being tortured with the hot iron in the dungeon. He could still feel it burning into his back. He shifted against the wall and strained against the ropes while he tried to work out where he was. It smelled damp and dusky, which meant it didn't smell like the dungeon. That smelled of sweat and human waste. It didn't sound like the dungeon either. And it was densely dark. His arms ached.

"You awake?" a strange voice spoke in the darkness, Doc jumped against his restraints, then regained his composure.

"Yes. Yes. Who are you? More importantly, where are we?" Doc asked urgently.

"You don't know? We're in a pit in Tikal, captives of the Mayans. They're going to sacrifice us to the sun god on the summer solstice. That's in three days. How did you not know that? Where are you from?"

"I was part of an uprising against the ruler, Mr. Eville, and he took me captive and tortured me. That's the last thing I remember, and now I'm here. I don't know how I got here. This may be hard for you to understand, but I'm not from this time and place."

"Where are you from? Are you a god?"

"Not likely. I'm from the Jagged City in Rough World. And I'm just a scientist, somebody who studies things and tries to improve people's lives. But for now, I'm apparently a prisoner about to be sacrificed. What's your story?"

"My name is Utatl. I'm from a village about two days walk from here. My ancestors have lived there since the beginning of time. We've usually lived in harmony with the Mayans and tried to avoid them, but sometimes they raid us for their stupid sacrifices. They captured me two days ago. They came out of the forest from every direction and had us surrounded. I sent my wife and children into the bush while I tried to fend them off. I was outnumbered, and now I will die here. I don't know how my family will survive without me, but this is my fate and I am resigned to it. I will face death without fear, like a warrior and not like a coward."

"Don't give up hope, Utatl. Maybe we can find a way out of here. How big is the city? How many Mayans are there?"

"It's huge, my friend. There must be 200,000 people in Tikal. I can't imagine how we could escape. The only way out of this pit is the hole they lower food and water into every day. Have you gone mad? You have been unconscious since I arrived here. Perhaps it doesn't really matter. You might be better off not being awake for the ceremony. It is not fun. They will take all the other prisoners to the top of the highest temple. There the high priest will relieve us of our heads, and the crowd will cheer as they bounce all the way down the great steps of the temple and our blood spills everywhere. Then they will fertilize their fields with our bodies. That is our fate, my friend. It is how they please their sun god and grow good crops. The celebrations will start tomorrow."

"Not exactly how I planned to spend my summer," Doc muttered. "Still, don't give up hope. I'll do whatever I can to save us."

"I appreciate that, my friend, but I think we will soon be making the journey along the underground river to paradise together."

* * * * *

Tannic took a couple of steps away from the shore and winked at SRG. He shouted, "I think my greatest fear is the unknown. Like seeing the Rainbow Star in the middle of a grassy meadow, all by itself and mysteriously unguarded. Walking through a meadow without any monsters, fearing the unknown the whole way, is the single thing that frightens me the most. Can you imagine how scary that would be? Just the thought terrifies me! I would be paralyzed in fear!"

SRG nodded his head. *Good one, Tannic. Who knows, maybe he'll fall for it.*

They walked on in silence under the tropical sun, flies buzzing around their heads. Swatting them away, SRG noticed a strange line of clouds emerging from the horizon. After a second he realized that they all had one of two shapes—either a long line or a circular dot.

"What is it?" Tannic asked, following his gaze. After a moment he said, "It looks like Morse code."

"It does . . . hang on, write this down in the sand," SRG replied, watching the clouds closely. It was hard to keep track of which one he was on, so he spelled slowly. "N . . . i . . . c . . . e . . . t . . . r . . . y . . . . . h . . . a . . . l."

They looked down at the message Tannic had scrawled in the sand. "Nice try. —Hal."

"Guess he didn't fall for it. At least we know he's listening in on us." SRG sighed. "He's learning as we go through this."

"Yeah, well, it was worth a try," Tannic answered. "Come on, let's go. We know what we need to do."

They walked in silence for the better part of an hour. There were trails all over the island, weaving in and out of the bush and crisscrossing everywhere. They all looked pretty well traveled. Tannic was thinking about being captured by yet another primitive tribe, and SRG was thinking about Danika. He couldn't get her out of his mind. The realization set in that he would never see her again, and he wasn't sure that he had ever told her she was his best friend—apart from Tannic, which was still saying a lot. Now he would never get the chance. *She never even got to go to a prom. It's all my fault.*

The spear caught their attention by landing in the dirt between them. Tannic dropped into a wary crouch and raised the Dragonwrigley. He turned in every direction but there was no visible enemy. SRG held up the ugly stick uncertainly, waving it around as if he expected it to do something, but nothing happened. Then the second spear hit, squarely between his shoulder blades. He fell face forward without a sound. Tannic spun around and sent a nonstop stream of fireballs in every direction, but mostly in the direction of where the spears had come from. He kept this up until SRG was sitting up, staring at him. Then he stopped and studied his friend.

"Did you see where it came from?"

"No. But there are obviously people here. So what now? Should we look for them? Should we just explore at random?" SRG asked.

"I think we should hike to the highest ground we can find and see if we can see anything."

"That sounds good. Unfortunately, I think the place to hide the star will be with a tribe again."

"Okay, so we agree. Let's go upland and see if we can spot a village or something."

The vegetation varied from low grasses to waist high

bushes and short trees. The trails were clear, but the bush was thorny and thick, often impenetrable. They took a trail at random, and then picked the direction at every intersection that seemed to lead uphill. At length they crested a hill from which they could see the whole island. They sat down and took in the view. They could see meadows, patches of high forest with a canopy, and a couple of spectacular waterfalls. But there was no sign of a village, no smoke, and no rainbow light.

"It could be anywhere. There's a big waterfall over there," SRG noted.

"Where do you think the village is?"

"It has to be here somewhere. It's probably close to fresh water. We could start with the streams and waterfalls."

"Good point. Might as well start with the biggest."

They retraced their steps until they found a path that led in the direction of the waterfall. As they neared it, the sound of the stream crashing eighty feet into a pool grew louder and louder. So loud, that they didn't hear the hoof beats of the wild boars charging toward them. SRG screamed when the first one struck him from behind and sent him flying into the brush. Tannic turned just as another knocked him down. He held tightly to the Dragonwrigley as the beast spun back and gored his thigh. He took a swipe at its head and delivered a fatal blow, but not before taking a serious wound and losing consciousness.

SRG picked himself up. The herd had passed on. He was unharmed except for a few scratches from the thorns, and he picked his way back toward Tannic. Tannic eventually stirred, and SRG helped him up.

Tannic picked up the Dragonwrigley. "I didn't even hear them coming." He looked at the lifeless beast on the ground.

It was dark, almost black, and covered with coarse hair. It had a bristly mane, and large ivory tusks curved up from its lips. He delivered a satisfying kick to its severed head, which rolled off into the bushes.

"Me neither. I'm just glad we're doing all of this in the daylight. I can't imagine how scary this place would be at night. Like the night Danika and I spent in the Amazon. And spiders. Ugh, I hate spiders." He said it mindlessly, without thinking. Tannic shot him a desperate look. "Oops," SRG whispered. "Hopefully H . . . a . . . l . . . didn't hear that."

They continued until they reached the top of the waterfall. They looked over the edge but could see nothing remarkable about it. It was just a strong stream flowing fast and shooting over the edge until it dropped into a dark blue pool below. They left and continued down the trail, and before long the waterfall was just a distant noise, then it was drowned out by the rustle of the leaves in the warm breeze. Then SRG noticed something strange. The sun had been high in the sky only minutes before when they were looking at the waterfall, but now it was setting. The sky grew visibly darker as he watched it, and Tannic shot SRG a worried look.

"Well, it looks like you-know-who overheard your comment," Tannic said. "Apparently he can make the sun set whenever he wants."

"Yeah, sorry about that. I'm sorry I mentioned"—he dropped his voice to a whisper—"spiders, too, but at least I didn't talk about—" SRG stopped short. He was thinking about the video from his zoology class, the one with the Komodo dragon eating a deer while it was still alive. *Nature can be cruel. I'm just glad we haven't ever seen a Komodo dragon with its prehistoric reptilian brain. That would totally creep me out!*

"Well, no worries, Compadre. Whatever our friend Hal has to throw at us, we'll deal with. We're a team, and we're smarter than some stupid computer," Tannic declared angrily. "Hey—do you smell smoke?"

"I do."

It was getting dark, and the wind was crackling through the parched vegetation like a dry cough. It was a spooky place in the gathering night. They walked slower as they tried to find the source of the smoke. It might lead them to an ancient tribe. It might lead them to the Rainbow Star. It might also lead them into a fatal trap.

In the shadows behind them, a dark creature crept slowly along. Its forked tongue flickered into the air every few seconds as it took a bearing on them. The Komodo dragon was well over eight feet long and covered with black scales. Its powerful front legs ended in grizzly-like claws, and its broad mouth had rows of razor-sharp teeth. The dragon's lumbering movement gave no hint of its real running ability—it was fast enough to catch any creature on the island, including humans. And now its reptilian eyes were focused on two young men stepping slowly forward as the darkness enveloped them. It waited patiently to make its move.

"I think I can see the smoke. Over that ridge. But it's so dark I can barely tell," SRG said. Then his foot slipped on a rock and he stumbled backward into Tannic. They both tumbled to the ground, the Dragonwrigley clanging on a rock as they fell. The Komodo dragon made its move at the same instant and leapt from the bush to the spot where SRG had just been standing. But it missed him completely. Now it turned its menacing head and faced them both. Its black tongue shot out of its mouth as it took a quick assessment, and before they could move, it had SRG's leg locked in its jaws and was applying a crushing force. SRG screamed as the Life Wedge glowed above his head.

Tannic scrambled to his feet with the Dragonwrigley in hand. He took careful aim and delivered several fireballs at the creature, careful not to hit his friend. They sparked, but the beast's scales deflected them. Tannic then stepped to the side and shot a flurry of crescents at the lizard. Again, they hit their target but the black scales deflected them as well. The sword seemingly had no effect on the beast.

The Komodo dragon had its long claws wrapped tightly around SRG and was chomping on his leg as it tossed his lifeless body back and forth. Tannic stepped alongside the dragon and brought the Dragonwrigley down swiftly on top of its head with all of his might. The sword bounced back, but he heard the skull plate crack. He was about to swing again when the creature paused. It opened its mouth and spit SRG out. Then it turned away and lumbered back into the bush, its long tail leaving a drag mark in the ground spotted with blood.

Tannic rushed to his friend's side as SRG lifted his head. "What was that thing?" Tannic asked.

"Komodo dragon," SRG replied. "While you were studying people, I was studying animals in my biology class, and that's one I'll never forget. We watched a video where a Komodo dragon ate a little deer while it was still alive. I was just thinking about how it's about the scariest creature I've ever seen, and I was relieved we hadn't run into one in Rough World. The next thing you know, there it is. Do you think Hal's reading my mind?"

"I don't think that's possible, Compadre. It has to be a random coincidence," Tannic replied, shaking his head.

"Okay, so where do you think we are? Primitive tribe,

Komodo dragon, wild pigs, any ideas?"

"That puts us in the South Pacific. That and the plant life we've seen."

"So what primitive tribes could we be dealing with here? What do you know about them?"

"Well, the worst tribe would be the Sentinelese. But that would put us in the Indian Ocean, in the Bay of Bengal. They live on North Sentinel Island and still have basically no contact with the modern world. The few times people have tried to contact them, they've attacked the visitors. So they could be described as hostile and war-like. They're hunter-gatherers who live in small groups and use spears and bows. They also have crude tools of stone and whatever metal debris drifts ashore. We don't know much more about them, because all the observations have to be made at a distance. That's about all I know about them. I'm pretty sure we don't want to be taken captive by them."

"It sure is handy having you know so much about primitive tribes. But to be honest, if we make it out of here alive, I hope we never need this information again. Danika . . . " his voice cracked as he paused. He wiped away a tear. Tannic put his hand on his shoulder to reassure him.

"Compadre . . . I know. But it'll be okay. Right now, we just need to finish what we came here for. We need to find Doc. That's what she would have wanted. If we get that far, then we'll figure out what to do next."

"You're right, I know you're right, it's just . . . " SRG's voice faltered again.

"Come on Compadre, this is Level 9! We've come this far, we can't let Doc down now. Let's go find this star!"

SRG wiped his eyes, nodded and let Tannic lead the way. He was still carrying the ugly stick, which he still hadn't figured a use for. He felt like throwing it away, but his instincts told him to keep it.

The trail wound along a ridge and eventually led to the source of the smoke. The smell kept getting stronger as the two walked along in the dark, stumbling occasionally over a rock or a root but vigilant for any moving creature. Finally they reached a sharp ridge with a steep drop-off on the other side. In the canyon they could see a campfire with men, women, and children dancing in its light. Faint rhythmic drum music completed the scene as they studied the encampment from their perch above.

An assortment of crudely built structures were connected in a circle around the central campfire. The circle was open at one point, in the deepest part of the canyon, where the hillside abruptly jutted up almost vertically. In the center of the hillside was a large opening. Emanating from the cave was dim, rainbow-colored light.

SRG slapped Tannic on the back excitedly. "Do you see that? The cave? The Rainbow Star must be there. Come on, let's go get it," he exclaimed.

"Hold on, Compadre. Let's come up with a plan first. There's a lot of them, and they have spears and bows and arrows. They're not going to let us just walk in and take it. And we don't have Danika to help us. It's just me and you."

"Point well taken, Tannic," SRG answered. They watched a minute longer while they thought. "Okay, we sneak down to the outskirts of the village and try to get a look into the cave. If the Rainbow Star is there, one of us acts as a diversion while the other one sneaks in and grabs it. I've lost two Life Wedges while you've only lost one, so I don't have any margin for error with the villagers. You also have the Dragonwrigley. So I think you should be the diversion."

"But if there's an Ender Dude, and you know there will be, the ugly stick seems pretty useless. Don't you think I should go in? I'd have two shots at the Ender Dude, and I'd just have to get it done before the tribe does something terminal to you. Based on our previous experiences they'll probably tie you up for a while and hold a meeting while they decide what to do with you. That would buy me some time."

"And if they don't?" SRG asked.

"Then we go to plan B."

"Which is?"

"I don't know. I don't have a plan B. Plan A has to work."

"Okay." He nodded. "Your plan makes more sense. You'd just better get that star before it's too late for me."

"No worries, Compadre! When have I ever let you down?" Tannic smiled.

"Uh, there was that one time we dug the hole in Mrs. Kibbitch's back yard. You let me take the fall for that one. Then there was the time you convinced me I could fly—"

"Okay, okay. It was a rhetorical question. Come on. I've got your back on this one."

SRG grinned as he nodded his head and slapped Tannic on the back. They slowly made their way down the steep slope and toward the village. It took about thirty minutes of careful stalking, but they finally arrived at the outer edge of the shelters. Tannic peeked between two canopies and signaled to SRG.

"This is it. You run into the opening and get their attention, and I'll sneak into the cave. If everything goes according to plan, I'll see you in Doc's lab in a few minutes. If not, well, I'm proud of you, Compadre, and what we've accomplished so far. No matter what happens, we did the right thing."

"Yeah, yeah. Just go get that star, Good Buddy!" SRG whispered. Then he ran between the two lean-tos and started screaming like a madman. He ran straight at the natives, and they all stopped dancing and stood in shock as they watched him streak through the opening to the other side. It took a couple of seconds, but they came to their senses and picked up their weapons and followed him into the darkness.

SRG was running into the wind, and he was trying to run like the wind. He stumbled now and again but managed to keep his feet. He had stopped yelling when he exited the compound, and now he was just running for his life. The tribe's warriors were behind him, but it wouldn't be long before they were close enough to reach him with their arrows. Even in the dark, they were probably expert marksmen. SRG felt the rush of adrenalin in his veins and it made him run faster.

* * * * *

Tannic stepped into the cave unnoticed. There was just enough light from the rainbow source to let him see where he was going. The cave zigzagged back and forth like a meandering hallway, the light getting brighter bit by bit, until it opened into a cavernous room. In the center, on a rock pedestal, stood a Komodo dragon far bigger than the one that had attacked them. This one was fourteen feet long at least. It was jet black, and large horny projections swept back from both sides of its head. Its scales were larger than coins and shone like black mirrors. It turned to look directly at him and hissed fire. Its open mouth revealed long fangs in addition to the many rows of sharp reptilian teeth. Hatred burned in the Komodo Ender Dude's eyes. It was standing on three legs, with its tail coiled neatly around its hind ones, and in its upturned right front foot it was holding the Rainbow Star tightly with its grisly claws.

Tannic stepped back for a second. He didn't see the Sentinelese warrior watching his shadow from around the corner.

* * * * *

SRG ran until he was out of breath, knocking branches and leaves out of the way with the ugly stick. He paused for a second and glanced behind, as the first arrow hissed in his ear as the air rushed past his shoulder. He heard it stick in the ground, followed by a second and a third. He swung the ugly stick wildly back and forth, but nothing happened. Frustrated, he broke the stick over his knee. The broken ends instantly blazed to life like strong flares, and his eyes widened.

As arrows and spears fell around him like a hailstorm, SRG ducked low, ran, and used the flaming sticks to set the surrounding bone-dry brush on fire. He worked fast, like a mad arsonist, and in seconds it was exploding into life, the wind sweeping the growing flames toward the Sentinelese and their village. Now they were turning around and running for their own lives, chased by a thirsty wall of flames. He looked at the glowing ends of the ugly stick and laughed. No longer fearing the Sentinelese, he ran after them through the ashes, screaming again like a madman. "Is that all you got? You got nothing! You hear me? You got nothing!"

* * * * *

Tannic crept slowly into the chamber. He noticed the shadow move on the floor just as the warrior hit him with his adze, and he screamed as the bones in his shoulder snapped. His left arm hung uselessly from its socket. He spun and swung the Dragonwrigley one-handed in a horizontal arc at the man's stomach. The sword jolted as it hit flesh, but it didn't stop until the man lay in two pieces on the floor.

Tannic turned to look up at the Ender Dude, who was watching the scene with interest but still hadn't moved. It hissed fire at him again, and struggled to move down while balancing the Rainbow Star in one foot. It paused for a second as if in thought. Then it suddenly dropped the star. As it turned to attack Tannic, the star fell toward the ground. The beast's tail accidentally whipped around and cracked as it connected with the star like a Louisville Slugger ripping the leather off of a baseball.

The Rainbow Star hit Tannic so hard that it knocked him down, and the Ender Dude charged with incredible speed. It was almost on top of him when he dropped the Dragonwrigley from his good hand and grabbed the star. The last thing the beast saw was the smile on Tannic's face.

Chapter 13

WORLD THREE LEVEL 10

The Tikal Sun Temple

Darwood burst through the door. "They've done it, Sir. They completed Level 9!"

"Excellent news! What happened? How did they outsmart Hal?" Mr. Eville asked eagerly.

"I'm not sure yet, I just heard from Nosrac in the programming lab. They're writing the wrecking-ball code to shut down and destroy World Three the moment the players defeat Level 10, Sir. Nosrac isn't holding out much hope for that, but they want to be prepared just in case."

"Excellent!" Mr. Eville exclaimed. "Is there anything we can do to help the players defeat Level 10?"

"No, Sir, not according to Nosrac. They don't even know where the code for the level is. And Hal seems to be encrypting things, sealing them off with passwords, and changing the code literally every second. Their hope is to catch him off guard, use the one second when he'll be inactive to break in and initiate the wrecking ball code. After that, every second that goes by that Hal doesn't know how to respond diminishes his ability to control the program. Nosrac thinks it will only take a couple of seconds for the process to become irreversible and put us in control again. They don't know if it will succeed, but it's our only hope. Of course, the players still need to defeat Level 10, Sir, and I'm sorry to say that's not very likely."

"Very well. Keep me informed. You may go now," Mr. Eville said, somewhat deflated.

* * * * *

SRG and Tannic were standing in the lab looking at each other. Jody walked in with the laptop.

"Danika? Danika?" SRG shouted.

"She's not here," Jody replied. "I haven't seen her at all. After what we saw of Level 8, I think we know what happened. I'm sorry, SRG."

"Yeah . . . I was just . . ." SRG replied softly.

"What happened on Level 9? I missed it," Jody asked.

"It was so cool!" He perked up a little. "I finally figured out what the ugly stick was for!"

"Really, what did it do?" Tannic asked. "I was in the cave fighting off the biggest Komodo dragon in the world."

"The warriors were catching up and started firing arrows at me. I just got frustrated and broke the stick in two, and the broken ends caught fire like a flare. So I started setting the bush on fire. The wind was blowing from me to them so in seconds they were facing a wall of fire. You should have seen them run for their lives. It was awesome! I wish Danika . . ."

"Yeah, me too, Compadre. But you did a good job fending them off. The Komodo dragon Ender Dude was holding the Rainbow Star and had to drop it to attack me. Its tail swung around and accidentally knocked the star right to me. It was beautiful!"

"So now what, Jody?" Tannic asked. "It's on to the last level. This is what we came for. Doc has got to be there. I think it's a waste of time looking at the laptop, but I guess we should, just to be safe."

Jody opened the laptop and booted it up. Tannic typed in the password for the last time and watched the screen come to life. He clicked through to World Three Level 10. It was an empty folder.

"That's weird," Tannic mused. "There's nothing here. Do you think Hal erased Doc's computer file? Could he do that?"

"I don't know," SRG said, "but it creeps me out. Hal's worse than Mr. Eville ever was. He listens to everything we say. And now it's like he can read our minds and what? Delete things from Doc's laptop?"

"Let's not jump to conclusions," Tannic said. "It could just be a coincidence. Maybe Doc misplaced those files or was rewriting them. Besides, does it really matter? None of the last few levels resembled what was in the files. I say we go out there and wing it. It's worked so far."

"You're right. But it still feels creepy. I mean, Level 10 has to exist, right? Doc's being held captive there. Cody said it was a dungeon in some kind of castle. But now all traces of it are gone? Something's up."

"I know, but what can we do? We still have to go out there and get him, wherever 'there' is," Tannic concluded. "I guess our special weapon is a surprise too. But it should be waiting for us next to the sword at the door."

They crossed the lab to where the Dragonwrigley leaned against the corner, waiting for them like a faithful dog. But it stood there alone.

"Perfect!" SRG grimaced. "No special weapon, either!"

"Okay, that is weird. I mean, it's a first. But come on, we'll do it. We've got to."

They waved goodbye to a worried Jody and exited the lab into a thick jungle. It was hot, but not too humid out. The bushes were dense, and there was a canopy of lush green trees. Ahead of them ran a well-used trail. They exchanged glances, and SRG shrugged his shoulders.

"I guess we follow it?"

"I guess so. The bush is too thick. We could really use a machete here. Where do you think we are?"

"It kind of reminds me of the Amazon, but we've been there a couple of times. Maybe somewhere close to that?"

"Central America, then? If it's a primitive tribe, that would mean we're probably facing Mayans."

"That's not bad, is it? Weren't they really advanced—art, architecture, calendars, astronomy, agriculture, all that? I mean, I don't know a whole bunch about them."

"They were. They left behind some spectacular ruins. Tikal is famous for its pyramids. The Maya were great astronomers and built their pyramids to display their knowledge. They'd set up groups of temples and other buildings so that when you stood in the right place and watched where the sun rose, you could mark off the solstices and equinoxes. It's almost the summer solstice at home—that's the longest day of the year in the northern hemisphere, around June 21, right after graduation. They also had a writing system and recorded their entire history, but a lot of that was destroyed as heretical when the Spanish discovered them. We do know a lot from their art, though, including the fact that they had some really brutal religious practices and wars."

"Oh . . . "

"They had a very complex social structure that involved a political elite class which controlled much of the wealth, and then a large group of commoners who provided most of the labor. They were also at war with most of the surrounding tribes, and they would actually wipe out whole neighboring civilizations, killing a lot of people and taking the rest prisoner, to use for slave labor and human sacrifice in elaborate ceremonies. The high priest was in charge of those. Their favorite weapon was the atlatl, the spear-thrower. They also used bows and arrows."

"So more atlatls and bows and arrows . . ." SRG paused.

"There's more. The king came from a royal bloodline but also had to be a successful war leader, and he proved that by taking lots of captives. Their king was considered divine, and the enthronement of a new king was always a spectacular event involving human sacrifice. Each king had an elaborate scepter representing a different god, and a headdress with long feathers and a large jade stone to represent the jester god. Sounds like the perfect place for the Rainbow Star."

"Anything else?"

"Just two things that I found really interesting. First, they had a number system and were one of the earliest people in the world to have a zero. The other thing was their ball game. There's a stadium in literally every city: a long court with two end zones, with vertical stone hoops about ten feet off the ground. They used a stuffed leather ball that would fit through the hoops. So we don't know the exact rules or even the name of the game, but I kind of imagine it was like the first version of basketball."

"That sounds really interesting . . . care for a game of horse?"

"Uh, it wasn't exactly like that. They had teams of players, usually a Mayan team and a team of random captives, and the losing team would be sacrificed afterward."

"Wow! You're like a walking Wikipedia, Tannic. If we run into Mayans, at least we'll know what to expect."

"I think that's more than you wanted to know. Besides, we don't even know if we'll find any Mayans. But I'm really thinking that's where Hal is leading us. I mean, it seems the most logical, and his circuits are all based on logic. Maybe we can use that to our advantage. Maybe he's stuck in a logical mode and we can use something illogical to beat him? I mean, that's the difference between real humans and artificial intelligence—we're not bound by logic. We have opinions, we can change our mind. We're unpredictable. Compadre! I think we're on to something here. We need to do the unexpected to defeat him. What do you think?" Tannic whispered.

"Sounds good to me—unless his logical systems expect us to do the unexpected."

"But he won't know what that is until it happens! Neither will we! Come on, let's see where this trail leads."

They followed the path for nearly an hour. The sun was high in the sky and it was getting hotter, but the lush green vegetation offered some relief from the punishing solar rays. They stopped in a shady spot to rest for a second. SRG wiped the sweat from his brow. They stood transfixed, as a large jaguar stepped from the bush and into the middle of the trail. It looked at them for a moment with its large green eyes, then it yawned, stepped back into the bush and was gone.

After a moment, Tannic spoke slowly. "Well, Compadre, I think that nails down where we are. I'd bet money we're in Central America, and even more money that we're going to see Mayans sooner rather than later."

"I think you're right. What's our plan if we do? I'm unarmed!"

"Just get behind me quickly and I'll turn the fury of the Dragonwrigley loose on them. I don't know what else to do. If we go down, we go down swinging."

* * * * *

Doc tried to see his fellow prisoner in the dark. The sun was getting higher in the sky, and there was almost enough light now to make out the shape of Utatl, who was tethered to the wall in the same fashion about ten feet away.

"I just realized something Utatl. How is it that you understand my language?" Doc asked.

"I don't. I thought you understood my language," Utatl replied.

"No, I don't speak Mayan. That's strange. It must be something with the programming on this level," Doc mused.

"What is that? Programming?"

"Oh, uh . . . it's nothing," Doc shook his head. "Forget about it. Listen, I've been working at these restraints all night, but I've haven't made any progress at all."

"It's no use, my friend. I worked against mine until I started bleeding. There is no escape. I am resigned to my fate."

"Trust me, Utatl. I'll think of something, just follow my lead when I make a move."

A Mayan guard lifted the wooden grate and lowered a ladder into the pit. He then climbed down carrying two gourds filled with water and a rough loaf of maize bread. Bits of corn kernels stuck out through the crust. Doc's mouth watered, and his stomach growled.

The guard held the gourds for Doc and Utatl and then he broke the loaf in two and handed them each half. They bent down to eat. Doc was ravenous. He couldn't remember when he'd eaten last. The water tasted sweet. He could have drunk three gourds of the cool liquid. In a matter of minutes, the meal was over and the guard retreated to the ladder.

"I will feed you again tomorrow. Today begins the festival of the Summer Solstice. Tomorrow will be a day of dancing. The next day will be the ball game, and afterwards the sacrificial ceremony to the Sun god, Kinich Ahau. There we will remove your heads. Then the high priest will remove your beating hearts, and we will spill your blood on the temple steps. Your bodies will make great fertilizer for our crops, to raise the maize like in the bread you just ate," the guard explained. Unceremoniously he climbed the ladder, pulled it up, and closed the grate. In the distance Doc could hear music, a flute and some drums. He hung his head. He woke up to find the sun was setting.

* * * * *

SRG looked at his friend. Then he signaled up the trail and the two of them continued their journey into the unknown. After another hour, they came to a substantial opening in the forest canopy. It was a meadow blanketed in waist-high grass and wild flowers. It was beautiful. They looked at it suspiciously for a moment. Their trail led through the meadow and out the opposite side.

"I think we should cross fast to avoid being seen," SRG suggested.

"I agree, Compadre. I'll go first."

Tannic ran out into the sunlight and was in the middle

of the meadow, with SRG on his tail, when he suddenly stopped. SRG almost knocked him down.

"What is it?" SRG asked.

"I swear I saw something in the grass as I was running. It . . . it looked like rainbow-colored light."

"No way. What would the star be doing out here, unprotected?"

"It would be the unexpected thing. But I think we should look really quickly anyway. You never know."

Tannic led the way, and they could both see rainbow light beneath the densely matted grass. He bent over to part the grass, and their whole world collapsed. The dirt below them gave way and they fell twenty feet into a carefully dug pit. At the bottom, sharp poles jutted up from the ground six feet high. They narrowly missed being skewered, but they were stuck twisted between the poles. The Dragonwrigley lay in the dirt just out of Tannic's reach. In the center of the pit was a large prism. It wasn't the Rainbow Star. That was when the net descended upon them.

A dozen Mayan warriors peered over the edge of the pit. They wore finely woven tunics accented with brightly colored feathers and knee-high sandals. Their long black hair was tied back with jaguar headbands and had more feathers hanging from it. The leader was wearing a headdress topped with the skull and antlers of a small deer. They chattered excitedly as they lowered a ladder into the pit and descended one by one. The leader picked up the Dragonwrigley and turned it over in his hands, admiring the fine craftsmanship. He had never seen the materials this weapon was made from.

Two Mayans pulled SRG loose and lashed him to a pole. Others did the same with Tannic. Then they started the slow process of lifting them out of the pit. Once they were all above ground again, the Mayans carried their new captives away. SRG and Tannic were both speechless.

It took them an hour to reach the city. Then they carried Tannic and SRG to a row of pits covered with wooden grates. The Mayans tied the boys' hands to their feet and looped the loose ends around their necks like nooses. Then they lowered them one at a time into a pit. Tannic and SRG lay side by side at the bottom. If they moved too much, the nooses would tighten. Tannic didn't know how long he could stay in this position.

The leader of the band spoke. "Congratulations! You've arrived just in time for the ceremony of the summer solstice. Tomorrow will be marked by dancing and music. The next day will be the great ball game. You two will play on the captive team against our Mayan all-stars. The losers of the game will be sacrificed in the afternoon to honor the sun god, Kinich Ahau. We will be pleased to use your bodies as fertilizer in our fields." He laughed as he turned and walked away.

"Are you okay?" Tannic asked.

"Yeah, I think so. Although that's a relative term at this point. What are we going to do?"

"I don't know, but you heard him speak English, right? It's not just me, you understood him too."

"Yeah I did. That's weird. Has that ever happened before, it's kind of creepy. What do you think it means?" SRG asked.

"I don't know, maybe Hal wants to be sure we understand what is going to happen to us, which can't be a good sign. What are we going to do now?"

"For starters I'm thinking we'll have to win that ball game!"

"We don't even know how to play!"

"So we'll learn. You have a better idea?"

"No. I was hoping you had a plan. You always do."

SRG was silent for a minute. "No. None. Nada. I'm fresh out of ideas."

"And at the end of your rope?" Tannic asked.

SRG couldn't help giggling, even though it constricted the rope. "Don't make me laugh, Tannic! I don't know how you always find humor in situations like this. I'm feeling pretty hopeless right now." And then he laughed some more, and Tannic laughed too.

The two boys spent the night in the rope restraints. In the morning, when the guards came to untie them, their bodies were so stiff that they could barely move. The guards stood them up, tied just their hands, and tethered them to the wall. Then a Mayan woman came in with a length of string. She wrapped it around their chests, arms, and waists, then wrote down some notes and then left.

"What was that about?" Tannic asked.

"We either just got measured for our uniforms or for our caskets," SRG replied.

"Now look at who's the funny man!"

* * * * *

The first dance consisted of four women in long white gowns. They wore colorful headdresses that radiated with long flowing quetzal feathers in all the colors of the rainbow. Each of them held a different jade carving: a jaguar, a frog, a deer, and a wild boar. Musicians played flutes and beat drums while they danced in a circular pattern on a raised stage of rock slate in the center of the plaza. When they finished they set their carvings in the middle of the stage, and the crowd of fifty thousand Mayans cheered in unison. The women bowed and four men took their place.

These wore jaguar pelts and headdresses made of wood carvings and sparse feathers. Strings of shells were strapped to their calves and clapped out a rhythm as they danced in time to the music. They too danced in a circle around the stage, with a small torch in the center. At one point the flames grew higher and the dancers took turns leaping over them. Each time, the crowd cheered.

* * * * *

Doc woke up to the sound of the crowds cheering. He could hear the music too and surmised that the celebration had begun with the dancing. It might have been interesting to watch, at least as a Mayan, but not as a prisoner.

"Psst. Utatl. Are you awake? How long does this dancing go on?" he asked into the darkness.

"Yes, I'm awake, my friend. This will go on for hours. I have never seen it, but I have been nearby in the jungle and heard the music."

The guard interrupted their conversation by opening the grate and bringing food and water down. He moved efficiently in the dark, giving them two gourds of water and another loaf of bread divided in two.

"Enjoy your last meal, men. Tomorrow you will join a line of one hundred people who will be sacrificed. You should be proud, for you two will be at the front of the line. That is the place of highest honor."

The guard then left and closed the grate.

"Listen, Utatl. Tomorrow? Let me go first. Trust me, and be ready for anything."

* * * * *

The next group of dancers were women. They wore bright, rainbow-colored tunics and danced gracefully in a circle as the crowd delighted and a dozen flutes played a haunting melody in a minor scale. The lone drummer beat the wood-and-leather drum softly and slowly. The crowd swayed in a slow rhythm to the music. The lead dancer started twirling in the middle of the stage, followed by each of the others in succession. The crowd erupted when the dance ended. They were anxious for the final act.

The women were escorted offstage and four muscular men climbed up. They stood in the center of the stage and raised their arms. The crowd cheered louder than ever. Assistants brought up a pair of stone hoops mounted on stands and two leather balls. The four players broke into two teams. One man would roll the ball to the other, who would kick it into the air with one foot and then through the hoop with the other. They managed to get the ball through the hoop on about half of the attempts. Every time, the crowd cheered. Finally, they danced around again with their arms in the air, and the crowd cheered one last time.

The final dancer was a woman. Beautiful jet-black hair flowed to her waist. She wore a solid white gown, and as she moved gracefully about the stage, her hair flowed with the wind. In the center of the stage was a small statue of the sun god, Kinich Ahau. She danced lovingly over and around the statue. The drum stopped beating, and one by one the flutes stopped playing until only one remained. A reverent hush blanketed the crowd as they silently watched the beauty of dance displayed in its finest form. When the flute player reached the final note, the dancer stopped, wrapped her hands around the statue, and raised it high over her head. The crowd erupted again into cheers that went on for several minutes. Then the dancer lovingly set the statue back down, took her final bow, and disappeared off the stage. The crowd slowly dispersed to various feasts. There was a growing sense of anticipation for the next day and the ball game.

* * * * *

SRG and Tannic were roused from their sleep early. The Mayan guard gave them each a gourd of water and some maize bread. He was also holding their uniforms for the ball game, blue tunics with gold trim. The guard had them change and then tied them together before they climbed out of the pit. They were stiff from being tied up, and they stretched their arms as much as they could. The sunlight blinded their eyes, and it took them a minute to get their bearings as they were led to the stadium. They could hear the murmurs from the spectators.

They entered the field through the south entrance and were met by ten other players who looked as confused as they did. The stands were full of spectators. Everyone had turned out to watch the Mayan all-star team defeat another group of captives, who would then be led to their sacrifice.

A tall Mayan in a blue tunic stood in front of them. "This is the K'uk' Mo' stadium, named for Kinich Yax K'uk' Mo', the first king of the Mayans. The divine king is sitting over there, in the purple tunic with the large headdress and mask. He will officiate the game. But first I must explain the rules to you. There are two teams of twelve players each. The object is to kick the ball between the other players and through the stone hoop that is the opponent's goal. The team that scores the most goals wins. If there is a tie, the game continues until one team scores, and then that team wins."

"The game is played in two halves with a break in between. The divine king will throw the ball into play at the beginning of each half. There is a timekeeper sitting just below the king. He has a bowl of sand with a hole in the bottom. When all the grains of sand have drained out, that half of the game is over."

"You may not use your hands at any time. If you fall down during the game and your hands touch the ground, you will be removed from the field for that half. There will be two officials on the field who will regulate play. Good luck, gentlemen. Enjoy the game, which will be your last experience in this life."

SRG and Tannic looked at each other. Their teammates were silent. One was crying. They all looked up as the crowd started cheering. The Mayan team was entering the field at the opposite end, in red tunics. They walked in single file onto the field and assembled in front of the Divine King. He stood up and raised his hands. The crowd cheered more. Then the Mayan players started chanting. They crossed their arms and slapped their elbows, then their legs. It was an intimidating display and reminded SRG of an All Blacks Haka. In fact, the players looked so big that he was reminded more of a World Cup rugby team, not a group of Mayans, who historically were not that tall.

"Those guys are huge!" he whispered.

"Yeah, but maybe they're big and slow too. It could be to our advantage. Is it legal to trip them? Or hit them low? How physical is this game? It looks like it'll be pretty hard to kick that ball through that hoop. It must be ten feet up. Will the ball bounce?" Tannic asked.

"I don't know. I guess we're about to find out," SRG replied.

The coach ushered them to the center of the field next to the Mayan team. They stood in front of the divine king, who addressed them all.

"I now sanction the official Ku'it ball game of the summer solstice. The losers will be sacrificed this afternoon, along with the other captives, to honor the sun god Kinich Ahau. May the best team win!'"

The divine king threw the first ball into the arena, and the Mayans quickly scrambled for it and began kicking it back and forth, moving it efficiently toward the goal. It took a couple of tries, but one player finally kicked the ball through the stone hoop. The crowd stood up and cheered. Tannic shouted something over the crowd, but SRG couldn't make it out.

The referee threw the ball into the middle of the field, but this time Tannic was there. He passed it to SRG, and they played a fast break soccer move to the other side of the field. The Mayans were scrambling on defense now. They had never seen opponents move the ball so well. Tannic and SRG's years of soccer practice were finally paying off. SRG kicked the ball to Tannic who was met immediately by two Mayans and kicked it back to SRG, who gave it a good square kick at the goal. To his amazement, the ball sailed through the hoop. He was jumping up and down and wanted to high five Tannic as the other players looked on in amazement.

Without delay, the official threw the ball into the field again. A Mayan seized control of it and passed it to a teammate. SRG cut in front of the pass and stole the ball, but his pass to Tannic was picked off and the Mayans pushed the ball in the other direction. SRG stepped up to the man with the ball and didn't see the Mayans set a screen behind him. As he ran into the player, he fell forward and hit the ground. The official halted play, and SRG was ejected for the rest of the period and sent to his team's end zone.

Play resumed immediately, but Tannic had a hard time defending against the Mayan team by himself, with little help from his teammates, and after a few tries the Mayans scored again. The captives were now down 2 to 1, and they were outnumbered too. When the official threw the ball in again, Tannic quickly took control, but he got tangled up with a Mayan player. The Mayan player went down and caught the turf with his hands. The official stopped play and the Mayan went to his own end zone.

The other captives soon caught on, with Tannic shouting instructions on the field, and it became a defensive battle for the rest of the first half. The Mayans took several shots on the goal, but they all missed. The score was still 2 to 1 in their favor when the timekeeper stood up to signify the end of the period. The captives joined SRG in their end zone. He wasted no time giving them more defensive instructions and encouraging them.

"Listen guys, we're only one goal behind. I'll be back in the game, and I won't fall down this time. We just need to play good defense, keep them from getting shots at the goal, move the ball well ourselves, and get as many shots on goal as we can. Don't be afraid to be physical. We're playing for our lives here. Give it all you've got, leave it all on the field. We can beat these guys!"

The coach brought them water, and then they jogged back to the middle of the field. The timer lifted the bowl and sand began dibbling from the bottom. The divine king threw the ball into the field again, and SRG immediately picked it off and was kicking it ahead of himself as the Mayan's best player contested for it. Another Mayan player set a blind screen and SRG ran into him. He fell forward but caught himself in a squat and stood up. Tannic let out a sigh of relief and ran into the star Mayan player, knocking him to the ground. That player leapt up and lunged for Tannic with his fists raised. It took both officials to stop the action, but after a short conference they agreed that the Mayan player had fallen during normal play, and he was removed from the game. He stomped his feet, swung his fist, and shouted as he went to his end zone. The crowd jeered. The divine king stood up and quieted the crowd.

The official threw the ball into play, but despite being without their star player, the Mayans' defense kept the captives from scoring. Both teams had several shots on the goals, but they all missed. Time was running out, and tension filled the stadium. People were on their feet and cheering. Their team was about to win yet once again.

SRG made a sudden move and stole the ball. He passed it to Tannic, and they passed it back and forth between themselves as they crossed the stadium toward the goal. It was a fast break, and they had only one Mayan player between them. SRG kicked the ball back to Tannic, who took his best shot at the goal. It hit the top of the hoop and flew wide. The timekeeper was starting to raise the bowl. SRG ran desperately after the ball, spun around and gave it one last kick. The Mayan team were already raising their arms victoriously in the air. The crowd was cheering so loudly that they didn't see the ball sail gracefully through the hoop as the last grain of sand left the bowl. While the Mayans celebrated, the officials met at mid-field. They ruled that the goal had indeed been scored before the time expired, and the game was tied at 2–2. The teams would need to play until one of them broke the tie.

The crowd was jeering wildly when the divine king stood up and raised his arms. They reluctantly quieted down to listen to him. "The game has ended in an official tie. I now sanction the tiebreaker. The first team to score a goal wins. The losing team will be sacrificed. May the best team win!" He threw the ball back into the field, and the Mayans were already there to take control. The captives took a minute to get organized as the Mayans drove the ball to the goal. The star player took an uncontested shot and the ball sailed at the center of the hoop. The excited crowd jumped to their feet but then sat back down as the ball rattled around and bounced back out.

SRG grabbed the rebound in the confusion and passed it outside to Tannic, who pushed it up the field. He kicked it to another captive, who kicked it to another, and then SRG came running as fast as he could to catch up. They were working well as a team, with only two Mayans between them and the goal, when Tannic finally took the shot. It sailed over the hoop, but SRG had positioned himself on the other side to catch the rebound. A Mayan player rushed him, and SRG used the opportunity to take a headshot. He butted the ball off his forehead, and it went straight through the goal.

The crowd gasped and then began to boo in unison. A conference was called among the officials at mid-field. After several minutes, a murmur ran through the crowd. An official went to the wall to confer with the divine king. The goal was determined to be fair because the player had not used his hands, and while it had never happened before, nothing in the rules specifically said that you couldn't use your head to move the ball. The divine king explained the result to the crowd, who stood in shock. It took a couple of seconds in the confusion for the captive team to realize that they had just won the game. They started jumping and whooping and celebrating with each other. SRG hugged Tannic, and they were all smiles. The Mayan team stood sullenly by, watching the celebration of life, realizing what defeat meant for them.

"We did it, Tannic! We beat the all-stars! We get to live!" SRG screamed.

"Yeah, we did it, Compadre!" Tannic answered, still in a daze.

The teams were then escorted to mid-field, where the divine king addressed them again. He stood up and removed the wooden mask. SRG gasped.

"C . . . C . . . Captain Killbeard! I thought you were dead!" he said.

The king smiled. "As you can see, I'm not dead yet." He turned to face the crowd. "I have also changed my mind. To honor the sun god Kinich Ahau, today, the winning team will be sacrificed instead of the losing team." The crowd cheered wildly.

"But . . . but . . . " SRG shouted.

The king turned back to face SRG and winked. "Never trust a pirate!"

The Mayan guards filed onto the field and grabbed the victors. They tied their hands together and then tied them all into a line and led them off the field to the main plaza and the Temple of the Sun. The crowd parted and followed them to the plaza, cheering and hurling insults at them. Eighty eight more captives were already tied together there, waiting in desperation. The guards brought the ball team captives to the front of the line, where Doc and Utatl stood. Doc look at SRG and Tannic in shock. He wanted to rush over and greet them, but he couldn't. He was tied to everybody else. Then he let out a deep sigh and hung his head. His one last hope shattered.

The guards put SRG, Tannic, and the rest of their team in the line directly behind Doc and Utatl. Then they marched the entire group of prisoners to the temple and started them up the hundred steps to the top. The prisoners walked on the right-hand side of the stairway as they climbed. They could see Captain Killbeard standing over the sacrificial altar at the top. As they ascended slowly, the crowd cheered. In the divine king's headdress was a jaguar-skin headband, and in the center of the headband was the Rainbow Star. He smiled like a pirate, leaning on his wooden leg, the Dragonwrigley shining in his right hand.

"I'm sorry Doc," SRG said just loud enough to be heard. "We failed you. We came back when we heard that Mr. Eville had taken you hostage. We were determined to save you. We even won the ball game today, but Captain Killbeard cheated us again. I'm sorry." Doc shook his head.

Utatl looked back at him. "My friend, do you know these captives?"

"Yes, Utatl. They are friends of mine. Like me, they don't belong here either. They come from even yet another place, and they shouldn't have come here at all." He turned to SRG. "Where's Danika? Please tell me she's safe?"

SRG looked at Tannic and then frowned. "I wish I could, Doc, but . . . she . . . died on Level 8," he answered, choking the words out.

"I'm sorry that you came here because of me. I fear we have no escape. And Killbeard has the Dragonwrigley—you know what that means." Doc dropped his head again.

SRG swallowed hard. Tannic was still silent, climbing

the steps in a trance, resigned to his fate. The crowd roared in anticipation as the captives reached the top. Two guards cut Doc loose and led him to the altar. They held his head down against the stone. He struggled, but they were too strong for him. He took one last worried glance at SRG and Tannic, and then closed his eyes.

Captain Killbeard stepped up with the Dragonwrigley. The crowd went wild. SRG couldn't watch what was about to happen. He looked out at the crowd. The mass of people extended as far as he could see. The plaza looked like a brightly carpeted sea of Mayans.

Captain Killbeard's voice interrupted his train of thought. "I, the divine king, give you the first sacrifice. I offer this life for the pleasure of the great god Kinich Hal!" he shouted. The Mayans cheered at the top of their lungs. Captain Killbeard stepped forward and raised the sword as high as he could. The Rainbow Star bathed the entire temple and steps in brilliant colored light. The Dragonwrigley vibrated in his hands and emitted a green glow from the logo on each side. As he moved the sword forward, it caught for a moment in the quetzal feathers of his headdress. He stumbled a step and then caught himself. Then his wooden leg went out from under him. He lost his balance and fell end over end, bouncing down the stairs. His headdress came off entirely and the Rainbow Star flew through the air and landed on the upper platform. SRG strained against his tethers and the other captives, and suddenly the long line collapsed like a string of dominoes. He stretched an arm out, but the star was just out of his reach. He only managed to knock it down the stairs . . . where it bounced twice . . . and landed in Tannic's outstretched hand. Tannic closed his fingers around it with a death grip.

Chapter 14

Back to Mr. Eville's Office

Darwood burst through the door. "They did it!" he shouted. "They did it!"

"They did?" Mr. Eville leaned forward. He was shaking, but he took a deep breath and composed himself. "Excellent! Do you know what this means? We're back in charge! Wait a minute, what about the wrecking ball software?"

"I just came from the lab, Sir. Nosrac's team uploaded it the second Tannic grabbed the star. Hal was momentarily confused, just as they had hoped. Nosrac thinks the program has progressed too far for Hal to stop it. World Three is about to go down, and Hal will be no more!"

Mr. Eville took another deep breath and let it out slowly. He could feel his heart pounding in his chest. "Okay. Go tell Nosrac and his team, 'Great work'! Whatever he wants is his for the asking. Have you got that, Darwood? And tell them to take some time off with pay after World Three is gone. We'll deal with that later. In the meantime, I need to turn my attention to SRG, Tannic, and Doc."

"Yes, Sir! Got it, Sir. And might I say, Sir, you composed yourself well and dealt with this problem brilliantly, Sir."

Darwood turned and closed the door. Mr. Eville opened the bottom drawer to pour himself a whisky. His hand was trembling.

* * * * *

"Danika?" SRG called out. "Danika!"

"She's not here, Compadre. She's gone," Tannic said sullenly.

SRG exhaled deeply and looked at Doc and Tannic, who were still shaking from the ordeal. Tannic still had the Rainbow Star clutched tightly in his right hand. "How random was that? Killbeard got the Dragonwrigley tangled up in his headdress and fell down the temple stairs!" SRG crowed.

"I thought my heart was going to stop; watching you guys! I'm still shaking!" Jody said.

"I thought for sure we were goners," Tannic blurted out.

"I knew I was a goner. I was just hoping something would happen to save you two. I didn't have a plan, I had run out of options . . . I'm sorry, boys. You should never have come back here. Now, Danika . . ." Doc's voice wavered.

"Now we take the Fortran Sword and focus on dealing with Mr. Eville once and for all. Then maybe we can go home," SRG added. "If Danika . . . " He took the Rainbow Star from Tannic and set it on the bench next to the other nine. He looked at their cache, thinking about what it had cost them. Then he looked at the corner next to the door, where the Fortran Sword stood. It hadn't changed. It was still beautiful.

"So what's the plan, Doc? Last time we cut the electricity to his office and shut down his force field. Do you think he'd fall for that again? Do you still have contacts at the power company?"

"I do, SRG. I'll contact them and see what I can do. I don't know if it'll work, but it's been a few years and maybe he's forgotten. Besides, you can be sure he's been panicked about World Three. By the way, what happened? How did I end up in a Mayan village on Level 10? I was in a dungeon, and next thing I knew I woke up there?" Doc asked.

"Long story, Doc. Apparently Mr. Eville programmed some artificial intelligence into World Three which eventually learned to take control of the game and rewrite the levels. It named itself Hal. So Hal did all of that to us," SRG replied. "We were playing against a computer that used all of our own fears against us and learned as we progressed through the game. But we managed to defeat it in the end, by being unpredictable."

"Wow! I warned Beezil about that happening. Obviously he didn't listen. But then, he doesn't listen to anybody," Doc replied. "Okay, here's the plan. Give me fifteen minutes. I'll contact the power company and have them black out his office like before. Tannic, you take the Fortran sword, and when the lights go out I'll turn on a flashlight and you attack Mr. Eville just like before."

"Perfect!" SRG answered as Doc left the lab. "Jody, set your watch for fifteen minutes."

They didn't say much while they waited. A somber tone hung in the air. Eventually, Jody signaled them and they walked to the door. SRG had the ten Rainbow Stars in his arms, and Tannic picked up the Fortran sword admiringly. He sliced it through the air a couple of times. It was longer and heavier than the Dragonwrigley, but it had great balance and felt lighter in his hands. He could see his reflection in the finely polished blade. He thought of Mr. Eville and smiled. He would avenge Danika's death. This was for Danika now. Then he nodded at Jody, who opened the door and they stepped into the hallway leading to Mr. Eville's private office.

The hallway was brightly lit, and they recognized the large wooden doors with the hieroglyphics carved into them. The ten slots to the right of the door were empty. They could faintly detect the odor of Mr. Eville's cigars and whisky as they approached. Tannic stood ready with the Fortran sword as SRG set each star into an empty slot. The door creaked as it opened.

"Come in, come in! I've been expecting you. So nice to see you both again. It's been years. What can I help you with this time?" Mr. Eville asked insincerely.

"You know why we're here. So let's make this easy. We want to go home, and we want you to leave Doc alone. And no funny business this time!" SRG said tersely.

"Oh, gee. I really wish I could do that. I really do," Mr. Eville sighed. "But you see, I just don't have to, so I won't. There you have it."

"You should be thanking us. We saved you from Hal. You wouldn't still control this kingdom if it hadn't been for us . . . and Danika."

"Oh, yes. Poor, dear Danika. She's dead. I'm very sorry about that. Well, no, actually I'm not. And I won't be sorry to put the two of you in the Transport Chamber and be rid of you, either! I'm going to send you off into the great unknown in the space-time continuum. I'd send Dr. Denton along with you, but I'm afraid I'm not done using him yet. But I won't be seeing you two again, that I can assure you."

Tannic raised the Fortran sword and charged at him, but it clanged and sparked when it hit the invisible force field protecting Mr. Eville's desk. He stumbled and then caught himself.

"Oh, Tannic, Tannic, Tannic. I thought for sure you would have remembered my force field. You disappoint me, lad."

Doc stepped through the door just as the lights flickered. He pulled a flashlight from his pocket and turned it on, but the lights only dimmed for a second and came back on. Tannic rushed Mr. Eville a second time, but the Fortran sword simply sparked against the force field again.

Mr. Eville let out a sinister laugh. "Oh, you thought I'd fall for that again? You amaze me, you really do. This time I was prepared. My backup generator kicked on when the power went off. I am really disappointed that you all underestimated me so badly."

The door burst open again, and several Minotaurs stormed in and seized Tannic and SRG. They took the Fortran sword away from Tannic, and Mr. Eville reached under his desk and turned off the force field. One Minotaur took the sword and leaned it up in the corner behind the desk.

"Now let's see, where was I? Oh, yes, I remember. I was about to load you two irritants into the Transport Chamber and get rid of you for good," Mr. Eville beamed.

"Please, Beezil! Send the boys home. You've done enough damage. They saved your empire! They lost their friend. I'll do whatever you want. Just let them go home," Doc pleaded. "Have a heart."

"Sorry, Doc. We both know I can't do that. I never want to see them again, and this time I'm not taking any chances."

SRG and Tannic glanced at each other and then at Doc, who looked utterly defeated. They were out of options. It was finally over. None of them noticed the Fortran sword slowly rise into the air. No one noticed until its tip stuck Mr. Eville in the back. He winced, and Danika slowly re-pixelated out of thin air.

"Just for the record, I'm not dead yet!" she announced.

"Danika!" SRG and Tannic shouted. Doc stood there

dumbfounded as Mr. Eville squirmed.

"We thought you were dead!" Tears welled in Tannic's eyes.

"Yeah, funny thing about that. I was almost dead. As I sank into the water after losing my third Life Wedge, I landed on a Heart Gem. How random is that? Then I decided I could be more help to you if I stayed invisible and Hal didn't know I was alive," she continued.

Mr. Eville reached for his desk drawer, and Danika pushed the sword against his suit jacket and shirt until the blade broke the skin and he started to bleed.

"Okay, okay. Easy now, child. No point in being unreasonable." He raised his hands in submission.

"Wait! You helped us?" SRG asked.

"Who do you think kicked Captain Killbeard's wooden leg and pushed him off the top step, Einstein? Yeah, I've been following you. I've been with you the whole time."

"You could have let us know you were alive! We've been worried sick!"

"Yeah, I know. Sorry about that. It was hard, but I really didn't want Hal to know I was there."

"That's okay. I'm just so happy you're alive, I can't believe it," SRG responded. Tannic was too choked up to talk.

"So, Mr. Eville, it looks like the tables have turned. Make your Minotaurs leave now! Do it!" she demanded as she pushed harder on the sword.

Mr. Eville winced and signaled to his henchmen, who hesitated, but then left the office.

"Now walk slowly over to the Transport Chamber. And just in case you're thinking about trying anything, remember this, it would make my day to skewer you with this sword."

Mr. Eville walked carefully to the Transport Chamber.

Doc appropriated the skull and roses key from his vest pocket, inserted it in the slot, and twisted. The door squealed as it opened. It hadn't been used since the last time they'd been here. Mr. Eville stepped reluctantly inside. His head was spinning. He was trying to think of a plan, but he couldn't come up with anything. He was beginning to panic when the door closed. Doc took out his little black box and plugged it into the controller.

"Where should we send him?" he asked the others.

"Just someplace random, I think. Just push a bunch of buttons and let it fly," SRG said, smiling contentedly.

Doc randomly punched a bunch of buttons, fog leaked from under the door, there was the loud bang and a flash of light. The door opened. Mr. Eville was gone. The smell of heavy air hung in the room. They exchanged high-fives as the fog dissipated.

"Now it's time for us all to go home, Doc. You and the people of Rough World won't ever be bothered by Mr. Eville again," SRG added.

"Not just yet," Tannic interrupted. He turned to his sister. "Last time I was here, Doc figured out where Fairhaven is and how to send us back home, to our real home, Danika. And I've realized something from my experiences here. I like being a whole person. I want to go home. And I need to take my rightful place on the throne and we have to deal with Queen Diana. We owe that to the citizens of Fairhaven. I promised myself that if I ever had the opportunity again, I'd take it. I know I haven't talked to you about it, but my mind's made up." He turned to SRG. "We'll miss you too, Compadre. You're truly my best friend, and I am grateful I ended up in Albany, Oregon. I'll never forget you, but I must do this. I don't know what else to say."

He took Danika's hand and led her into the Transport Chamber. She looked lovingly into her brother's eyes, kissed him on the cheek, and stepped back out.

"I'm sorry, Tannic, but my real home is Albany, Oregon, now. I want to go back there, to the only family I really remember, and to SRG," She said tearfully. "But I understand and I will miss you too."

Tannic let out a deep sigh then nodded his head in approval. "I know I'll be leaving you in good hands. Take good care of her, Compadre!" Then he nodded at Doc, who held up his hand to say goodbye. Doc turned the key and the door closed. Then he turned the black box on and set its destination. Fog leaked out of the doors, followed by the familiar loud bang.

"That all happened so fast. I didn't have time to really say goodbye," SRG said sadly.

"I'm sure he wanted it that way," Danika said. "He was probably afraid he would change his mind."

"I understand. Are you ready to go home Danika?"

"I can't tell you how badly I want to. Doc, I'd love to come and visit someday, but I don't think I'll ever play Rough World again. Can I take the Fortran sword home with me?" Danika asked.

"I don't see why not. I'm really going to miss you two. Thank you for everything you've done, for me and for the people here!" Doc said. "I'll never forget you either!"

He opened the door to the Transport Chamber one last time, and SRG waited for Danika to enter. Then he gave Doc a manly hug and stepped inside. He looked at Danika as the fog started to fill the chamber.

Chapter 15

The New King

Tannic plugged his ears and closed his eyes. He'd made the journey often enough that he knew the drill. He held his breath and waited for the flash and boom. He didn't really like leaving Danika behind, but he knew she deserved to be happy, and he was certain his best friend would make sure that happened. In any case, he needed to go home to Fairhaven and set things right. Their father would have wanted that. The good people of Fairhaven deserved that. He'd have a lot of work to do, and he wasn't sure where to start. He had to get to the castle and make his identity known, and then he'd go from there.

He was engulfed by the dense fog and the familiar smell of the heavy air. When he opened his eyes, the air was starting to clear. He was in the royal forest. He recognized this tall stand of trees. It all rushed back to him, and he was overcome with emotion. His father. His mother. Danika as a small child. The smells of the castle, the noises of the crowded market on Saturdays. All the random things he remembered flooded over him as he walked through the forest. He touched his own arms—he was whole again. And his stomach growled for the first time in years. He was hungry. In fact, he was starving.

Eventually Tannic reached a clearing and a road. He wasn't certain exactly where he was, but there were noises in the distance, and in a minute a horse-drawn cart came into view. He waited patiently by the road for it. He had a lot of questions.

The driver noticed Tannic and pulled to a stop. His cart was loaded with fresh produce and towing a milk cow behind. Tannic waved him down.

"Can I help you, stranger?" the driver asked.

"I hope so," Tannic answered. "Am I in Fairhaven?"

"Are you lost, young man? Yes, you're in Fairhaven. But from your clothing, I can't tell where you come from."

"I'm from Fairhaven, but I went on a long journey. Now I'm back. I need to find my way to the castle. Would you be so kind as to give me directions, good sir?" Tannic asked.

"I can do more than that, young man. I can give you a ride. We're headed there now. Today's Friday, and we're headed to the castle for the market tomorrow. We have a cartload of produce to sell, as you can see."

"I'd be most grateful, Sir." It was then that Tannic noticed the driver's wife, who looked like a good stout woman, and his daughter, who was beautiful and about Tannic's age. He climbed aboard and found a place to sit in the back among the vegetables and potatoes. The cow looked at him quizzically. He caught the girl staring at him and he felt a bit shy.

"I'm sorry, I forgot to introduce myself. The name's Wardroff. Barce Wardroff. This here is my wife Milgred and my daughter Amily."

"I'm so happy to meet you all, and I really appreciate your help. My name's Tannic."

"Have you got a last name, Tannic?" the driver asked.

"Oh, I'm sorry." He hesitated, but it was as good a time

as any. "Silveren."

The driver and his wife looked at each other with a serious gaze. "That's not funny, son. The good prince Tannic disappeared more than ten years ago and hasn't been seen since. His sister disappeared with him. Everyone said it had something to do with the queen, but there was never any proof. Anyway, he's long gone."

"I'm not sure how to explain this, sir, but I'm him. I'm the rightful heir to the throne."

"Oh, I see. Well, this will be interesting indeed," the driver answered. He rolled his eyes and gave his wife a knowing nudge and a wink.

"If you could just take me to the castle, I would be forever grateful," Tannic added.

"Oh, indeed we will, son. We're headed there now, and it should be an interesting trip."

They rode in broken silence for the rest of the day. Tannic asked a few questions about Fairhaven and received polite but curt answers in response. The whole time, he couldn't keep his eyes off Amily.

Late in the day they reached the castle gate. Two guards stood in front of it wearing amber-colored doublets and bright blue trousers. Over the doublets they wore purple frocks with the Silveren family crest embossed on the front. Their black boots were highly polished, and each was armed with a sword and a spear. They smiled as the cart drew near.

"Good day Mr. Wardroff, Mrs. Wardroff, Miss Amily," the first guard greeted them. "Here for the market? I trust you had a safe journey."

The second guard looked at Tannic. "I see you've got a stranger with you, Barce."

"Yes, we picked up the lad on the road, offered to give

him a ride to the castle," Barce replied. He shot a glance at his wife. "He says his name is Tannic Silveren."

The comment made both of the guards break out in laughter. Barce and his wife started laughing too. Only Amily and Tannic were quiet. She smiled demurely and looked at him with empathy. He kept his composure and stepped carefully down from the wagon. He walked up to the closest guard.

"I don't mean to interrupt, but could you just take me to the Queen's Court? I have some business to attend to," Tannic stated.

"Hah, hah. That's a good one, son. But nobody, and I mean nobody, gets to see Queen Diana without an official appointment. Do you have an appointment? An invitation? Anything? I'm guessing not!" the guard asked and answered, becoming more serious.

"No, I don't," Tannic confessed.

"Well, I'm sorry 'Mister Silveren.' You'll need to get an appointment," the guard answered with a touch of sarcasm. "In the meantime, you're welcome to stay in the village and enjoy the market tomorrow. 'Mister Silveren.'" They all laughed tauntingly again. Everybody except Amily.

Tannic turned away, dejected. Then he had a thought and reached into his pocket. "I don't have an appointment, but I might have something better," he offered. He slid the gold ring onto his finger and showed it to the guards. It had a round red stone polished flat, with a seal engraved in its surface. The emblem matched the crest on the guard's frock. "My father gave it to me before he died. It was his official seal."

The laughter stopped abruptly. The guards were stunned. They looked worriedly at each other. Barce looked anxiously at his wife, and she returned the gaze. Amily leaned forward, fixated by Tannic.

"Young man, I don't know who you are or how you got that, but I'm taking you to see the queen immediately. You're under arrest for impersonating the royal family and stealing the king's ring. I hope you understand the seriousness of this offense."

Tannic swallowed hard. His mouth was dry, and he felt his heart racing in his chest. As the guards grabbed his arms and marched him through the gate, he took a last look over his shoulder at the Wardroffs. They still looked surprised. Amily wore a worried expression.

Tannic was led into the castle, through the inner courtyard, and to the main entrance of the keep. It hadn't changed at all. People were setting up booths for the morning, and no one paid any attention to the guards taking their prisoner through the crowd. There Tannic's guards conferred with others before escorting him up two flights of stone stairs, stairs that he and Danika had played on as children. He tried to smile as they led him to the antechamber. He tried to calm himself as they explained their situation to the court guard, who in turn explained it to the court clerk at the desk. Tannic thought he recognized the clerk, and was about to say something when the clerk abruptly stood up and left through the large door leading into the royal court. It shut behind him, and Tannic stood nervously between the two guards. He took a deep breath. It was good to be home, but he wasn't really home just yet. He had no idea how this would play out. Diana was evil, after all. Evil like Mr. Eville.

* * * * *

In the royal court, Queen Diana sat on the throne. She was flanked by the royal court guard and the royal book-keeper. Below them sat the royal secretary and the commander of arms. The court clerk bowed as he approached.

"Your Majesty, Queen Diana; I'm sorry to interrupt, but an urgent situation has just developed that you should be made aware of," he explained.

The queen rose from the throne. "What situation could be so urgent that you need to interrupt me?" she demanded.

"I'm sorry Your Majesty. The guards have brought in a young man who claims to be Tannic Silveren, the heir to the throne. He must be an imposter, but he is also in possession of the royal seal. It's most disconcerting. What shall we do with him?" the clerk asked.

"He is obviously an imposter and a thief. Arrest him and place him in the dungeon! We'll interrogate him for a confession before we execute him!" the queen shouted. "And bring me the seal!"

"Yes, Your Majesty. I thought you would want to know. We have already arrested him. We will take him to the dungeon master and place him in a cell."

* * * * *

The court clerk reappeared with a serious expression. He whispered to the guard on Tannic's right arm, and guards began moving Tannic toward the dungeon staircase. Tannic knew exactly where they were leading him. He felt his heart pounding.

"Oh, one other thing," the clerk added. "I need the royal seal."

The guards looked at Tannic. "You heard him, boy. Take

the seal off your finger."

"It's tight, I need you to let go of my arms to get it off," Tannic explained. The guard looked at the other one, who nodded. They both let go of his arms. Tannic tried to pry the ring off his finger, but it was stuck. He had one other chance. He bolted for the door to the royal court and dashed through it with both guards and the court clerk fast on his heels. Everybody in the court rose to their feet. The guards caught him by the arms and started dragging him away again, but Tannic saw the queen. She was older now but, he would never forget that face. He caught her eye and saw that she recognized him too.

"Your Majesty, I'm sorry for this interrup—"

"Take that man to the dungeon! Now! Have the dungeon master cut his finger off to get the seal. He won't be needing it anyway!" the queen demanded.

"Wait!" Tannic shouted back. "I can prove I'm Tannic Silveren. I know the combination to the royal safe!" The courtroom grew quiet. Everyone was staring at him.

Finally, the court bookkeeper spoke up. "Young man, the last person who knew the combination to that safe died almost twenty years ago. It hasn't been opened since."

"If I can open it, will you believe me? Will you accept that I'm Tannic Silveren?" he asked.

"Take this imposter away and throw him in the dungeon immediately!" the queen shrieked.

But the rest of the room was silent. The court sage spoke softly. "If he is in fact Tannic Silveren, gentlemen, Your Majesty, let him prove it by opening the safe. If he can't, then he has proven his own guilt and we don't need a confession. We can execute him publicly during the market tomorrow. With Your Majesty's permission?" And he gestured to the guards.

Before the queen could form an objection, the guards led Tannic to the safe. It was built into the rock wall next to the throne. Its face had a large dial, with letters instead of numbers. Tannic stood facing the dial. His breathing was shallow and his hand trembled. He would only get one chance, and then it would be the gallows. The queen watched him with a tense expression, but when she saw his hesitation, a small, knowing smile spread across her face and confidence began to burn in her eyes. She glared mockingly at him.

He simply stared at the dial for a moment. Then he took a deep breath. The courtroom was dead silent. As he put his right hand on the dial, it all came back to him, and he suddenly had a strange feeling, a random realization he'd never had before. He turned the dial three times clockwise and stopped on the letter S. Then he turned it counterclockwise twice and stopped on R. He heard a faint click. Finally, he turned the dial clockwise one more time and stopped on G. He pulled down on the handle. It didn't move.

"Place the imposter in the dungeon!" the queen announced gleefully.

As the guards approached, Tannic panicked and pulled harder on the handle. There was a groan, then a sharp squeal from the lock mechanism as years of dirt and rust gave way, and he felt something click into place as the bolts retracted. The safe door creaked as Tannic pulled it open. There was a collective gasp behind him.

Queen Diana bolted for the door. The two guards grabbed her by the arms.

The court sage looked seriously at Tannic. Then he bowed. "King Tannic. Welcome home, Your Majesty!"

The court erupted in cheers. Everybody was shouting and hollering at the same time. They had just witnessed firsthand something that would become a legend in Fairhaven. The day King Tannic returned.

The court clerk indicated Queen Diana. "What shall we do with her?" he asked Tannic.

"I'm not sure yet. Remove the crown, gown, and shoes. Leave her in her undergarments and escort her to the chamber at the top of the tower. Lock her in and post a guard around the clock. Nobody is to visit her."

"At once, Your Majesty!"

"One more thing. Is Rufus the wizard still alive?"

"Indeed he is, Sire!"

"Good. Bring him to me."

The guards removed Diana's crown and jewels over her protests. Then they took her gown and shoes and led her down a long hallway to the tower, where they fulfilled the king's orders. Behind the locked door, she screamed her fury. "This is not the end of me! I'm the queen! You'll pay for this! I demand justice! I'm entitled to a fair trial! Do you hear me? I'm entitled to justice!" Her guard chuckled to himself. *Yep*, he thought, *and with any luck you're going to get it.*

* * * * *

The court clerk escorted Rufus the wizard into the Court Room. Tannic was seated on the throne now. Bells were ringing in the towers, the castle was abuzz, and soon the entirety of Fairhaven would know Tannic had returned to assume the throne. Tannic looked closely at old Rufus. He hadn't been much of a wizard to begin with, and now he was older. He was hunched over, his beard was long and white, and there was a milky glaze in his eyes. He started to speak in a quiet, gravelly voice.

"Master Tannic, I am deeply sorry for what I did to you and little Danika. I was acting under the orders of the queen. I was afraid . . . I have lived with my regret all these years. Whatever you decide to do with me, I deserve it. I'm resigned to my fate."

"Rufus, you old fool. I forgave you a long time ago. I know better than anyone that the real villain here was Diana. But I will just ask one thing of you. Please come here."

Rufus slowly approached the throne. Tannic leaned in close to his ear and whispered, "Do you remember the potion you gave us? I want you to fix another like that and bring it to me. After that, your debt to me is paid in full." Rufus nodded anxiously and quickly left the room.

By the time he returned, it was late in the day and Tannic was getting settled in as king. Word had spread to the market square, and people were celebrating. The singing and cheering could be heard inside the castle.

Diana listened to the ruckus from her tower cell. It would be dark soon, and she hadn't had anything to eat or drink all day. She fumed as she paced the floor.

Tannic looked at the chalice in his hand. He could serve it to Diana and never see her again. But he paused. The best punishment, he realized, would be to let her live out the rest of her life in Fairhaven as a peasant, knowing she wasn't the queen anymore and never would be again. Everybody would disdain her. He smiled and poured the potion out onto the floor.

* * * * *

The guard knocked and entered Diana's room with a tray of food and a glass of wine. He set them on the table and left, locking the door behind him. She approached the table hungrily and started to take a bite. Then she stopped. Would they poison her? No. Whatever they did, they would do it publicly. They would want to humiliate her as much as possible. But she would survive. Yes. She would survive whatever they did to her, and then she would return. And she would get even. With Tannic, and then with all of them. They would pay for this.

Diana ate the food as fast as she could and vigorously gulped down the wine. It tasted excellent. She ate so fast that she didn't bother to taste the food, not that it mattered. She suddenly felt tired. It had been a most stressful day and she laid her head on the pillow and fell into a deep slumber. While she was sleeping, she dreamed about her revenge.

* * * * *

Tannic looked over his court. He smiled. Now he had his work cut out for him. He needed to set things straight. He needed to make up for any damage Diana had done to Fairhaven and provide the people with good and fair leadership. He called to the court clerk.

"Yes, Your Majesty?"

"Three things, if you would be so kind. First, please call me Tannic. You can be formal when people are around and it's necessary, but otherwise just call me Tannic. Second, go out to the market square and locate the Wardroffs. Please bring them to me. I want to return their kindness for escorting me here. I'd like them to join me for dinner. And if you would, please seat Miss Amily next to me. Finally, I have a new food I would like the cook to prepare for dinner. It's called pizza. Let the cook know that I'll come down to the kitchen to show him how to prepare it." Then his stomach growled again. He could almost smell the pizza already.

"Yes, Sire." He nodded and winked at Tannic as he left the room.

Chapter 16

The Prom

When the fog cleared, SRG and Danika found themselves alone in the family room. They could hear
his younger brothers upstairs, arguing over something. The
television still showed Rough World on the screen, and it
said "Game Over." SRG got up and turned the television and
game system off. Then he took the disc out and put it back in
its case. He looked at Danika quizzically, but she didn't say
anything. She sat quietly on the couch, the Fortran sword in
her right hand. He laid the case on the stack of other videos
games and returned to the couch. Danika still hadn't said
anything. The pizza box was on the ottoman in front of them.
It was empty with just crumbs and strands of cheese left. The
knuckleheads had eaten all of it. They looked at each other
and still didn't speak. It was almost eleven o'clock and time
for Danika to go home. SRG's parents weren't home yet,
and the rest of the house was dark. Finally, they got up and
walked to the door.

"That was crazy," SRG said quietly. "But I'm glad we
did that. Doc needed our help. Hopefully Rough World will
be okay now. Are you okay?"

"Yeah, I'm fine. I'm going to miss Tannic, but I would
have missed my life here more. I'll be okay."

"I'm going to miss him too. He's been my best friend for so many years—most of my life, really. But he's doing what he needs to do. I'm happy for him. And who knows, maybe we'll see him again someday."

"Yeah, who knows . . . "

Danika put her coat on, picked up her purse, and walked up the front hall. Their conversation was interrupted as SRG's parents came in.

"Everything okay while we were out?" his mom asked.

"I think so," SRG replied. "Danik—uh, Katie and I were just playing video games. I was about to walk her home."

SRG's dad shot his wife a look with raised eyebrows. "Okay, honey," his mom said. "Don't be too long, it's already late."

"*Mom . . .* " was all he said as he and Danika walked out the door.

SRG's mom looked at her husband. "What?" she asked.

"He's never done that before. Never walked her home," he noted.

"Well, he's never asked her to the prom before either." She winked as they walked upstairs.

* * * * *

Prom day arrived and SRG was busy getting ready for his big date. He had picked up his grandpa's vintage Mustang early that morning and spent most of the day cleaning it. His grandpa had been more than happy to lend it to him, especially because he was taking Danika. The Mustang was always pretty impeccable, but he spent a couple of hours detailing it anyway. Now it was shiny and ready for the prom. He went upstairs and took a shower and put on the rental tuxedo laid out on his bed. His mom had helped him pick it out. It was a classic black tux with a white shirt and a black bowtie. He had originally just wanted a plain black necktie, but his mother had convinced him to go with the bow. Now as he looked at himself in the mirror, he realized she had been right. His dad had shown him how the buttons on the shirt worked, the cufflinks, and which direction to put the cummerbund on. When he was completely dressed, he stood in front of the mirror. "Bond . . . James Bond," he said softly to his reflection in his best James Bond voice. Then he smiled and went downstairs, where his mother was waiting with the cream-colored corsage in the clear plastic box. She had helped him pick that out too. She gave him a big hug, and he drove the spotless Mustang over to Danika's house.

Mrs. Karsten opened the door when he rang the bell. "Wow, Stevie! Don't you look dapper?" she asked. "Come in. Katie will be down in a minute. I want to get a couple of pictures of you two before you leave. This is so exciting!"

SRG waited anxiously until Danika appeared on the stairway. She normally wore her long blonde hair down, but tonight she had it up in a French braid. She had a few well-placed bunches of baby's breath flowers in her hair, and she was wearing a flowing turquoise gown with a fitted bodice and a low-cut neckline, with a white pearl necklace of her mother's. SRG gasped and almost dropped the corsage. He lost whatever train of thought he had.

"Wow . . . you . . . you . . . you look beautiful," he choked out. "I, uh . . . wow, I never . . . just, uh . . . wow," was all he could manage.

"Here Stevie, I'll help you pin the corsage on Katie, and then I want pictures," Mrs. Karsten stated. She showed him where the corsage went and helped him attach it to Katie's gown. Then they stood in front of the fireplace and Mrs. Karsten took a couple of the obligatory prom photos—the kind you look at thirty years later and laugh because you remember looking much cooler than you actually did. Danika stood proudly next to SRG and took his hand in hers. She was glowing. He appeared somewhat shell-shocked. They would both laugh at the photo thirty years later.

SRG escorted Danika out to the Mustang and opened the door for her. He made sure not to catch her gown as he closed the door. Then he got in and started the engine. It had a nice deep-throated resonance to it.

"Wow, who are you?" Danika asked surprised at his chivalry.

"Bond . . . " he smiled. "James Bond."

They both laughed as he drove them off to the prom and into their future.

Chapter 17

Mr. Eville's Landing

The flash of light was blinding and disorienting, and it was followed by a thunderous boom that rang in his ears for several seconds. When he opened his eyes, he was surrounded by a dense fog, and the air smelled strange. He stood still for a moment, confused and not sure what to make of his surroundings. As the fog dissipated, he saw that he was standing in a field of thick, knee-high grass. The foliage was lush and green and the sky was bright blue without a cloud in it. The sun shone brightly overhead, and the temperature was really pleasant. Beyond the meadow was tall forest, and he could hear birds singing in the distance. *This definitely isn't Rough World.*

Mr. Eville looked down and was pleased to see that his favorite three-piece suit, bright red tie and alligator boots had survived the journey intact. He smiled briefly. He didn't know where he was, but he would be all right. He'd get Dr. Denton for this, of course. It wasn't over yet. It was just a matter of time, and he was a patient man. He would get even.

On one side of the meadow was a road. He waded through the grass to reach it. It was just compacted dirt, with patches of grass in the middle separating it into two tracks. But it looked well-traveled. There were hoof prints and what looked like wagon marks.

Which direction to go? After a moment he realized it didn't really matter. There had to be civilization at both ends. He turned left and started walking.

After about an hour, Mr. Eville was warm and starting to perspire. He loosened his tie and found a nice tree to sit beneath and cool off. He was getting thirsty, too. He'd need to find water and shelter before night came. He grumbled under his breath. *I'll definitely get even with Dr. Denton for this. No doubt about that.*

His thoughts of revenge were interrupted by a young boy walking along the roadway, and he looked up. The boy was wearing medieval-looking attire. He stopped and smiled at Mr. Eville.

"Hi, Mister. Are you okay?" he asked.

"Yes, I'm fine. Thank you for asking," Mr. Eville replied. "Say, son, maybe you could help me out. Can you tell me where I am?"

"Are you lost, Mister?" He looked him up and down. "You're not from around here, are you? I've never seen anyone dressed like you before."

"Yes, um, I don't think I am from around here. You see, that's the real problem. I'm not sure exactly where I am presently."

"Well, Mister, you must not be from around here, everyone knows where you're at. You're on the Castle Road," he answered.

"And what castle would that be, young man?"

"Wow, you're really not from around here, are you?" he repeated, shaking his head.

"Yes, I think we've established that. Now, what castle we talking about, my boy?" Mr. Eville asked again. He was starting to lose patience with the lad.

"Why, *the* castle, Mister. There is only *one* castle here in . . . Fairhaven."

The End